REALM OF KINGS

THEA ATKINSON

Chapter 1

I almost died twice before I was twenty.

The first time was the night Kit found me hanging from a rafter in an abandoned school gymnasium, cranked out on whatever drug I'd stolen from the dealer who strung me up.

I barely remember what he looked like, but I remember Kit's face when she saw me hanging there. The image of her face gutted me each time it floated up from my memory and took me unawares.

That moment should have been enough to sway me from my drug addiction. It should have been my rock bottom. But it wasn't. It was a match to the pyre beneath the wicker man.

Kit suffered for months after that, as I stole out in the middle of the night and found some drug-addled escape from reality in the more derelict houses of our city, digging myself into a hole as deep as the graves my parents were buried in.

It was Gideon who saved me the next and last time, and I was never sure if Kit felt jealous that he was able to pull me from the pit of addiction, or if she just hated him because he was much older than me.

I was a kid without power then. The same as I'd been with the dealer. Weak and untried in the ways of life and love, I surrendered my power because I didn't realize I could keep it. And my weakness made Kit weak in the face of her love for me. Over those years, I came to see power as might and strength, as callousness and distant, buried emotion.

I'd spent nearly a decade trying to make up for the horrors I'd heaped on her. I was the thief of her youth, her beauty, her sanity. And none of the monsters I'd killed, the vampires I'd staked, the damn witches I'd neutered could salve the wound because she had no idea I was applying any ointment.

I realized that truth now. In an effort to shield her from the frightening things that hunkered in the dark places, I'd kept my hunter's life from her. Her ignorance meant she thought I was doing all the horrible things I'd been doing all my horrible life.

In the days when I was using Bloodmist to get through the kills and hunts, I was an addict but a functioning one. I did good things. She just couldn't know that. All she had to go on was the sister who had failed her over and over again.

That was about to change. And as I stood in the hallway outside of Terran's suites, wearing my own pants and Stone's shirt that he'd flung over me after bursting in on Blade and me, I considered just where in the manse she might be.

Flint had brought her to Fae on Terran's orders because he'd thought I'd tried to escape when I'd been fighting for my life in the Catacombs of Dread. I wore the tooth of the leader, Slavin, around my neck. A wearable trophy that Blade had collected and had made into a necklace. I felt it nestled between my breasts beneath Stone's shirt. It was meant as a reminder for me, to know I had survived, that I could survive again. My fingers went to it as I considered the courage it would take to find my sister and face her with the real truth of my life.

In the few moments we'd had to speak to each other, there had been no time for anything except to let her lob a dozen years of frustration at me in words so painfully true I had no defense against them. I deserved every single syllable of shame and guilt and hatred that exited her prim mouth.

I couldn't change what I was or what I'd done, but I'd be damned if I'd let her be a sacrifice to it any longer.

It took me ten excruciating minutes to scout the hallways of the wing after Stone and Blade left me to answer their father's call. I'd memorized enough of the layout that I knew to head to the part of the manse I'd never seen, save for the short bit of time I'd been ordered to Terran's wing.

By the time I stood at the head of a corridor guarded by three short, but muscled Fae males, my palms were clammy. As a plan, I didn't have much. A ferryman coin that I didn't know how to activate, and no way to get rid of the guards lurking outside the pair of gilded doors, growling Flint's name every thirty seconds.

I ducked back out of sight, laying my back along the wall to think things through. The quick glance I'd captured played again through my mind, showing me a landing that looked very familiar. I had the feeling that if I retraced my steps in my mind, I could almost believe that landing was the top of the stairs where Terran's apartments were.

The image behind my eyes overlaid the one from my memory when I'd been brought to Terran's quarters to discuss my wayward nature of getting abducted and nearly killed in the catacombs. I was sure I'd come straight back around to his wing.

This section of the wing was fairly sparse, without much that a girl could use as a weapon. A couple of statues too big for me to lift, a vase stuffed with dried blooms, and a large, life-sized painting of a woman with bright red hair. Her skin seemed to glitter faintly in the wolfish-looking face, and the eyes possessed an uncanny sentience. Predator through and through, that Fae female. I doffed my imaginary hat to her.

"What do you say, lady?" I whispered so low I barely heard the words brushing along the currents of air. "Do you think if Terran called for Stone and Blade, he'd also call for Flint?"

She held her counsel, but I didn't need an answer to presume I was right. The guards outside the doors suggested the occupant of the rooms needed guarding, and it was easy to tell myself the powerful third hand to the boss wouldn't require so much backup if he was within.

I fished into my pocket and pulled out the ferryman coin I'd slipped from the pouch of cursed objects before Stone could notice. If the coin worked by touch alone, I was sure I'd have been whisked out of Fae already, so I wasn't sure exactly how it worked. But it was all I had, and if all I could do for now was get the coin into Kit's hands, then so be it.

As Gideon was wont to repeat, opportunity comes to those who are patient enough to watch for the moment it appears. And if the hunter didn't have time to wait, she created the opportunity.

So either the guards had to get rousted from their sentry, or I had to find a way past them.

I hated the thought of it, but a direct approach was the best I had going for me. I'd have to use what I had.

So, with a bracing breath, I swung around the corner of the wall and put haste in my step as I approached the male guards. I recognized none of them, which was a good sign. If they weren't familiar to me, then I wouldn't be to them. All the same, I kept my head down, eyes downcast, hoping they'd overlook my clothes and take me for one of the mortal indentured.

All three of them stiffened at the sight of me. I felt the shortwaves of acute attention focusing toward me, marshalling the energy of a magic that smelled like pine needles and sulfur.

I forged ahead just the same, plastering a look of fearful respect on my face.

"I'm to clear away the woman's bath," I said, pulling the information Blade had given me about Kit being ordered to be bathed and pampered in preparation for her presentation.

A content and happy woman would go to her death like a lamb to the slaughter, or at least that was what these Fae seemed to think.

"And I'm to help her with her hair," I added, knowing it was a risk to add anything on that could be questioned, but I needed to make sure I had enough time.

They both ran a suspicious gaze over me. The urge to reach for my karambit was so strong I had to clutch at my shirt to keep my hands occupied.

Finally, one of them nodded curtly and stepped aside, pushing open the door. My palms went clammy as I angled through the doorway. My heart hammered in my ears as I closed the door behind me. Our last words echoed beneath my heartbeat like a bass rhythm, thick and full and discordant.

The room was tiny compared to the suites I held. A large beach stone fireplace took up the entirety of the exterior wall. It possessed a large slate mantel festooned with branches and rushes that lent a forested aroma to the air as it crackled merrily along, tossing the occasional spark onto its flagstone hearth. The floor was made of white pine and was pitted by hundreds, if not thousands, of footsteps through the years. It was cozy, but it was no suite. With a double bed that rested along the left wall, covered in a thick patchwork quilt tucked up neatly to the turned spindle headboard, it looked more like a heritage room from a pioneer cabin than a room in a wealthy Fae's manse.

She was sitting next to the tub instead of in it, back to me, her white shoulders slumped downward. Wrapped in a large white bath sheet that somehow made her look small, my sister didn't look up when I entered. Instead, she dropped her head backward, resigned, it seemed.

"I told you," she said. "I'm not eating the chocolates."

I blinked in confusion until I noted the silver tray sitting on a cross-legged table situated beside the tub. It held a slender bottle of what looked like champagne and a delicately blown glass candy dish that looked like Noah's Ark with a menagerie of creatures the human world would never have seen peeking out from dozens of tiny, round windows.

It seemed the little things were made to slide out of their windows should someone wish to eat them.

"I don't blame you," I said. "I don't think I'd have the stomach to bite the head off a unicorn either."

If she was expecting someone other than me, she made a great show of appearing unsurprised at the sound of my voice. There wasn't a beat of time before she swung her head to peer at me over her white, oh-so-painfully white shoulder. The sight of it, how untanned, soft, and innocent looking, put an ache in my belly. I knew she worked in her garden with a large floppy hat, gloves, and a long-sleeved shirt. It pained me that I knew that about her, but that she had no idea that I could conjure the image at will.

Then again, maybe she'd known all along and all that clothing was her way to hide from me.

"It's me," I said, my voice thick with emotion.

Stupid. Of course, it was me. But I couldn't stand the tension in the air anymore, and I couldn't wait to see if she'd fill the silence. I almost expected her to curl her lips back the way I'd seen her last. What I got was so much worse. A facade made of wood where the artist hadn't bothered to carve even the faintest smile. Not to be deterred, I stood there, waiting as she rose slowly from her stool, clutching the bath sheet where the knot formed at her cleavage.

She was large-breasted like me, like our mother, but while my chest was muscled beneath the fat, hers was rounded over the towel like bowls of ice cream. She'd grown trim in the time since I'd last seen her in the mortal realm. The heavy-set woman I'd known had changed in the last weeks. Her cheeks hollowed out like tiny gourds, as though the weight had come off too quickly.

I'd faced hundreds of monsters in my day, but I was never so nervous as I was at that moment. My back was rigid. I twisted my fingers around each other as I stood there, doing my best to force myself not to run straight back out the door and down the hall. I was a hunter, for pity's sake. I could stand in front of my own damn sister.

"Are you alright, Kit?" I asked softly.

Her chin trembled. It was slight, and it was very subtle, but I saw it.

"I don't think I've ever heard you ask me that before," she said in a rasp that suggested she too, was having a hard time speaking.

"Things change," I said. "People change."

Obviously the wrong thing to say. Her face screwed up and there came that curled back lip. A flash of anger rose in her eyes.

"Yes, they do," she ground out. "I imagine it's difficult for you to see your doormat of a sister growing a backbone."

"I never said you were a doormat, Kit," I said. "I never thought you were." This so painfully soft I wasn't sure she heard the words until her jaw went white and she approached me, step by step, stopping close enough that I could have pulled her into an embrace.

I didn't. I knew better. What I did was take a step backwards, involuntarily, feeling like a broken teen again.

"I didn't come to argue," I said.

She cocked her hip. She made a tsking sound behind her teeth. "You never argue. You just call with some sob story that means I have to fix things again. What am I fixing this time, Ava?"

My arms went round my belly, hugging tight and clasping the fabric of my shirt. "I haven't asked for your help in three years."

Her left eyebrow rose into a sharp arch. "You called me just weeks ago."

My fingers clenched around the material of my shirt. "That wasn't what I called for."

She blew out a long, almost moaning breath from her nose. I took a step toward her and her eyelids narrowed angrily. I thought better of it and retreated. Blew out my own long sigh.

"I thought they gave you a luxurious suite," I said. "This is so..."

"Modest?" she asked quietly. "I asked for a small room. Flint knows what I like."

"Do you know where you are, Kit?"

"Of course, I know. I'm in some other world, impossible as that may be, but here I am. And if I'm not mistaken, it's because of you. Again."

The words were a razor against my heart. "Do you know what I do for a vocation?" I asked.

This question was trickier. I had no doubt she understood in some capacity that we were in a Fae world, with beings who possessed magic, but I didn't think she understood the violence of the place. Hell, I'd not truly understood it myself until the last couple of weeks. I doubted even Gideon knew how bad it was here.

But the thought that there were creatures that could do her harm in her *own* world, that I committed violence to keep that harm from other innocent people like her...I wasn't sure how she would take that knowledge.

Her chin moved sideways a hair as she considered me. Finally, she shook her head, and I imagined she didn't want to say what she thought I did—or didn't do--for a living. But it didn't matter. I was here to tell her, to warn her, to try to get her the hell out of here.

"I'm a hunter," I said, and this time when I took a step toward her, I did not back up again when she flashed a warning look at me. "And it's not deer or game I hunt."

"Is it...is it people?" she asked as she tugged the knot higher up her bosom. I might have laughed, but the tone wasn't teasing. It was tremulous and afraid.

"What did Flint tell you?" I asked, the shock lacing my voice. "For fuck's sake, Kit. What do you think of me?"

"He said you were an assassin." She lifted her chin. "Don't assassins kill people?"

I ran a hand through my hair, catching the locks in a clump at the back of my head. "Sweet baby Jesus," I said.

She scowled at the use of the curse, but I didn't feel the least bit chagrined. This was my sister. She thought I could actually kill a human being without qualm. I closed my eyes and gave myself a beat before I spoke again.

"A hunter and an assassin are two different things," I said, opening my eyes to see she had gripped the rim of the tub. "Please, Kit. Sit down. Let's talk."

She shook her head. "I don't need to talk."

"Yes, we do," I said. "If you think I could kill someone—"

"But you are going to kill someone," she said. "A king. You're going to kill the king of this land." Her voice was both shrill and low, too impossible things for one voice to accomplish, and yet she managed it with such aplomb I was amazed her voice didn't crackle into shards of glass.

I held up my hand, not surrendering, but resisting.

"Yes, I'm being sent to kill the king," I said. "No, I don't do this on a regular basis. I kill monsters, Kit, for Jesus' sake. Vampires. Ogres. Werewolves. Black magic witches and worse. Not people. Never people."

She sank down so that her bottom rested against the lip of the tub, and I realized she was so relieved she couldn't stand anymore. I edged forward.

"Vampires don't exist," she whispered. "Or werewolves. Or ogres or witches or any other ridiculous euphemism for your targets that you think I'll swallow."

That stopped me short. She wasn't relieved; she was shocked. "You don't believe me," I said.

Her hand waved in front of her chest. "Flint said—"

"Fuck Flint," I said and was about to storm toward her, grab her by the hand and drag her by her hair until I could beat the truth into her, but a masculine voice behind me froze me to my spot.

"I'm not so sure I'd oblige that," the voice said, and Kit's gaze traveled over my shoulder. And damn if her face didn't go soft, her body all saggy.

"Flint," I said, not needing to turn around to know it was him. Just knowing that when I did, there was going to be a hell of a fight.

Chapter 2

The energy of Flint's presence behind me was like standing beside the electric chair. He all but buzzed with threat. Sudden movement of any sort, offensive or defensive, would be foolish, and I knew it. I had to let him make his play first, even if I was at a disadvantage.

So I watched Kit's face instead of spinning on my heel to face him. I took that risk of leaving my back exposed to a male of power when I knew he could cut through me with a single gesture, even though it was a painfully disquieting play.

I had to trust that I still knew my sister. She'd always let her feelings scoot around her face like an egg in a greased pan. It took a great deal of will to wait and take my cues from the play of emotions that ran rampant over her features.

Worry teased her features first as she realized he'd slipped noiselessly into the room without either of us noticing. She was calculating how much he'd heard in that second, filtering through the words she'd uttered to see if she'd said anything that might make her seem less desirable to him.

That left quickly, replaced by a sense of righteous anger, that emotion she pulled on me every damn time she'd caught me succumbing to one drug, one party, one youth's arms after another until she'd honed that emotion into a weapon. I was used to that look, and gaunt though her face might be, it hadn't changed in all these years. That one was for me because I'd put her in a position once again of having to examine things she'd done for dishonorable actions.

It was the third thing I watched for, though, the thing that told me I needed to duck and lunge sideways out of harm's way because she'd realized he wasn't just going to stand there and let me be in her presence without penalty.

All of it, all three emotions took no more than a heart-beat. That anxiety flickered across her face so fast, I almost missed it because she pulled a shutter down over it as quickly as her mouth formed the O of surprise.

But I saw it anyway, and my body responded the way it had trained itself to do. Hours of sparring with Gideon, of battling beasts more primal than myself, put a fluidity in my muscles. I ducked smoothly, lunged to the side, and swung around all at the same time with an ease that felt oiled. In a single instant, I was crouched on the floor, facing him.

The karambit was in my hand, the blade tucked behind my forearm out of sight. I could drag it in an arc to the left, across my chest, and slash through his shins in a heartbeat. I could bring it back with a twist and spin and cut through his throat with the next swipe.

I did neither. I was too afraid to move. I'd expected him to charge me, maybe land a blow, and so was poised to defend against attack. I hadn't expected him to cast magic. Not with Kit in the room, in the way. But he had. He still stood with his palm out, caught in the gesture of casting, frozen in place by the sight of whatever lay behind me. His handsome features twisted into something ugly as he looked past me.

In that instant, I knew what the problem was even as the hair lifted on the back of my neck and on my arms. The stink of sulfur and ozone pricked my nostrils.

"What have you done?" I whispered.

A glance behind me. That's all it took, and even then I didn't need to look to know what I'd see.

A blast of purple magic sizzled around Kit's head, lifting the ends of her hair with invisible fingers as though examining the color and texture in a leisurely inspection. At first, that was all the magic did, playing with her hair, a soft crackling sound skipping over the length of each strand.

Then, as if the power enjoyed being watched, it took hold of clumps like an errant wind had blown up and taken her hair in a tight embrace, whirling about in a dervish dance. Her eyes went round and wide, the whites so bright in her surprise that I could almost trace each thread of vein that ran through them.

That was when the smoke rose from her towel, soft as cashmere, as it twirled into lacy threads that rose to the ceiling.

Even as I watched, paralyzed by the thought that if I moved, it would free the magic and give it rein, the power zigzagged along those locks in a march to her scalp that was so painfully slow I knew without a doubt that time had found a way to stand still. I stood gaping at her, unable to do more than pray that the flames I feared would spark to life would not do so. I was still hoping, terrified to move when I smelled the scorching of fabric and knew I'd waited too long.

"Sweet Jesus, Flint," I said, the words slipping free in a breath. "What have you done?"

His palm was still raised, but he wasn't looking at me. He was terrified, too, I realized.

But one of us had to do something.

"Pull it back," I said.

He blinked. "I can't."

Can't. Not a word I expected. Not when a single blast of his magic had set Lilah, the black magic witch's cupboards on fire.

The memory of that moment lit my muscles into action finally, freeing them from the gooey paralysis of fear. I had one thought. Get to Kit.

Beyond that, I wasn't sure what I'd do. I just leapt to my feet. I might have dropped my blade. All I knew was that in less time than it took for me to take a breath, I had knocked her into the tub. I sailed right along with her, tumbling onto her body as it sank beneath the water.

The splash, her cry of surprise, the shock of water gone cold soaking me through.

The tub was massive. Room enough for two, deep enough for a giant. I went under, tangling my limbs with hers as I fought to pull us both back up to the surface. Soapy water burned down my nasal passages and scorched my palate. My hands flailed through the water, feeling for her, scrabbling to get hold of her and push her to the surface. I felt her legs land on my head, pushing it down.

I gasped. Swallowed water. Coughed and inhaled and flat out panicked. Fighting my way to the surface felt like wrestling a kraken. Inky blackness washed into the sides of my vision as I tried desperately to keep them open against the sting of soap. Still, I fought through my own terrified sense of self-preservation, trying to shove her back up and over the side to freedom. Something landed a strong whack along my cheek. Behind my eyelids, stars lit up and went out.

And then strong hands yanked me free. I sucked at air so hard my lungs near exploded from pain. When I fell, it was to the pock-marked wooden floor. I opened my eyes to see black knots and gouges beneath my face as I hung there on my hands and knees. I coughed up a burning gush of water loaded with soap. It burned up through my nostrils and trailed out onto the floor in a mix of snot and spit.

"Kit," I said in a rasp when my throat disgorged all the liquid and gave me the space to speak. "Is she alright? Where is she?"

I blinked rapidly, trying to clear my vision of the residual bath water. A swing of my gaze showed my sister lying on the floor on her back, Flint stretched out alongside her. Rage surged through me as I caught sight of his black hair hanging down in curtains, keeping me from seeing her face, her eyes. Without a good view, I couldn't tell if she was hurt by the fire or if I'd drowned her while trying to save her. My heart squeezed hard enough to hurt.

I tried to crawl toward them, ready to peel him back like a banana and squish his very life right through his eyeballs.

A hand held me back. A hand I hadn't realized was lying between my shoulders until the moment I tried to move.

I scraped it off with an irritable brush of my hand as I rose up to my knees and faced Blade, ready to do battle if I had to, just so long as I got to Kit.

"He killed her," I said, and somehow my voice sounded like it was coming from someone else's throat. "Damn you all to hell he killed her."

I knew my lips were curled back, that my teeth were bared like a dog's. I was soaked and dripping and my throat burned like a brand had been shoved down past my tongue, but none of that mattered. Kit was dead. This was all for nothing. I thought I would shrivel like a leaf and crumble into dust.

Strong, warm hands cupped the back of my neck, pulling me toward his chest. That hot cinnamon fragrance of him swathed me. Over his shoulder, I caught of glimpse of Stone by the door, of Mica just beyond him. The buzz of Blade's nearness tickled my cheeks and chest, trickling along my wet skin like a dancing butterfly. The wet shirt clung to me like an onion layer.

I fought him. I had to. I didn't know what to do with myself if not commit violence of some sort. And so he took the blows I landed as I tried to wrench out of his hold. Managing to win myself a little slack, I threw myself once more toward Flint and my sister and found enough freedom to swipe the floor for my karambit. Because Flint needed to die. And the moment I found the metal with searching fingers, I was going to hack and slash my way through the room until either I was dead or he was.

"Ava," Blade said in a voice so soft, so gently insistent, that I halted my search. "Ava, she's not dead."

My hand fell flat on the floor, fingers splayed against the pine boards of the floor.

I whirled on him. "How do you know?" I yelled. "Flint hit her with his magic. I saw her combust. I saw the smoke...the flames. Oh god. The flames." My throat tightened so it was impossible to say more through the choke hold the memory had on me. It took a moment to swallow down the clump of what felt like wool before I could speak again.

"She's gone. Just look at him." I pointed to where Flint was tapping Kit's cheek, maybe a little too hard, as though he didn't expect her to feel it. "She's fucking dead and he knows it."

Somber, flat-toned words from Blade. Carefully neutral of emotion. Careful, neutral expression.

"She's not dead."

My throat made a horrible sucking noise as I gasped for air and realized I was crying.

"You don't know that," I said. The air felt like a fist closing around me. "Someone has to do something."

"Someone already did," Blade said.

"Yes. Me." This said too shrilly as the words squeaked out of me. "*I* did something. He just stood there like a dolt while she caught fire. I had to dunk her." My voice caught on the next words. "I had to dunk her so she wouldn't burn to death. Oh, sweet Jesus."

My hands went to my face, covering over the twist that contorted my face until it hurt, and I sobbed out the last. Drowning. So much better than burning to death.

"Ava," Blade said, and this time he grappled my wrist and pulled me away with enough force that I slid backward on the floor toward him.

I was wet and growing colder by the second as the fabric chilled, and my hair lashed against the bare skin of my neck. The inky blackness of it looked stark against the shock-white of my skin.

Kit was gone and all I could think was I'd give anything to turn the clock back and never go to Lilah's lair, never meet Gideon at the Rot Gut Tavern. Except never meeting Gideon at the Rot Gut would mean I'd never have met Blade. Oh, the complexities of all the warring emotions...it was too much. I just wanted to bury my head in the darkness of his arms, out of sight.

And the guilt and shame of it--even if I wanted Kit alive-- was enough to make me cling all the more.

He enveloped me with his arms, pushed my cheek against his heated chest. His heart hammered in my ear. His lungs carried his words to me like an amplifier.

"Mica saved her," he said softly as he ran his palm over my hair. Once. Softly. Then he cupped my cheeks with both massive hands. "Mica pulled the power back."

I could swear I heard my heart stutter. "Mica?" But he was sick. My gaze cut to the doorway as if to answer my own question. Yes. I'd seen him there earlier. I was sure of it.

He was gone now. Stone too. And yet, I thought I heard the rustling of clothing, the muttering of voices, but I couldn't be sure. I squinted as I tried to look through the door into the hallway. It was too dark. Shadows moved in hulking, hunched shapes along the wall.

I pulled my gaze back to Blade's face. I needed to hear it again to be sure.

"Mica pulled the power back?"

He nodded, his expression pained. "I need to go to him, Ava," he said, bringing his face closer so that his eyes trapped mine. The silver limning them flared. "You understand? I need to go to him. I need to know you won't do anything foolish while I'm gone."

It was impossible to tear my eyes away. No matter how badly I wanted to steal a glance at Kit as she lay on the floor, with that shadowed hulk of Flint leaning over her, I found Blade's eyes far too magnetic. All I could do was nod stupidly.

Mica had pulled the magic back. I didn't know what that meant, but I was sure it meant Kit was alright. It had to mean that because I wasn't sure I could get through the next moments if it didn't.

"You'll return to your rooms," he said in that hypnotic voice. "Stone will take you."

I swallowed hard, the lump in my throat making it difficult to speak. He was asking a lot if he expected me not to retaliate.

"He struck her," I said. "Blasted her with his magic."

He'd been aiming for me, but I'd moved. That fact raced through my mind and back again like it was doing sprints. It was as much my fault as Flint's, I knew, but that didn't negate the fact that he'd blasted magic without considering what might happen.

"He didn't care if she was there. He just shot at me."

"I know," he murmured. "And he will suffer for that mistake. But for now, she's alive. Mica took the magic. It can't hurt her anymore."

Anymore. Meaning there had been some damage. I knew it, just wasn't sure how bad it was. As a moan came from Kit's direction, I lifted my face to his.

"I'm not leaving her."

"I will heal her before I go to Mica," he said in a tight voice. "But it's best you're not here when it's over. I don't want you getting in the way."

That rankled, but a furtive glance at Kit and catching sight of the scorched skin that showed above her wet collar, choked off any retort I might want to deliver. This wasn't the time for my own hurt feelings or ego. And maybe he was right after all. I knew the level of healing he could do, and I trusted him, didn't I?

I nodded as my eyes eased closed. I knew he needed to get to Mica, and all I was doing by arguing was delaying Kit's recovery and keeping him from Mica. The youth had only just been saved by Blade from the withering of using too much magic all at once. The boy would probably need more blood to heal.

The best thing I could do for them both was to obey. It gutted me to leave, but I knew it was best.

A sigh fled my lungs as I nodded. Lifted my chin. What I saw in Blade's face made me avert my gaze again. It was too intense, all those emotions battling each other for first place, and I wasn't sure which would win. I wasn't even sure what all of them meant.

His arm slid around my waist as he pulled me to him, standing, settling me on my feet. "I'll get Stone to take you back to your rooms. He'll light a fire. You'll take a hot shower. Warm yourself up." His hands rubbed mine, and I realized at some point he'd pulled my fists into his massive hands. I also realized I was shivering. My teeth chattered, and I wasn't entirely sure it was because I was cold, but I didn't argue.

Blade stood with me and tugged at the blankets that lay across the bed, careful to keep me angled away from Kit's view. I could hear her moaning softly, and each quiet sound fanned my heart with hope. She was alive. Hurt. But alive. I had to concentrate on that.

And yet still, I shivered. Convulsively now. He tossed the blanket over my shoulders. I felt the handle of my karambit as he pressed it into my hands.

"You're so cold, Alathir," he said. "But trust me. Everything will be alright." His glance over my head, directed at Flint, was filled with rage. "Even if I have to kill my brother to make it so."

Chapter 3

The trek to my rooms seemed to take forever, and Stone was silent the entire time. I didn't need his escort since I'd memorized the hallways, and the landmarks were easy enough after I'd committed them to the data banks within my brain that I could have found it alone. But I was glad of the company, even if both of us walked the hallways with a wooden stride, our thoughts filled with concerns and worries. He, for Mica and me, for Kit.

When we reached the door, the guards were gone. He turned to me and grasped my hands beneath the heavy blanket.

"I'll let you know how she is," he said, and I nodded.

"And Mica," I added, and he nodded.

He held my eyes for a long moment with his gaze. His hands were warm and soft and comforting. I wanted to thank him, but before I could, he pulled away, letting me go so he could open the door.

"I'm fine without the fire," I said before he could worm his way past me to do Blade's bidding and light the fireplace. He cocked his head at me, the steely color of his eyes flashing before he had a chance to lower his gaze. I saw his throat bob, a suggestion of protest climbing his vocal cords.

"Really," I said. "I just want to change and shower."

He nodded silently, and standing to the side, gestured me into the room. "Sleep well if you can then, Ava," he said, and there was a tightness around his lips, a cloud in his gaze.

A long blink and a half sigh, and he shoved his hands into his pockets. The awkwardness was getting too strained for both of us, I knew. His eyes had a pinched look at the corners that suggested he both wanted to stay and wanted to leave.

I was already aching all over from the trembling. I needed that hot shower. I needed a space, alone, where I could unleash the pent up emotion I had only walled back with sandbags, and they were getting far too soggy. I needed to get inside and forget at least for the night, about all the things I would have to do in the next days.

I offered him a kind, but curt nod, and his lips pressed together as though he wanted to speak. Then he shook his head and dropped his gaze.

"Goodnight, Ava," he said and turned away.

I watched him go, feeling strangely despondent, and almost called him back...except a sound from within my rooms caught my attention. Like something heavy falling.

No one should have been in my suite, and nothing should have fallen on its own. The hair on the back of my neck rose.

With a fluid movement, I swirled the blanket from around my shoulders and dropped it at my feet so I'd be able to move freely, speedily, if I had to. If I was still cold, I didn't feel it. Just the prickling sense of being watched.

Then I leaned around the doorjamb, my hand going automatically to my sheath. My senses buzzed with information: the cold, wet sensation of my jeans sticking together, making it hard to move. Stone's shirt, wet and clinging to my skin. The breeze touching my face that told me something in the room—a window, a door—was open and letting in a draft. The rustling sound of movement that wasn't my own. The scent of cinnamon and something else in the air, a strange perfume that hadn't been there before.

As swift as those things rang through my senses, the sight of movement by the armoire immediately clapped out everything else. The door had just shut, I was sure of it. In front of the closet, lying splayed open, was a thick book.

I raced to the armoire, ignoring the book for the moment in favor of yanking open the doors to see who was inside.

Empty. Nothing but the dresses and a change of clothes the same as there always had been. But now, the scent of cinnamon was stronger. Narrowing my eyelids, I strained to see within the depths of the armoire, pushing aside the dresses and the shirts and trousers. Far more glittery dresses than I remembered, all covered in sequins and shards of delicate but sharp crystals. As I shoved one flimsy bit of lace and ribbons aside, my thumb caught one of those crystals and the bite into my skin made me yelp.

I yanked my hand back and automatically stuck my thumb in my mouth. Blood. Of course there would be. Because why not?

At least my inspection satisfied me that no one had come out of the closet or gone back in. There wasn't a single seam in the back wall of wood to suggest a door of any sort. I leaned sideways, noting that the armoire itself wasn't even pushed against the wall.

Squinting at the space, I decided to run my hand over the back of the closet. Just in case I sprang loose some hidden door.

Nothing.

I did the same for the wall. Again, nothing.

Chewing the inside of my cheek thoughtfully, I looked from one to the other. It may not look like there was a way in and out of my room, but this was Fae. I couldn't be certain some magical portal didn't exist between the two. I decided to give it a hard shove, crab-walking it side to side until it was several feet away from the wall and several feet sideways to a new spot. If there was magic between the two, I hoped that would be enough to break the energy.

The exertion was enough to make me breathe heavily. I leaned against the armoire's doors, my head against the wood as I caught my breath. My gaze fell on the book lying open on the floor. I was sure I recognized it.

I dropped to a crouch beside it, my arms over my knees as I eyeballed it. I was sure it was the book I'd taken with me as the excuse to search for Kit. Of course, it was blank. It had been blank ever since I'd seen it in the room upon my return from the Shadow Trail. Blank like the book Terran had given me when he'd wanted me to learn about the endowments. I was beginning to think every book in Fae was blank.

It was evident the thing had some sentience. The more I looked at it, the more I thought about it, the more I decided the damn thing was following me. I'd dropped it back there in Mica's wing. I distinctly remembered that. Blade had kissed me and I'd...well, I'd dropped it and not thought about it again.

But here it was.

Back where it started.

On its own steam.

I swallowed nervously. I scanned the fireplace hearth where it had been when I'd picked it up to take it to Mica's, the wing back chairs where I'd seen it when I'd returned from the trail, the floor where it now sat, and even if every synapse in my brain was screaming at me to kick the damn thing under the armoire, I reached for it.

Breath caught in my throat, I ran my fingers over the edge of the cover, just an inch or so, to nudge it to the side.

Nothing happened. My breath let go in a whoosh of relief.

Magical, and perhaps sentient, but not harmful at least. I laughed beneath my breath at my foolishness and plucked the thing from the floor. My thumb laid on the blank pages while my fingers curled around the cover and spine.

By the time I stood up, I realized I'd left a bloody print on the corner of the page.

"Damn," I said. If there was anything I didn't want to do, it was to leave any of my blood here in Terran's lair. No telling what could be done with it or to me if anyone noticed. I certainly learned enough in Fae to know proceeding with caution about leaving anything of myself to chance in this realm of vindictive creatures.

The thought struck me that I'd have to make sure everything that could be left behind of me was gone before I
left. Blood, hair, skin. Kit's too. I couldn't leave anything
behind that could be used against us later. Presuming we
survived the king's harem, at least.

So lost in thought, staring down at the pages and cursing
myself for being so stupid, I slowly noticed words had
begun to appear on the blank pages. Words and gilt illumination and gorgeous pictures of gemstones so realistic I
thought they were real gems sitting atop the pages.

I even scraped at the drop shadow of the one on the
left-hand page. Ink. Not hologram or authentic stone sitting atop the vellum. Just plain old vellum and ink and
paint. But magnificent. So realistic my eyes fought to see
the lines of ink instead of the hard edges of real stone.

Whoever had drawn the gems and illuminated the lettering had been a master artist. I couldn't help flipping
through the pages and tracing the drawings with my eyes
from one to the next.

As I turned, more and more phased onto the vellum in
a leisurely way, as if the illustrations wanted me to take
my time with them. As they came, writing appeared as
well. Tidy, angular notations in letters and symbols that
I recognized as English only if I squinted at them. But I
had to squint, and it made reading the words an effort of
determination.

Narrowing my eyelids, I scanned a bit of lettering alongside
a gorgeous multi-colored crystal. Snow Stone, it read. Part of
the crown jewels of the Court of Skin and Bone. Capable of
crumbling mortals to dust. I shuddered. Whatever court that

was and wherever it lay in the realm, I did not want to ever see the crystal in person.

Page after page was filled with such information, and as I scoured the pages and squinted to read more, it dawned on me that this was the book Mica had stolen from Terran's library. He'd mentioned reading a book of sacred gems, and this couldn't be anything but the same tome, but he'd not mentioned it was enchanted.

Maybe he had no idea. Maybe taking it off Terran's shelf triggered the magic. But why was it here? Mica couldn't have brought it; he'd confessed to never having been in my rooms before I'd returned from the journey to Erachne's shop. In fact, it had been lying on the seat of this very chair that day. Lying open as if someone had been caught in the middle of reading by some other activity and left it at the page they last read.

Oh my God. Maybe it wasn't left open, but opened on its own? What if each time I saw the book, it was open to the same pages?

That would indicate the book or the person who kept leaving it wanted me to see specific information.

I sank into the chair nearest me, the large wingback chair in front of the fireplace, the book in my hands. I flipped through again, thinking there was no way I could remember a specific page when the book had always shown as blank.

I stared down at the vellum, letting my eyes un-focus. I wasn't sure what language the notations were written in, but I suspected part of the enchantment was to present the information to the right reader in the language they understood, else why would English show when I squinted?

Sitting back, I closed the book with a thwack, then gripped it by the spine. I blew out a decisive breath with an utterance to the tome to forgive me, then flung it across the room.

It landed on its covers, pages splayed open like a trollop. A grin stole my mouth, both because the thought made me think of Blade's comment to me back in the tavern on the trail, and because I was sure the book was telling me something in its own way.

"Gotcha," I muttered and pushed myself from the chair to cross the room to where the book had landed in front of the door.

I caught a glimpse of a blue stone drawn multiple times from different angles on the verso side. Before I could stoop to pick it up and examine the words or pictures closer, a sharp rap sounded beside my ear. I cocked my head.

"Who's there?" I asked, instantly on alert.

"The big bad wolf," said Blade. He sounded both impatient and concerned despite the teasing words.

I grabbed for the door handle too quickly to even pretend I wasn't excited to know he was on the other side.

He looked ragged. A gauntness dogged his features that wasn't there when I'd left Kit's room, but when he saw me, whatever my own expression said to him, he smiled. Wanly. But smiled just the same. It lifted my spirits.

"Ponytail," he murmured.

I stepped aside, kicking the book with my foot so that it slid across the floor to lodge beneath my bedside table.

"You're still wet," he said. "Normally, that would excite me, except you're also cold as a fish's belly."

I couldn't help rolling my eyes. "Trust you to turn a horrible situation into a joke."

He brushed my cheek with the back of his fingers. "Who said I was joking."

Despite the last hour of worry and anger, my stomach tightened way down low in response to his touch. To disguise it, I took a step back, out of reach, and angled my body so he could enter the room. My eyes, however, seemed starved for him, and they followed him as he crossed the room to the fireplace. "I thought Stone was going to light you a fire," he said.

"I told him I'd be fine without one."

The pivot of his body was sharp and noisy as his boots scuffed the floor. "That's no excuse," he said.

I shrugged. "Did you expect him to muscle his way into the room?" An accusation, perhaps, a commentary on what these Fae were capable of, but I kept that to myself. I was just so glad to see him, and I wasn't about to ruin that for myself.

"Kit?" I asked, giving him no time to argue.

He sighed. "It took longer than I thought, but she's fine. Resting."

It was such a relief that I slid down the wall to the floor, thrusting my legs out in front of me. My head dropped back. My eyes closed. "Thank sweet baby Jesus."

He was there in front of me before I could open my eyes again. I felt him there, knew he was looking down at me. The softness of his voice so clear, it could only come from right above me.

"No thanks to me, then, eh Ponytail?" There was something in his voice, not pique or anger, but a tightness that sounded very much like a part of him was bound and being held in a dark well.

I blinked my eyes open and lifted my face upward. He did indeed stand there. With a rake of his fingers through his black hair, he revealed himself more fatigued than he probably wanted to show.

"Mica?" I asked.

His chest rose and fell twice before he reached down for me. I met his hand with mine and let him pull me to my feet, but I was not going to let him avoid the question.

"How is he?"

Silently, with such careful movements I might have been an egg about to crack under a sudden blow, he tugged me against his chest. His massive hand covered my cheek as it pressed up against his heart. It was hammering, I realized. A hummingbird fighting a hurricane wind, terrified its wings would snap against the force.

That was the moment I realized I wasn't the egg that might shatter, but him.

Suddenly, my throat ached too much for words. My arms coiled around his waist without being bid, and the moment my hands slid over his shirt and met each other on the other side, he crushed me tighter.

I held him, felt the racking of his body as he fought for control of whatever emotion was storming through him at such speeds it created heat that burned through the cold of my wet body.

I said nothing, just let him clutch me ever tighter, the knowledge that all I had, my body, my silence, a silver thing of sterling understanding was what he needed. That I could give it to him when I could offer nothing more. I didn't ask again if Mica was alright. I supposed he wasn't. I supposed those moments Blade gave to Kit stole the time Mica needed, and regret and shame for my joy rose to my throat like bile.

I swallowed down my own emotions. He needed me, and whatever it was he required, I'd let him take it. And he did. He held me closer, so close I thought our bodies might meld together through some atomic energy that would dissolve our clothes, the skin between us, and let our cores find each other.

After a while, his shuddering halted, and he took a deep breath.

I lifted my face to his, my eyes searching his own. A half smile played at the corners of his mouth, one I recognized as a deflection, as though he might crack an inappropriate joke. Then it disappeared. I thought I caught sight of a sheen of tears in his eyes.

"I'm sorry," I said, braving the silence finally.

His throat worked over a reply, and when I thought it would at last croak free, his hand cupped my back side and lifted me off my feet. His other hand cupped my chin.

"Show me," he rasped out.

And then his mouth was on mine and I didn't have the heart to struggle.

CHAPTER 4

There was nothing of the Blade I knew in the way his mouth moved over mine. Rather, he explored me with a sense of wonder instead of the sort of fevered demand he'd forced on me before.

The kiss was sweet and tender. My heart stuttered and strained against my chest at the way his lips erased the ache in my throat, released the pent up energy that coiled in my stomach. There was joy in the kiss, both his and mine. I thought I might come apart at the seams if I didn't mold myself to him, use his solidity to hold myself together. I worried that if I let him go, I might disintegrate.

My hands let go of his waist to creep up his back and cradle the back of his head, holding him there. The moment my thumbs met his occipital bone, pressing inward, massaging the knot of tension there, he gasped. His hold on me grew tighter. And yet...and yet, his kiss remained languid.

I couldn't remember a time when I enjoyed such tenderness in a kiss. Gideon loved me, I knew he did, but I took him so often in need, I never gave him a chance to make love to me. I never thought I could deal with the emotions that might consume me if I did.

It was far worse right then, with my entire body melded to Blade's, the only thing separating us, the solid length of his excitement rising against his trousers. The room was too hot. I was sure steam rose from the back of my wet shirt and coiled around us like a kundalini serpent. I couldn't breathe for the intimacy.

And so, because I knew nothing else, I intensified the kiss. I ground against him, desperate to ramp up the encounter, to feel passion and need over the ache he was eliciting from me.

It was he who broke away, and I might have cursed as his lips peeled away from mine. When those bright green eyes stole over my face, the silver rode the crimson serpent around his irises so hard I almost couldn't see the colors change.

"You're afraid," he murmured.

I lifted my chin, only to realize I'd not done so on my own power. His finger had hooked beneath it, raising my face for his exploration. I knew what he saw there, even if I didn't want to admit it. Fear. Desire.

His embrace loosened to allow his hand to search for mine. I let him tangle his fingers in mine, knotting our hands together so tightly I knew I'd not be able to let go.

"Say nothing. No protests. No excuses," he said. "Just come with me."

"I don't think I can walk," I confessed, and for a second, surprise played over his features. Then, the specter of a smile teased the corner of his mouth, and he nodded.

"I feel the same, Ponytail," he rasped. "But I'd drag myself over the hot coals of hell on my hands and knees if that was what it took to have this moment with you."

He scooped me off my feet again, this time using just one muscled arm as his hand tucked in between my legs and hitched me onto his waist. I didn't need to hook my ankles around him; because he gathered me so that his elbow, his forearm, took the weight of my legs. The other hand cradled the back of my neck, his fingers teasing the fine hairs and making my spine tingle.

Settled there, I laid my head on his neck, burying it in his warmth, laying down kisses across the cords of his powerful throat, touching down on the pulse and feeling mine race to meet it. I might have murmured words of encouragement, filthy things, things that might make a warrior pale, because I didn't know how to react except with crudeness.

Dark chuckling, deep-throated and hoarse, was my answer, and I clung to him all the tighter as it filled the air between us.

His stride was swift enough to carry us to the bathroom without me sensing his movement. All I felt was the electric hum of his body against mine, and if I was worried about Mica, I told myself this was what Blade needed right now. He needed a distraction. He needed to feel as though nothing else existed except this moment. And it felt good to be needed. To be the balm for someone's pain.

The warmth of heated basalt enveloped me, and I knew he'd carried me to the bathroom. When he set me down almost reverently atop the vanity counter, I hooked my ankles around his waist, trying to bring him closer. My hips strained for his. I would distract him right then. Take his pain as mine for a while, not the way he might have done for mine back in the tavern, but the way a woman can for a man.

I might have managed it, except he eased my legs down to hang alongside his thighs. When I tried to protest, he placed a finger against my lips just as firmly, just as gently.

"You're shivering, Ava," he said, his eyelids shuttering pensively. "I intended to put you into a hot shower to warm you up, but dare I believe it's desire that has you trembling, and not the cold?"

I didn't trust my voice. A nod was the best I could manage.

Something moved in his eyes, that serpent again, this time rising like a cobra's head around the silver limning his irises. For an instant, I wasn't entirely sure the serpent wasn't real, that it wasn't mesmerizing me instead of the other way round.

"You want me, Ava?"

Another nod. God help me, I did want him, and I couldn't find the voice to say so.

"Then to hell with the shower," he said in a hoarse voice that sounded as if the words had been dragged from depths too dark to plumb. "I'll peel those wet things from you and warm your skin with my tongue and breath till it's flushed and hot and ready for me."

At that, his jowls transformed, revealing the hound in his face for just a second. A dare, I thought, a challenge to see the monster and change my mind.

I didn't. I took his hand and placed it on my breast over the wet shirt and bra. At his touch, my skin hummed. He altered his face back to Fae again, the hound nowhere to be seen except in his eyes. I watched, still in a trance of desire, as his gaze slid with the ease of hot oil over my face and down to my throat, where the rope scar from that horrible night so long ago tainted my skin. His gaze could have been fingers caressing the mottled and rashed flesh.

"That mark," he rasped. "Someday I will kill the man who put that on you, who marked you as his without your consent."

"He's probably already dead."

"But his mark still claims you." He dragged his eyes to mine once more and locked them there. "I aim to change that, Ava. And I aim to do so this night. Before you go to the king."

I blinked at him, thinking he was going to find some way to heal the scar, and for a second, my breath hitched.

To be free of that memory every time I brushed my teeth or combed my hair. To have the liberation to remember it only when I chose to and not every damn time I caught my reflection in an unguarded moment. The hope was too precious. Even if I never left the king's harem, even if all I had to live was one more night, I wanted that freedom.

But before I could admit as much to him, his eyelids shuttered. Desire saturated his glance, making me feel drunk.

"Turn around, Ponytail."

Turn around. Put my back to him and face the mirror. For an instant, I balked, and my hesitation pulled a growl from him because he knew the reason I resisted. A hunter never showed her back to danger. She faced it head on.

"Do it," he said. "I want you to see yourself when I take his claim from you. The moment it's gone, I want you to know it in your eyes, the expression on your face, the hammering of your pulse in your throat. I want you to understand his claim on you is finished."

My throat went tight at his words and the ferocity in them. I turned, my shod feet scuffing the floor tiles as I spun. I caught sight of myself in the mirror and of his face behind me. We both looked alarmed, tense, but while nerves played at the crinkles around my eyes, his face was smooth. A rush of heat bloomed in my cheeks.

I felt like a virgin again, like the very first moment Gideon had brushed his mature fingers between my innocent thighs. I was terrified and eager all at the same time. That moment had hurt when I'd foolishly expected it to be pleasure from the start. This would be like that, I knew. The anticipation, the hope, was almost an agony.

With his eyes locked on mine in the mirror, Blade toed the heels of my shoes until they scraped away from my feet. I slid free, lifting my sole so he could kick the shoes aside. They skittered somewhere unseen.

"I'm going to undress you, now," he said against my cheek, those eyes still holding mine. "And no matter how badly I want you, I'm going to take my time as though we both have an eternity ahead of us. You understand?"

It was a long way till dawn, and yet it wasn't long enough. "Yes."

Those lips, hot and swollen, touched down on the back of my neck the same moment his arms came around me to find the buttons of Stone's shirt. But instead of slipping the hole over the bit of wood that formed the closure, he flattened his palm over my chest. It was massive, that hand, and the heat in the belly of his palm made me gasp. Electricity sang down to my navel, tugging at the finer nerves lodged even lower still.

A simple touch, and yet more intense than a moment of entry. I caught my breath, willing my pulse to slow. I was sure he felt it against the crook of his neck where it met mine, that both of our heartbeats were scavenging energy from the other.

Instantly, my shirt was dry. The warmth of it cocooned me where his hand touched, and by the time he pulled his hands away and dropped one to the side of my thigh where the sheath held my karambit, I realized what he was going to do.

For the first time in my life, I let someone disarm me. But if I expected him to just lay the blade on the vanity, discarded as unimportant, I was wrong. He held it up to the light where it caught the glint of illumination cast by the blacksteel oil lamps lining the walls and over the mirror.

I inhaled slowly, drawing in the smell of fragrant oil as my eyes tracked the stars that winked on the knife's edge. My mouth parted, thinking I might urge him on, because already the ache in my chest, my throat, between my thighs was unbearable. I wanted to feel him inside me, easing the tension in my shoulders, eliciting a sweeter, more lustrous tension in other places.

Then, the blade disappeared behind my back, and for a heart stopping moment, my instincts blazed to life, screaming at me that this was wrong. All wrong. There was no way I should be standing there, letting a predator—and I couldn't deny Blade was a predator—hold a knife at my back and do nothing.

But I did. And it wasn't just out of trust that I allowed it. It was the way the fabric of both shirt and bra razored open behind me, a sound that sent a delirious shiver through my body, intensified because I knew it was Blade holding that knife.

By the time my shirt fell away to my sides from my back, clinging to the silkiness of my bra as it fell apart, I realized just how right he'd been when he said his breath would warm me. It cascaded over my flesh with such heat, it went straight to my core.

I shivered for an entirely different reason than from cold, then.

"Yes, that's it," he murmured. "You feel it. That connection. That part of yourself deep inside that knows it's made for me."

The backs of his fingers skimmed each vertebra as his hand climbed my back while the material of my shirt fell away. It was such a sublime sensation that I had to bite down on a moan.

"Fuck," I said, unable to remain silent a moment more.

"Oh, I plan to do just that, Ponytail. And I want that lustrous hair in my hands when I do." He dropped his lips to the top of my head, bathing me in that cinnamon scent of his breath. "I want to bury my fingers in it as I bury myself inside you."

As if his own words unlocked some sense of urgency that he'd been keeping at bay, his hands moved to my jeans next, this time unbuttoning them, and with each second, they grew drier even as I grew wetter. By the time he slid them down my thighs, I wasn't sure if I could control myself any longer.

I kicked at the legs, impatient, and he held them still as he kneeled behind me, his breath washing my bare buttocks.

My knuckles whitened as I gripped the counter tighter. I swayed. My legs bowed, and when he cupped me from behind, his fingers finding the perfect, swollen seed of pleasure, I gasped out loud.

"Jesus, Blade," I said, the words tearing themselves from me.

"Which one?" he asked in a hoarse voice. "Because one of us is about to become your god, Ava."

I wanted it, oh how I wanted it. No stitch of shame kept me from thrusting my ass toward him, splaying myself like a trollop, urging him on.

"Not yet, Alathir," he said, but the words sounded as ragged as a tattered flag of truce. "I told you I wanted to take my time."

At that, he spun me around and lifted my knees over his shoulders one by one, forcing me to arch back against the vanity, bracing myself as his mouth clamped down on the whole throbbing fist of nerves between my legs.

On his knees before me. Head bent. His powerful body beneath me, he was submitting even as he took his mastery. Any other time, with any other man, I would have ground against the suction, digging in to find my climax and be done. I would have taken control, owned my pleasure, and moved on.

Not with Blade. He held the reins so tightly I cursed at him as he teased me, dragging me to the pinnacle on threads of gossamer, and leaving me there as his lips roamed my thighs and other, darker places with expert kisses. Even when I wound my fingers into his hair and tried to hold him there, he did what he wanted, where he wanted. I was powerless, and yet I never felt so free.

Time and again, the pleasure built and receded, and he paid keen devotion to each fold of flesh, tasting me as if I was a fine wine, murmuring his appreciation, all while I bucked back and begged for release.

"What in the hell are you waiting for?" I ground out more than once.

"Not this way, Alathir," he said. "This is not the way I claim you."

At that, he swept my legs from his shoulders, cradling my back with one powerful arm as my feet touched down to the warmth of the basalt tiles. So freed, I planted my hands on the counter behind me and hopped on.

When I spread my legs, he was already standing between them. His eyes glinted. Somehow he'd undressed in the seconds between untangling himself from my legs and the moment he dropped his hands down onto my thighs, locking me in place.

And fuck. He was magnificent. I couldn't stop myself from tracing each raised scar that peppered his flesh in brands. I'd seen each one in my dreams, knew how they'd feel, and yet touching them sent a shudder through him that echoed in me. He ran his fingers over my scars, whispering up to my throat, and when he touched that scar too, I felt as if a loop had been closed.

"Kiss me," I said.

With a growl, he came at me then. No hesitation. I thought he might swallow me whole, and I was ready for it. I parried his kiss like I might parry a sword arc, meeting him steel for steel.

Then, with a guttural, primal growl, he dragged his mouth from mine and swung me around to face the mirror again. I met his eyes there, watched as he kicked my feet apart, bowed me over.

"I have been wanting to heal that damn wound since the moment I saw you, Ponytail," he rasped. "Brace yourself. It's going to be a hell of a ride."

With that, he thrust inside, and the pain was its own searing brand. He was too big. Too rough. Too entirely, perfectly violent.

He dug his head into my back as he buried himself deeper with each thrust. As promised, his fingers trawled through my hair, gripping it, tugging it just enough to force my face to lift, to present my face to my reflection the way I presented myself to his cock. My skin hummed. I hummed.

"Oh gods," I said, because I could feel the climax building and it was going to crash over me like fire and ice at the same time. I was going to break beneath it. I stiffened involuntarily, instinctively, the way I might brace for a mortal impact. The tension in my core took all my energy.

"Let me in, Ava," he growled in a ragged breath. "Dammit, let me in."

The protest came before I could think through what he was asking. "No," I said, pulling back, trying to draw away. My fingers let go their grip on the counter and scrabbled for the blade because I had to escape. I couldn't do this. I wasn't ready. My thumb brushed the handle.

"Give it to me, Ava," he said, and I knew he didn't mean the knife.

I gasped beneath Blade's hold as he locked me in place. He thrust deeper, longer, forcing me to take every inch of him.

"Let me in, Ava."

"No. Not here. Not now. Not this way."

"Dammit, Ava. I can't hold on much longer. Let go of it."

So I did. There was no fight in me anymore. I went slack beneath his punishing thrusts and the pleasure came when I did. Not in quick-fire spasms, but in long, drawn out explosions. The oil lamps guttered. Cinnamon rose to the air and made my nose itch. Magic swelled in the air as if it were a great snake drawing breath after a winter of hibernation.

And as it awoke, memories roused as well and pounded on the door of the closet they slept in. They came as I did, fast, dizzying, dragging my breath from me like a silk scarf being pulled from my throat.

I was seventeen again, hanging from a frayed rope, being drawn up and held there for a long, breathless moment before being lowered once more so I could scrabble for footing with sneakered feet. Catching my breath as the rope went slack. Laughter. Barking orders. Being raised again, kicking. Unable to scream. Kit's voice. The sound of her weeping. Begging.

The terror of memory chased the pleasure of sin. It almost disintegrated it.

The guilt came then, in a wash of agony that brought tears to my eyes. I sobbed beneath Blade's body. This wasn't what I wanted. This was fear, not joy.

And then...

Then, the feeling of suffocation peeled back like a tsunami from the shoreline. My mind's eye rolled away like a long-distance video camera, taking with it the intensity of shame and pain. My feet became someone else's, the hands clawing, dug at a rope on someone else's throat. I watched those legs churn and kick the air. I heard someone else choke on breath that wouldn't come.

And I knew...

This last moment of shame. That's what he wanted from me. That moment of pain, of helplessness and guilt...he wanted that, and he took it.

I saw it leave my eyes in the mirror the way he said it would, and I knew as we joined in climax that he suffered the pain with me. For me. Instead of me.

And then...then it was all gone.

And all that remained was that crashing, consuming joy of mastering a pinnacle and tumbling home again.

CHAPTER 5

We sat together on the floor of the bathroom, silent, both of us lost in our own thoughts or afraid to speak. My back lay against the wood of the vanity. My pants lay in a puddle atop my shoes. My karambit was still atop the marble somewhere and for the first time in years, I didn't care that I didn't know exactly where it was.

Blade sat with his knees up, arms propped over them while he watched me. The glow from the lamps played with his features, softening them. Or maybe I just thought he looked gentler.

The peace that settled over me was like a baptism. And yet...and yet I was afraid for him.

"What you did..."

"I'm fine," he said, leaning forward to plant a kiss on my forehead. "My magics absorbed most of it. What I couldn't do on my own, you helped with."

I cocked my head to the side. "Me?"

He nodded. "It was an old wound, deeper than cutting through tissues or bruising skin. I couldn't have reached it, couldn't have taken it from you if you hadn't opened to me. That took trust, Ava," he said. "And it took more than that." A smile flickered over his mouth like a struggling neon sign. "That kind of damage can only be shared, only be erased, with a deep connection. I'm so very happy to know you feel the same way as I do."

My head dropped back, choosing not to touch that part of the conversation for now. It was too raw, yet.

"Still," I said. "It was selfish of me to want to be free of it. Selfish to ask it of you."

My fingers trailed to my throat, exploring the skin. I was surprised to feel the rough skin still there, but there was no echoing ache deep inside as I roamed the tissue. Instead, there was a flush of heat and a different sort of tightness in my throat, the kind that flooded your cells with the excitement about a looming kiss.

I supposed that was more than I could hope for. To think of Blade every time I saw the scar. To imagine his lips on mine when I touched it.

"I couldn't take the scar," he said, noticing the movement of my hand. "Only the pain. I'm sorry, Ava."

I stared at him in disbelief. That he thought he should apologize for such an incredible gift.

"It doesn't matter," I said. "It's your mark now. Not his. I'm sorry you had to suffer so to take it from me."

For the first time, I realized just exactly what he'd had to go through, not just to lift the shame from me, but to take all the pain I'd lived through in the catacombs. I understood just how much he'd given to me without being asked.

A strange sheen rose to his eyes, and he blinked as though he had something in his eye. He crawled forward on his hands and knees until he could plant his hands on either side of my hips. He loomed over me, all the emotions playing across his face, but being crowded out by a look that I knew was filled with something I'd never seen before, something I had no idea I was missing until that moment.

He nuzzled into my neck. "It was the most delicious pain," he said. "And I'd taste it a thousand times more to free you from it." He smiled and sat back down, pulling me with him so that my legs straddled his lap and I sat within the crook of space made by his thighs. "I touched your soul, Ava, and you touched mine. Is that what love is, Alathir? Agony and ecstasy?"

"If it is," I said. "Then it's perfect for monsters like us."

His hand skimmed my arms, peeling away what was left of the shirt. His touch sent a tremor through my belly. I almost closed my eyes again, just to savor his touch, but I preferred to drink in his face. To meet him touch for touch as his palm brushed its way toward my hand. When his fingers met mine, he turned my hand over, showing my tattoo to the lights above us.

"Fight like you're already dead," he murmured.

My eyes went to the ink. "A reminder to give it my all in the moment or that moment might be all I'll have," I said.

"Spoken like a true warrior," he said and his gaze skirted mine to drop to my legs draped over his thighs. He looked pensive, sadly so.

"How is Mica?" I asked.

"He's being stubborn." His throat bobbed. The cords of muscle in his neck straining against the skin. "He's refusing my blood and wants to recharge on his own."

I almost hated to ask. "Can he?"

His eyes darted back to mine. "Every Fae can recharge if given enough time. But he expended a lot of energy to siphon Flint's blast, and just as much to project his magic into you. Replenishing that power could take years on his own. And for a Fae with his power...well, it's like a wildfire on a hot August afternoon after a month of drought. Wrangling it takes focus and control. Neither of which he's practiced enough in. "

"Is he really that young?"

"He's really that strong, Ava. He doesn't know how to pull or push just enough. It's always a flood, and it's too much. It makes him ill."

I swallowed. "I'm sorry," I said. "If it wasn't for Kit—"

"It's not just Kit," he said. "It's something else. He's been wasting for a while and he keeps using his magic as though he has control when he doesn't. Something is exhausting his power and he can't recharge fast enough. He won't take anyone else's blood but mine, and now he won't even do that."

Leaning into him, I cupped the back of his neck with both of my hands. "Force him," I said.

"I tried that," he said. "He blasted me across the room."

My eyebrows climbed upwards. "Mica? Blasted you across the room?"

A small grin lifted one corner of his mouth. "To be fair, he knows I wouldn't hurt him, and I didn't fight the magic because I didn't want him pushing more into it. That fit of temper just took more stuffing out of him."

"Of course," I said as I laid my forehead against his. "But why is he resisting?"

His eyes met mine. "He said I was already weakened from healing your sister, and that I needed all my magic to help you," he said. "I tried to argue, but there's no more stubborn Fae than my youngest brother."

I dropped my head on his chest, listening for the thrum of his heartbeat. "I didn't think I'd find a Fae more stubborn than you," I said, and his chest echoed with his chuckle.

"We are brothers, Ponytail. It runs in the family."

"Some family," I said, and he gathered me in, his powerful arms coiling around my naked skin, cocooning us, and as if I couldn't get close enough to him, I wrapped my arms around his torso, strained for him so that each inch of my flesh could touch his.

"He'll be alright, Ava," he said. "I'll make sure of it. Once he knows you're fine, I think he'll let me fuel him and that will hasten his restoration."

"I hope so," I whispered. "What he did for her..."

"Mica is the best of us. While so many in the Iron Kingdom and the Shadow Court are vicious, power-hungry Fae, he is untainted by ego. If he helped her, it was because he wanted to. His heart is so damn tender; sometimes I want to throttle him."

I peered up at him. His expression was hard, but I knew it was worry that seamed it, and not anger.

"Go to him now," I said. "Don't wait."

He extracted one massive hand from my waist to stroke my hair, his expression a mix of lust that tightened my stomach, and worry. "If my brother had enough power to toss me into his bookcase with a flick of his wrist, I'm sure he's well enough to wait for my return."

The hand running down my hair halted at my shoulder and slipped beneath. I felt him start to rise and to pull me along with him. As if I'd done it a thousand times and it was cell memory moving my legs, they hooked around his waist.

"For now," he said as he carried me deeper into the chamber. "I promised I'd put you into a hot shower, and I mean to keep my word."

He dropped me feet first onto the tiles beside the stall and leaned sideways to turn on the faucets. Steam rose around us, somehow fragrant of cinnamon the way he was, and I inhaled deeply, taking the fragrance in like it was oxygen.

"A shower does sound good," I said and couldn't help fluttering my fingers beneath the stream. A little moan escaped me at the warmth that met my fingers and I was already stepping into the shower when he stepped in behind me.

"A shower sounds perfect," he said in a voice that made me look over my shoulder at him. He gave me a meaningful look. "You don't think I'm going to let you take all the hot water, do you?" With a mischievous grin, he stepped into the spray and held his hand out to me. "Come, Ponytail. Let me wash your back."

I agreed almost too readily for my ego, but it didn't matter anymore. I didn't need to hold anything back, and I wanted him again. Be damned with whatever ridiculous pride kept me from admitting it to myself.

And if my back didn't seem to need as much washing as my front, who would count that as an error when the soap lather was luscious and his hands as they worked over me, foaming my nipples, my belly, below all that, until I was moaning loud and we were both breathing heavily.

"I feel like I've stepped into the Twilight Zone," I said.

His dark chuckle moved over my shoulder as he worked the lather in my hair into something that made my scalp feel like it was alive and taking a first breath.

"I should have taken you face to face first," he rasped as his skin slid along mine. "But I was greedy."

"And this isn't?" I asked, sagging beneath the stroke of his fingers as they left my hair and moved onto the small of my back, and then lower to the curve of my buttocks.

"Greedy was wanting to see your face as you realized you were free. But I could have foregone that just to feel your breasts against me, Ponytail. What a fool I was to take you that way."

I grinned to myself as I pulled his face down to mine in answer, the water cascading over us like a warm rain. I was sure I even smelled the pine scent of a forest around us, the fragrance of freshly bloomed flowers. Slick with soap and surrounded by the smell of a spring rain in a young glen, I gave myself to him again, and this time, there were no horrible memories. Just the feel of him, the drive of our passion, and I rode the waves of desire like I might never get a chance again.

When we were done, he dried me off with one of the thick, plush towels and wrapped me in his embrace. He sighed over my hair and we stood there coiled in each other's arms for a long moment before he sighed heavily.

"I need to return to Mica. Now that I've done what I can for you, maybe he'll take my blood." His lips touched down on the tip of my nose. "And you need some rest."

"And you?" I asked, shifting my head so my ear moved away from his heartbeat. "Don't you need rest?"

"I sleep less than you think," he said. "And I do have other things to attend to before I take my rest."

Other things. Like Mica and his father and probably a whole list of nasty things his father expected of him as the don fueled the City of the Dead in the basement dungeons.

I pulled away, realizing suddenly that I'd not been called to Terran's the way I'd expected. I was beginning to worry now exactly why.

"I thought I was supposed to meet you all below to get my orders."

He shook his head. "My father isn't feeling well. Stone suggested we get an early start in the morning."

I quirked an eyebrow. "I find it interesting he would admit to feeling unwell at all."

"Oh, he didn't. But it was obvious. He didn't resist Stone's suggestion to forgo the meeting with his assassin. We were checking on Mica when..."

His gaze skirted away, and I elbowed his ribs. "What?"

He shook his head. "When he screamed your name, Ava," he said. "He yelled it. Books flew off his shelves and everything."

"But how did you know I was with Kit and not here?"

He smiled that secret smile of his and tugged me back against his waist. "You think I don't know the scent of my mate?" he asked. "I could trail you to the bowels of Hades when the sulfur flowers are in full bloom."

I felt my chest flush, and not from lust, although that wasn't part of it. It was the warmth of feeling loved to that degree.

"You're blushing,"

With a shove, I wrestled my way out of his embrace. "I don't blush."

"But you are." He leaned in, and I could see his gaze traveling my skin in the mirror. "Am I embarrassing you, Ava?" The tease in his voice held just a hint of smokey desire and I had to turn away from the way his eyes blazed back at me.

I shook my head. "Just not used to this. To..."

"To having someone be willing to die for you instead of the other way around?" He caught my eyes in the reflection and held them captive. "Kit will never do that for you, Ponytail. Stone might. He is a good Fae. Dying for someone you love is not a hardship when you live a violent life like we do. It's the other things that measure the devotion. Stone will die for you, Ponytail, he might even kill for you, but he won't break his blood oath. That's his line in the sand."

"And you would?" I shouldn't ask it. I had no right. But it slipped out just the same. I knew what those vows meant. Consequences for an eternity for the fae who broke it and for those he loved.

His response was to cup my chin with his thumb and finger, aiming my face toward the mirror so he could force me to look at myself.

"The mortal you see in the mirror is the only match for the dark enforcer of the Shadow Court, Ava. You think I would stop at death to protect her? You are my blood. I touched your soul and you, mine. I wouldn't just break the blood oath for you. I would kill the males who own me with that vow. I would hold their lives in my hands and give them to you as a gift. I would take down the entire court I belong to, renounce every belief I hold, every promise I've made. For you. Only you. Except..."

I swallowed hard, trying not to let the stinging in my eyes bleed out of the corners. "Except what?"

His palm slid down to my throat, and his fingers curled around my flesh, warm and calloused, reminding me that his was a warrior's hand and that it could take my life in a heartbeat. And that it wouldn't.

"Except you don't need a protector, Ponytail. You're no damsel to be watched over. You are hard as diamonds and just as bright. You're not your sister. What you need is a lover. A match. An equal who sees you and knows you and loves every trophy hidden in your closets because you earned them and took them."

I had to tear my gaze from his because it was too intense. I felt awkward and unworthy and it was so joyful it hurt to breathe.

Running my hand through my hair, I eased out of his embrace and leaned into the mirror. The woman I saw looking back at me looked softer somehow. I caught a glimpse of Blade looking at me too, and grinned, sheepish.

"I look different," I said.

The backs of his fingers skimmed my shoulder above the towel. He was still naked, but not a bead of goose flesh raised his skin. "You look the way I have always seen you, Ponytail. Fierce. Magnificent."

A self-conscious laugh escaped me, and I tore my gaze away to busy myself with the towel as he nuzzled my neck. "I've never been called magnificent before." I lifted my chin, scouring the mirror for the scar on my throat. I thought it might not be quite so red and raised as it was just an hour earlier.

And while it brought Kit to mind automatically, the sight did not make me cringe the way it might have in the past. In the days before I'd come to Fae, I would have done anything to skirt the memory and the feelings that came with it. I would have lashed out in reaction to having them roused.

Looking into the mirror each day and seeing that scar was like hanging from that noose over and over. It wasn't just the terror of that memory that bothered me. It was feeling repeatedly and without relief, the knowledge that I'd failed the only person who loved me.

Now, I could scan it with an almost clinical scrutiny. This was new for me, this detachment. It was a gift to stand back from the awfulness of the memory and understand that the young girl who'd suffered that didn't exist anymore. The woman she'd grown into could find peace in the memory because it couldn't be changed. In truth, I wasn't sure I would change it now if I could. That memory made Ava Ashe, hunter of evil and protector of innocents who she was. It gave her the hardness she needed to face the evil of the world and do something about it.

Like it or not, that woman was a compilation of all those horrible things she had committed and all the beautiful things she had done since because of it. I was different because of that shame and guilt, and different in a way that made me a hunter.

Without that moment, I might never have been led here. I would never have met Blade. Never have found a joy and peace I'd thought belonged only to others. I wouldn't have found my mate.

Mate. A concept left in the human realm to explain away the connections between animals we considered less sentient than we were ourselves.

I found comfort in the whole complex nature of a primal drive to bond in ways mere human words couldn't express. It felt transcendent.

Just what that might mean later didn't matter. I had no idea how a mortal and a fae could find a life together and it didn't matter right then.

Right now, Mica needed him. And I knew what my mate needed was to be there for him.

"You better go," I said. "You need to see to your brother." I smiled, and, surprisingly, it held without faltering. I'd thought my awkwardness might bleed through my grin.

I watched him dress with great pleasure, his arms moving powerfully as he pulled on his shirt, the way his butt muscles clenched as he dragged his trousers over his feet and up his legs. My gaze caught on the trail of fine hair outlining the muscles of his abdomen, and I noted it was almost the only place on his torso that was clear of branding.

He caught me looking and winked.

"I'll be back in the morning, Alathir," he said and kissed me gently on the corner of the mouth.

I stood back, wrapped in the towel, and watched him prowl toward the door of the suite.

He paused, cocked his head, and then stooped to pick up the open book from the floor.

My hand went to my throat as he held it in his hands, his gaze skimming the pages.

"Where did you get this?" he asked, and his voice was filled with fear.

CHAPTER 6

"This isn't one of the books we brought back from the bookstore for Mica," he said.

I ambled out of the bathroom, clutching the towel against my chest. "No," I said, rubbing the corner of the towel over my hair. "I have no idea where it came from. It just keeps showing up." I reached for it, but he pulled it away, nestling it against his chest as his eyelids shuttered pensively.

"Keeps showing up?"

I nodded. "Was I speaking elvish?" I asked as I reached for the tome again. "I put it somewhere or drop it or toss it across the room, and it shows up somewhere else."

This time, he shifted the book in his grip so that the spine was facing out. "A book with no writing in it and nothing on the spine keeps *showing up*." His pull of air quotes was almost comical.

It was my turn to narrow my gaze. "It has writing in it," I said, surprised at his comment. "And pictures." At least it did now, while earlier I couldn't see them, but I was surprised he still couldn't. "You can't read it?"

His head cocked sideways. "Can you?"

I pointed at the spine. "Sacred Gems and Crystals of Ancient Faerie."

"Sacred Gems?" He coughed. "Sweet Jesus as you like to say. This is Mica's book."

Plucking the book from his grasp finally, I flipped it open. Of course, it splayed itself open to the same page as before, revealing a beautiful blue gemstone and spidery writing crawling over the white spaces.

"Actually," I said. "It isn't. He told me he stole it or one like it from your father's library." I ran my finger down the page, tracing the outline of the blue gem thoughtfully. "It keeps opening to the same page too. Strange."

"Ava," Blade said, splaying his hand down on the pages over the top my hand, pinning it flat against the vellum. "I know you don't understand how Fae works, but there is no book like it. All books in Fae are unique. We don't produce mass copies like you all do in your world. To be read and tossed aside and printed ad nausea for the sake of a few tawdry dollars."

There were no good responses to the disdain in his voice, so I merely lifted my chin. "You're saying that this is that book? The same book."

"It has to be. And if a book comes and goes of its own accord, it's more than what it seems."

"Be-spelled," I murmured. "Mica said he put a spell on it."

He tugged the book from me. "Mica can't put spells on things," he said. "He's not a sorcerer or a goblin. He's Fae.

High Fae. And no matter how powerful we are, our magics don't include be-spelling objects."

I thought about that and remembered that Terran had said Ferranus hired a Fae sorceress to cast a spell over the ballroom. That he had his soldiers out looking for a sorceress to break the spell but couldn't find her. Now it made sense why he'd needed to do that.

"I should have remembered," I said thoughtfully. "So I guess we can rule out Mica putting a spell on the veil to sort of auto-kill the king when he enters it and save me the trouble of assassinating the poor guy."

"If Mica could do that—if any of us could—don't you think my father would have done that instead of hiring a killer from the mortal realm. We don't like mortals knowing about us in general, and it would have been so much easier than pulling two human women into our business. Besides, the king is not a poor Fae. He doesn't deserve your pity."

"I'm not a killer," I said, my mind going automatically to the same argument because dammit, no one seemed to remember I was here under duress. So what if I'd fallen for a hot fae? I still wasn't doing this because I wanted to.

"And your comment about him not being poor has nothing to do with my aversion to assassinating him. Pity doesn't either. I swore to myself if I couldn't be a good person, I would do what I could to protect good people."

He snorted and brushed past me. "The king is not, nor has he ever been, what you might call good, Ponytail. He is not a mortal one might think needs protection." He prowled out of the bathroom.

I watched his movements the way one would a gorgeous panther. "I never said I thought he was mortal. And I didn't say he might need my protection."

"I know what you meant," he said. "It's just that the notion, the very concept of your values does not hold sway here in Fae. We are not the Spring Court. We are not the Summer Court. We are the Shadow Court and we are the Iron Court, and we are ruthless."

My hands found my hips, and I cocked them to the side in challenge. "You're not all ruthless, surely."

"If you mean I'm not ruthless, Ava, simply because I know how to be gentle, then you are forgetting the things I would do to anyone who plucks a hair from your head. You're forgetting the things I did when someone dared."

We both knew the things he'd done in the catacombs. Even if it was for the sake of saving me, there had been no pity in him for the creatures he'd killed. Some might call that something other than ruthless. Some might call it monstrous and we both knew it.

I crossed my arms. "I haven't forgotten," I said. "I meant Mica. Don't tell me he's ruthless because he's the farthest thing from it."

He sighed again, nostalgically, nodding all the while. "Mica. Yes. He is the best of us. Better even than some in the Summer Court and I've bedded a few of those creatures. So full of sweetness and light it leaks out their pores gods damn it." He glanced down at his crotch. "Do you know how hard you have to scrub to get fairy dust off your prick, Ponytail?"

He shook his head as he cupped his balls, as if remembering, and a slight quirk at the corner of his mouth teased it upward.

Then he coughed before he leveled me with that intense gaze again. The smile lurked at the edges of his mouth, waiting to take possession again.

I schooled my features into a neutral mask, refusing to rise to whatever bait he hoped to dangle in front of me.

His eyes rolled, and he became all seriousness again. "Some kinds of ruthlessness have no absolution, and our king doesn't deserve your pity for the things he's done."

I tapped my foot because we both knew that in the earthen realm, I'd have considered him a monster for the things he'd done, and I'd have fought to kill him or die trying.

But that was before. Now? Not so much. Even so...the suggestion was out there, and I would have done anything to not have that fact hanging in the air between us. I didn't want to think more about that or how I'd deal with all this once the hit was done and over, and I had to face it all.

"So you're saying Ferranus deserves to die?"

His hand sliced the air, indicting exactly what he thought of the question. "There isn't time to list all the reasons. Not if we had a century to do so. And I have better things to do with my time than conjure an agenda for you." His eyes sliced over my face in a too familiar glance that made me turn quickly toward the armoire.

As before, it was stuffed with shirts and trousers and tunics. I pulled a soft looking but shapeless shift from between a lacy nightgown and a woolen looking pair of men's pajamas.

Without a bit of compunction, I dropped the towel. His sharp intake of breath sent a shiver through me, and I spun around, holding the garment out to the side, giving him full view of my body. Testing, perhaps. Maybe I just needed to see that drunk look in his eye to soothe the craving for his touch that had already begun to coil inside my belly.

His reaction was exactly what I'd hoped. His eyes roamed my skin lazily, drinking me in. I felt like a large rippling bowl of sweet cream beneath his hungry scrutiny.

A smile took possession of my mouth as I slid my arms into the sleeves and pulled the tunic down over my head because I knew...he would watch every inch of my body as it disappeared beneath the fabric. As it fell around me, he blew out a long breath.

"Thank the gods for the small miracle of ratty clothing," he rasped and prowled toward me, letting each muscle carve his movements so cleanly I needed to hold my breath so I wouldn't give over to the ache lodged inside my throat that screamed it wanted his lips on me again.

When he reached me, that clump of desire had only grown and I pressed my back against the armoire doors, struggling not to pull his mouth down to mine. His throat bobbed as he swallowed. The electricity in the space between us sent shivers over my arms, trying to draw them upward. My heart beat sped up.

I waited, the hum in the air growing louder, until he reached over my head to pluck the book from the top of the armoire. The entire room seemed to exhale.

He stepped back, eyes flashing mischievously, my payment for teasing him, and he opened the book again.

The pages fell apart to what I knew would reveal that same blue stone.

"You said Mica broke the spell on the book?" He might have looked calm and collected, but the strain in his voice was evident enough that he had to clear his throat.

Hugging myself, I propped one elbow on top of the other. I felt better that way. More able to talk shop.

"Not exactly. It was the library itself that he said was under a spell. That was what he broke. The magical lock."

Blade made a thoughtful sound in the depths of his throat that could have meant anything. "I don't like that it seems to be following you."

I tugged the book from his hands and shoved it beneath my arm, so very loathe to give it up now that I realized there was some sentience to the thing. "If it meant me harm, it would have done something by now."

"You never answered my question," he said, crossing his arms over his chest.

"I did so. I read you the title, didn't I?" I back-stepped because I was sure he was thinking of taking the book from me again. "If this is the book Mica was reading, then why is it coming to me? Maybe he's sending it here."

"Why would he do that, Ponytail?"

My eyebrows climbed upward. "Great question. Why don't you ask him."

He snorted. "Oh, don't worry. I fully intend to. Now give it here."

I took another step backward. "No."

"Ava."

"I'm not giving it to you. It wants to be here and here it shall be."

I wasn't sure why I was being so stubborn about it, but I was not going to relinquish it. Not till I figured out what its constant appearances meant.

He gave me a stern look, and I lifted my eyebrow at him.

"If Mica asks for it back," I said. "Then he can have it."

"Don't make me wrestle you for it."

"Go ahead," I said, cocking my hip. "I doubt it will end in anything that remotely resembles taking a book from my hands."

He purred at the words, a very un-hellhound-like sound. "I'm not sure if you're suggesting violence or passion, Ponytail, but either one is fine by me."

A pause. A lengthy one where both of us were running through all the possibilities of how things might end. My cheeks flushed with heat. One outcome, I knew. And so did he.

I rolled my eyes and shoved the book at him, realizing we didn't have such luxury when we'd already used up too much. "Go on, then. Take the damn thing. I doubt Mica has the luxury of waiting much longer."

He nodded, and I shoved him toward the door once more, all but shaking my hands free of the electric hum that trembled up my fingertips with each touch. "Go see that he's alright," I said. "And if he's awake, tell him I hope he feels better soon."

He was almost through the door when he turned to look at me over his shoulder.

"Sleep well, Ava," he murmured. "Knowing the king will not rest his gaze on your sweet charms."

I grabbed his sleeve and caught the material just in time to keep him from crossing the threshold.

"What is that supposed to mean?"

Extricating my fingers from the fabric, his face softened. "It means you won't be going to the harem. I will."

Of all the reactions I could have had, I doubted he expected laughter, but it bubbled up freely enough that it suppressed me into explaining. "You're going to seduce the king?"

He shrugged. "He isn't exactly picky about gender, and I'm handsome, am I not?" He shot me a heart-stopping grin.

He was, and he knew it, but that wasn't the point. I wasn't even sure why I was arguing if it let me off the hook. Maybe it was curiosity. Maybe a bit of residual masochism. Perhaps it was worry for his welfare.

"But he knows you, doesn't he? He knows you are part of the Shadow Court."

"Indeed he does. And he won't be expecting such a frontal attack."

I slid my hand behind his neck, cupping his nape.

His voice lowered to a rasp that tightened my belly.

"I never had any intention of seeing you go to the king, Ponytail. But neither did I intend to go in your place as a Blood Gift using my own face. The raiment was supposed to glamor me into a mortal woman. In the end, I doubt my father will care who does the killing so long as Ferranus is dead, and I'm very good at killing."

So much info to process, I wasn't sure which point to attack first, but I chose the one that confused me most, and not the one that angered me.

"But why would you need the corset's glamor at all?" I asked, my voice thick with suspicion. "You wore Stone's face when your father sent me to you for seduction 101 classes."

No matter that I wanted to sink into his embrace, the hunter part of my body went rigid. I leaned back, just enough to pull away and look into his eyes. "If you could do that, then why would you need the raiment? Why not just use your own magics?"

His grin was sly and secretive. "I might be a shape-shifter, Ponytail, but I have only two faces: this and the hound's. I can't become someone else. I need a certain kind of magic for that, and the Raiment allowed me to wear Stone's form, the same as it allowed you to look like a pixie to the captain of the guard."

My jaw ticked sideways. Apparently, I had a lot to learn about Fae magic. "OK," I said carefully. "But that doesn't explain how the raiment was able to glamor you into looking like someone specific."

I paused, remembering that the damn thing showed the beholder what they wanted to see.

"Wait," I said in a pensive, peevish tone. "Maybe it does."

Maybe I'd wanted to see Stone then, and not Blade. Maybe I felt safer with the younger Fae brother, knowing I wouldn't be able to trust myself with the dark enforcer.

As if he read my thoughts, he said, "Don't worry, Ponytail. It was working correctly then, and no, it wasn't because you preferred Stone over me. Heavens forbid." He made a face. "The Raiment works differently for the Fae it was made for. It will glamor the owner into whatever he wants."

"You're the—"

He stopped the comment with a kiss and whispered the answer against my mouth. "There are ears here, Ava. I can't say more, but yes. It was made for me."

He drew away, holding my gaze with his. "I am going to the king as his Blood Gift. And you're going to go home."

The words stunned me. Home. Without having to kill anyone. Home. My chest felt too tight.

"But Kit," I said. "Your father will never just let us leave. We know too much." The words were nothing but a whisper even I could barely hear. "That's what your father said."

Again, a sly grin as he pulled back so I could look him in the eyes. "My father expects you to die. We will be sure you do."

I stared at him, trying to ask without asking because if the room did indeed have ears, I couldn't bear to have the secret known. In response, he clutched me tighter, laying his mouth alongside my earlobe.

"You will both die as Jasmine did. Violently and with much blood."

CHAPTER 7

For an instant, my skin prickled with imagined threat. Violence and blood. My mind reeled back to the moment of Jasmine's death in the dungeons below the castle. I heard her screams again, felt the impotent rage as I believed her dead at the dark enforcer's hand.

Then I watched the serpent flare to life around his irises, and I knew the truth. It grabbed hold of my throat, forcing the words from me whether I wanted them to be voiced or not. Whether or not those ears he spoke of could hear me.

"I knew it," I said. "She used the ferryman coin."

He touched the side of his nose with his finger. "My father bid me execute the occupant of the cell opposite yours, Ponytail. I did my father's bidding as I have always done." His eyes flashed. "Ferryman coins are a rarity even in this world, Ava. They ferry a mortal home and pull a demon from hell to take her place. A newborn or young demon, mind you. A changeling, if you will. And while it takes weeks for a demon to fully master the human form, I would never allow a demon to walk this world, no more than you would in yours."

His voice held a note I didn't understand at first. Not exactly coy, but filled with meaning, as though he was trying to tell me something without explicitly saying the words.

My mouth went dry as I mulled them through, and he watched me keenly as I did, giving me the time I needed to sort it out. He clearly couldn't confess to sending Jasmine home and was doing his best to explain what had happened.

But it meant she was alive. Alive! I couldn't help the joy that rose to my solar plexus as I realized that sweet woman had not been torn to shreds by the dark enforcer. He'd not done that horrible act. He'd enacted that violence against a demon. A young demon, but a demon none the less.

I felt less inclined to pity the creature he'd killed in the dungeons below. He watched my face for understanding, and it came as I remembered how he'd phrased his description of the things he'd done in the tavern on the Shadow Trail: no mortals were harmed in the making of this murder. So he'd sent the other women home and had executed the demons that took their place.

I thought of the coin in my pocket and how close I'd come to giving it to Kit. Not knowing how to activate it had saved me from what might have happened when her changeling took her place without me understanding just what I'd called forth. Flint's blast had interrupted us. I realized how grateful I was for that intervention now.

My hand went to my throat as I considered the consequences. And my fingers curled around my neck as I recalled his earlier words about Kit, that the demon pain that held her was dead. Awe flooded me as full comprehension settled in.

He'd ferried her home. A demon changeling now lived in her place, cuddling up to Flint, coming with me to the king's harem. I couldn't speak for the emotions flooding me.

"You say they're rare," I began, as I scoured the information for more details he tried to instill in his comments. "How many do you think are in the realm?"

His eyelids shuttered as he considered his next words carefully. "I'd say there is one more in the realm, Ponytail. And it just might be near enough to ferry the king's assassin home."

The king's assassin. More careful words. But I wasn't sure if they meant he planned to use that last coin to find his way out once he'd killed the king, or if he meant to send me home and take my place, leaving a demon to deal with the fallout.

In that moment, I was too afraid to ask more, and he took the silence that fell between us to sweep me into his arms. His kiss bruised my lips. It felt like a farewell. Tears stung my eyes at the thought. I wasn't ready. I should say something. But all that swamped my thoughts was the coin I held in my pocket, and the paralysis I felt over whether I should give it to him or keep it.

He drew back and sent me a wan smile before he spun on his heel and strode away. With that Fae speed, he was gone in a blur of color, and I was left standing there. My fingers trailed to my mouth, thumbing my lips thoughtfully.

I closed the door behind him and laid against it, my back pressed to the wood, my arms crossed over my chest. The sleeping tunic felt coarse all of a sudden as it bunched up beneath my fists. I laid against the door, surveying the room with my hands clutched against my breast.

I was more certain than before that his kiss had been a goodbye.

My gaze fell to the chair beside the fireplace. A familiar-looking book lay open on the seat, and I snorted my laughter. I wondered how long it would take before he realized the book had left his possession to find its way back here.

I pushed off the door and went to the chair. Lifting the book from the seat, I settled in with legs crossed to flip through the pages. In total, I counted a hundred pages of vellum with stones and crystals of all shapes and sizes. There was something called a Lilith Stone, a gorgeous ruby with what looked like a drop of blood inside. A rusty colored stone said to be the Eye of Agate, a dragon's blood crystal, and various others, but my fingers continued to shuffle back to the blue gem.

Something about it bothered me, and it wasn't just because the pages kept opening to this page. My gut told me I knew the stone. Tracing its outline was almost an echo of muscle memory.

I laid back, nestling my head against the back rest and let my mind wander where it would. Gideon always told me our guts knew the answers, but being so far from the brain, it took time to deliver the message. I needed to be patient if I was to hear the words. I had to trust that the message, like water, would find its lowest point and settle there, ready to be cupped and drank.

Staring at the room, I allowed my mind to open and my body to relax, all the better for the flow. My gaze traveled the spaces of the suite. It fell on my bed, the luxurious pillows. I took in the armoire and the chest beside it, saw inside to the interior where the clothes had no doubt changed already to supply what I would need in the morning. I trailed the wooden floor boards to the table and chairs not five feet away where I'd shared a drink with Stone and with Blade. Where I'd slid the coin free from the pouch of cursed objects.

That was where my gaze halted. That was where my breath exploded in a gasp.

It was there. Right there in front of me. The same gem I'd taken from Lilah's hand when I'd killed her. It had somehow ended up in the pouch of cursed objects and Stone had let me have it because he didn't know how it got mixed in with them.

I was on my feet immediately and grabbing for the gem. In my hand, it felt the same as always. I half-expected it to feel warm or vibrating. That it held no great energy when I'd so clearly solved the puzzle the book kept teasing me with disappointed me. I tossed it up and caught it again. Nothing.

A soft groan slipped free of my throat as I glared at the book.

"Really?" I asked it. "After all this, I get nothing?"

The book just lay there where I left it, the pages flopped open to the drawing that matched the stone in my fist. My fingers tightened around the gem. Obviously, I still needed to work out the meaning; otherwise, this was all happenstance, and there was no way this was coincidence.

With the stone in my hand, I dropped the backs of my knuckles atop my hips and chewed my lip thoughtfully. The stone had all the appearances of lapis lazuli with its seams of gold, but the gilt of the seams was too bright to be pyrite.

Frustrated, I stormed back to the book and grabbed it from the chair by its spine.

"Well, old friend," I told it. "I guess it's time for a story."

I carted the stone and the book over to the bed and propped myself on the multiple pillows. With legs outstretched and the book nestled in the crook of two large cushions, I squinted down at the writing on the pages that surrounded the illustration.

Through blurred vision, English letters showed through the foreign symbols. Letter by letter, I scanned the words, but it was slow, painstaking reading. Each time my eye moved to the right, the letters to the left transformed again. And it took ages to work out even a single word. Iron. It was short enough that I could remember it, but going backwards, I wasn't sure if the word before it was Prince or Princess, and going ahead, I couldn't work out if it read court or curse.

I scanned them again, slower, and discovered a smaller word between Princess and Iron. Of. So I managed to read Princess of Iron. Bully for me.

I was exhausted from the effort, and my head had begun to shoot razor-like jolts of pain each time I moved my eyes. Squeezing my eyes closed, tears of effort bled from my tear ducts and streamed down my cheeks. I couldn't keep this up. Already, I'd lost track of how long I'd been working on it and my eyes ached and burned from the strain.

What I needed was pen and paper. Whatever secrets or information the book held, relying on memory and blurry letters was not going to open the lock for me. My eyes needed a break. Judging by how hard it was to open my eyelids, I had a feeling even if I did, my headache would keep me from puzzling out a single letter more. I tried to think if I'd seen any writing materials in the room and decided I might have to dig through the bedside table...except I was so comfortable and my head hurt so much. Getting up to rummage seemed more work than I was ready for at the moment.

Something startled me awake from a sleep I had no recollection of falling into. The room was in a gleam of mid-dark, though, and the lazy fire had banked into the crimson and orange tiger stripes of coals in the firebox. A dream, perhaps. There were gooey threads of theta waves sticking like cobwebs to my thoughts.

But a hunter didn't leap out of bed. She listened first with every fiber of senses, even if there was no threat. Part of the training, the practice, to gather information with all your senses, to reach out with tenter hooks of hearing, touch, tasting the air like a snake. So that when a threat was there, the data would be automatic, and the reaction instinctual.

Had there been a sound knotted into the cobwebs of dreams, I wondered. My mind went to my karambit and my hands curled into fists. I realized I'd left it in the bathroom.

The gem had fallen out of my grip sometime during the night. I felt it wedged between my wrist and hip and dug for it, only to realize the book lay atop my stomach. Sweeping it aside, I braced myself to swing my legs over one side of the bed or the other, depending on where I needed to drop down.

But there wasn't another sound in the room, and I wasn't entirely sure now that I was awake that I'd really heard anything. A hazy sort of sensation coated my mind with images and emotions that told me I'd been dreaming. Vague images and even vaguer threads of emotion played at the fringes of my mind, challenging me to remember.

I yawned, wondering what time of the morning it was and if Blade had managed to help Mica.

I had just decided to roll over and get up when the hairs on the back of my neck prickled. A smell of ozone wafted over me.

I froze. Regardless of whether I could see or hear anyone, I knew the smell of magic now, and I knew I was no longer alone.

CHAPTER 8

I jackknifed to a sitting position and swept aside with my arm, crooking my elbow to catch whoever was standing over my bed.

Bone met bone so unexpectedly that I yelped and drew back my arm, cradling it against my chest. I was scooting off the foot of the bed long before a small female phased into sight.

Her ears were the first thing I noticed, large and plate-sized. I knew at once that I'd seen her before.

"Phaedre," I said, climbing to the floor and drawing myself up to a full stand. My eyes sought the gemstone like a guilty kid trying to seek out a stolen cookie. It found a small, rounded curve peeking out from beneath the pillow. Sufficiently covered if I didn't linger there.

I cut my eyes away to her face again.

She swung her homely face toward me, gracing me with the most beautiful eyes I'd ever seen.

"You know my name?" she asked, then tittered in excitement. "Did Blade or Mica tell you about me?"

She looked so earnest, so pleased that one of those males would think to mention her, that I didn't have the heart to confess I'd spied on her with Blade and that no one knew I had seen her.

Instead, I backed away. Just in case. Distracting her away from the book and the gemstone. Habitual practices of deflection--something I couldn't avoid surrendering to.

"I don't remember," I said, and she cocked her head at me. Those gorgeous eyes swirled like a kaleidoscope.

"It's not nice to fib," she said. "Your words taste of dishonesty."

My shoulders squared defensively. "It's not nice to enter someone's room without asking."

"You're a clever human," she said.

Her smile showed very large, pointed teeth with multiple gaps, and even though that mouth could probably crunch down on bone, they did not elicit a feeling of fear in me.

I bowed playfully. "A lovely compliment," I said. "From a lovely fae."

She hugged herself. "I'm not fae," she said. "At least, I'm only half. My mother was a goblin."

I wasn't surprised, considering her looks. I stuck out my hand. "I'm Ava."

She nodded, giggling. "I know. Blade has told me all about you."

I couldn't help the warm feeling that suffused my chest thinking that Blade had talked about me. I grinned playfully, coming around the bed and standing before her. I had to look down to talk to her, but she didn't seem to feel uncomfortable.

"Just what has Blade said about me?" I asked.

She clapped her hands together. "Oh, lots of things," she said, and her entire face lit up. And then she cast her eyes downward, toeing the floor with old looking leather shoes that had scuffs on the top. "Mostly, he said to leave you be, and stop watching you so much." She peeked up through her hair. "But I couldn't help it." She pointed at my own bare feet. "Your polish is in such need of fixing."

I chuckled as I angled my foot upward to show off the badly chipped pedicure. "Alas, I have no polish to fix them, and it's not really so important to me here."

"Oh, but it's so important here," she said and with a flourish so grand a magician would be envious, she pulled a bottle from the air above her. "I have just the right color."

She displayed it like a server would hold out a bottle of fine wine. The paint inside the ornate bottle was so deeply, richly red it looked almost blue in the undertones. The bottle itself was blown glass, but inlaid with gilt and raised carvings that looked for all the world like serpents intertwining.

"It's beautiful," I said, and meant it.

"It's the perfect shade for you. Mica loves bright yellows and oranges. Blade will only let me paint his black unless I beg to give him something more lively, but you are a rich, exciting red."

"Because I'm so angry all the time?" I asked.

She took a step toward me, shy, tentative. "Red is so much more than anger, Ava," she said in a soft voice. "It is one of the most primitive colors. The color of blood. And blood is life, is it not?

"But for you it's perfect because it's the color of protection. It's what you do in your realm, is it not? I admire your bravery."

My throat seemed to swell. I sank onto the foot of the bed, angled away from the pillow and the gemstone, and stretched my leg out. "I'm not so brave, really," I said. "I'm very afraid at times."

She made a move to sit beside me, and for a second I thought she'd fall to the floor, but a stool appeared to cushion her before she met the wooden boards.

"You're going to the king, aren't you?" she asked.

I nodded, not sure what to say.

"Then you are very brave indeed. I have to hide from him." She hid her face from me behind a baby blue fringe of hair and the sigh that escaped her moved the curtain of locks like a soft breeze. "I have to hide from everyone except Mica and Blade." Her fingers touched down on my bare foot, whispered down to the toes. Inspecting the old polish.

"You don't have to hide from me," I whispered and at the words, her face lit up.

I watched her, forming the most important question in a way that wouldn't spook her. I wanted to reach down and stroke her hair, maybe tuck it behind one of those massive ears, but I didn't dare move.

"Even so," I said. "I wouldn't think a goblin would be afraid of anyone, or have to hide at all." I leaned over, doing my best to catch her eye. "I've known a goblin or two, and they have very powerful magic."

I didn't tell her those goblins had been hunted down by me and killed for abducting infants from their cradles in the newborn wing of the hospital. I just knew when I found the babies, they had no eyes and no tongues. What the goblins did with them, I never asked. I just made sure the kidnappings stopped.

"Blade told me not to tell anyone." This said without looking up. "He said I'd be in danger if anyone knew I was alive. You aren't a danger to me, though, are you?"

Something caved my chest in at her words and I shook my head, wanting to comfort her. "What do you mean? If anyone knows you're alive."

She uncorked the bottle and pulled out a thick and lush polish brush. "I'm supposed to be dead." She hooked my foot over her lap as she said this so blandly I thought I'd heard her wrong. It took all my will to remain silent in the hopes she'd expand on the comment.

"You have pretty feet," she said, tilting her head to the side. Her hair brushed my instep, tickling the skin. "This is going to look beautiful on your toenails. Mica needs all the colors of the rainbow for his nails. And Blade..." she sighed theatrically as she peered up at me shyly. "He ends up cleaning most of it off except for one nail. I try to get him to wear it all but he just won't. He's very stubborn. Do you like this color?"

"It is a lovely shade," I said, willing her to keep talking by pursuing what she seemed most interested in.

She stroked the brush over my big toenail, the one without a single bit of polish left over. It tingled. "Sometimes I put protective magic in Blade's nail polish. He doesn't realize I've put a cloaking on him so his enemies don't recognize him."

"I suppose his ego wouldn't enjoy knowing differently."

She tittered. "I'm sure." She examined my nails and sighed. "It's not just pretty," she said. "I've put some magic in it for you. To give you red in the parts that need it."

I felt my brow furrow. "I don't understand."

She sighed. "You have enough courage. Enough passion, so the bright shades would just go somewhere they aren't needed and get wasted. I made sure it goes where it's needed."

She stroked again, letting the red cascade over the entire nail. The paint smoothed out into a slick puddle that was so deep it almost looked purple.

"Oh, look," she exclaimed. "I've never seen it stick so well before." She looked up, her face full of awe. "I've never seen the color take so very well before."

My throat tightened up. My eyes stung with unshed tears. I felt so damned unworthy and so damned grateful at the same time. First Blade and now this half-breed goblin.

"I do believe it's working," I murmured. "You're very good at magic."

She gave me a teasing wink with one large eye. "Of course it is. And I should be." She tittered. "I've been doing it for three centuries."

That she was of such an age surprised me. I'd thought her much younger.

I was glad I hadn't given in to my urge to stroke her hair. She wasn't a child, even if she seemed like one. Something was off about her, I decided. A beautiful, out of the ordinary 'offness' that only the very lovely-souled can possess.

"That's a long time to be practicing magic," I said. "You must be quite a master at it by now."

"Not as long as my father," she said as she ran her palm over the nails that still held polish. The old paint disappeared as if it had been rubbed away with an alcohol swab. "He is very powerful. I bet he could do the harder magics without even thinking about it."

She dotted the second nail with paint and watched it bleed toward the edges. "Although he can't do some of the things I can," she said with a hint of pride in her voice. "I think it's why he wants me dead."

That interested me. I leaned to blow a bit of air over the paint and smiled at her. She really was very ugly in a way that made the sweetness in her eyes that much more stunning. It was hard to tear my gaze from her, and soon, all I saw was the beauty of her nature and spirit.

"What things can you do that he can't?" I asked. "If he's so powerful, shouldn't he be able to do what you can?"

A grin split her face as she thumbed her chest with a fat digit painted in all colors of the rainbow. "Natal magics don't always pass down the way hair color or eyes do for humans. Sometimes it's a blend or an opposite. Sometimes it just lies inside like a little serpent coiled up in the cold. Many noble creatures of magic choose their mates based on the line needed to make it more powerful. Besides; he's not goblin. He's fae. Fae can't be-spell objects like goblins can."

I blinked as I regarded her, realizing she'd been watching me longer than I'd thought. "You spelled the armoire," I said. "The clothes inside. They change depending on what I need."

She blushed. "I wanted you to look pretty for him."

"For your father?" I guessed. Terran was obviously her sire. Back in the days when I'd had to meet Terran and his cronies for dinner, I'd worn a beautiful red dress, one that came from that very armoire.

"Gracious, no," she said, brushing her hair back so she could study her handiwork. "For Blade. I've been making things for him to help me find my brothers and sisters. So far, he hasn't found anyone but me. Besides: my father would never be interested in glamor made by a mud-blooded half-breed."

She blew on my toes before easing my foot to the floor and picking up the other. She settled it onto her lap and ran her hand up my instep. "Blade likes your hair," she said offhandedly. "He told me it was your best feature."

"You've discussed me." My eyebrow raised at the thought that the dark enforcer would discuss his love life with anyone.

She pulled the brush from the bottle again and gave me a long look through full lashes. "I asked him about you. He was so upset all the time after he spent time with you. Talking about you helped him, I think." She cocked her head. "He seems happier now. I asked about that too."

"I see," I said. "And how did he feel about being asked."

A long, crimson stroke painted the center of my big toenail as she sighed. "He got grouchy and sent me to my room."

I chuckled because that sounded more like the Blade I recognized. I'd overheard him say as much to her when I'd eavesdropped on Mica's room. "And is your room a nice place?" I asked, curious to know where that room might be, afraid it was the dungeons below, and the thought of her down there made me angry.

"Don't be angry," she said, with a toothy grin accentuated by pointed canines. I shuddered when I realized all of her teeth were pointed. I thought of those abducted babies again and had to force the image from my mind of her biting down onto tender flesh.

"It's a very nice room," she said. "I have all my paints with me and all the brushes and dresses and tiaras I could ever want. I even have a casting room," she said.

"A casting room?"

She nodded. "A place filled with treasures that I can pick and choose and practice with. I even made Mica a blanket that can smother all sound and magic except for what happens beneath it. He reads a lot at night and doesn't want to get in trouble."

The comment made me think of reading books under the quilts by flashlight, and I smiled to myself at the naiveté of them both.

"And what else did you spell, Phaedra?" I asked quietly, hoping she'd divulge more, fascinated by the lack of guile she displayed. The trust she seemed to give so easily.

"Oh you know," she murmured as she fluttered her fingers over the polish so that it moved as if alive over the nail. "Stuff for Blade, mostly. He takes too many risks." She jerked her head up, those bulbous eyes regarding me with all seriousness. "He thinks I don't know what he does, and he thinks he's keeping me safe by not telling me, but I know, Ava. I know what he's doing. He needs the things I give him. Just like you need this polish. Maybe more so."

The words were rushed as they flowed from her, her features so deadly earnest I almost didn't dare ask more.

But I had to. Because all of a sudden, my back went cold.

"What is he doing, Phaedre?" I wasn't sure why my throat had gone so tight, why my words sounded strangled.

It looked for a moment like she'd tell me, but then her lips pressed together tightly. I'd get no answer there. She loved Blade. She liked me. She might want to trust me, but this secret was far too important to her.

The next best thing, then, I decided, and my voice hushed.

"Who exactly is your father?" I asked.

She waited a long time before she spoke and her voice was so carefully neutral, I suspected she'd practiced the words in front of her reflection in preparation for some official speech. Either that or she'd heard it and repeated it many times to herself as a way to remove the sting of the words.

"I am mud-blooded," she said. "I am of the royal dynasty but a bastard. I don't deserve to live or carry the nascent magics of the line." Her eyes rolled up to meet mine. "I am the Iron King's bastard get."

I swallowed down hard on the clump of emotion that knotted up my vocal cords. Everything went hazy for a moment as I eyed her from the large ears to the fat thumbs and pointed teeth. Not Fae. Not goblin. Half-breed. Unworthy.

My heart hurt for her.

Her head jerked up, and she blinked with a long, heavy motion that seemed to take forever to close over the large eyes. "I've stayed too long," she said. "He knows I'm here." She looked over her shoulder toward the door. She shoved the polish bottle into my hands. "You'll have to finish. I can't stay."

Before I could do more than secure the bottle, she popped out of sight and the bottle fell to the floor.

The crimson paint bled everywhere.

CHAPTER 9

Dawn bled into the room with sticky light. I hadn't realized how close to morning it was when Phaedre woke me, but I presumed at the slants of crimson that filtered through the curtains that we had been talking for almost an hour.

Even as I drank in the coming light, an unearthly chime of sound shuddered through the room. It was a vibration of noise that ran up my toes from the very foundations of the manse and felt like bubbles popping over my skin and beneath my fascia. The full-bodied tone lifted the hair all over my body and resonated like liquid silver in the air, leaving traces of shimmer to slowly disappear the way steam does in a cold room.

Dawn had indeed come, and with it the ringing of the bells that initiated the Days of Endowment, calling to the Iron Court all the Fae of the realm. I had no doubt every Fae in the kingdom felt and heard the ring.

Not twelve hours ago, I believed I had no choice about attending that celebration. A reluctant assassin, I would do what I had to in order to protect my sister, even murdering a king with enough magic to rust the iron in my blood at a mere thought.

Now, that wedge had been pulled free. Kit was no longer in danger. I could let Blade mask himself as me to take on the job himself, and I could go home.

Twenty-four hours ago, I'd believed this morning would see me dressing in a magical gown spun by a kindly tree sprite so powerful, she'd been able to weave into the threads a magic that could disguise weapons beneath the skirts. I'd imagined being presented by Stone to a king in a grand room where I'd be considered a Blood Gift for his harem. I'd believed I would be plotting ways to use any one of the cursed objects delivered along with me in my trousseau.

All that had changed overnight with Blade's touch. Thinking about it sent a sort of exhilaration tingling through me. I had choices now that I didn't have yesterday. I could go home if I wanted.

And yet, the knock that rattled the door was a hateful reminder that I was not the master of my life here in Fae. Not yet. Soon.

And no doubt that was Blade coming from Mica's suites to either say goodbye or argue with me about staying.

"After everything that happened last night, you shouldn't have to knock," I said with a grin as I raced to open the door.

It wasn't Blade who stood there. And for a moment, my confusion made me stupid. I froze, all the emotions I wouldn't want to play over my face moving across it with a speed that made my muscles tight. My tongue was all but tied as Stone stood there in the hallway alone, balancing a tray filled with food.

He tilted his head at me. Just as bewildered, but affable and smiling.

"Forgive me, Ava," he said. "But after the last time I came in without knocking, I wasn't going to take the chance, even after last night."

My lips pressed together as I realized all the things I could have said presuming it was Blade at my door, and I swallowed down on the disappointment and confusion to stand aside. My movement reeled in the air currents, bringing with it a strong fragrance of coffee and warm bread.

"I have sourdough toast and quail eggs from the kitchens," he said. "Not the breakfast of champions but something to settle your stomach before we meet with Father."

"Oh," I said, not surprised but not pleased either. "And what time do we meet the Godfather?"

He tilted his head at me. "Godfather?"

I waved the comment away. "Never mind," I said. "Bad joke."

He shouldered his way past me, and I had to raise on my tiptoes to see what laded the tray. Not just toast and eggs, I didn't think. Orange slices and something that looked like custard in tiny, opaque bowls with ruffled rims.

The coffee, though, that was in mugs as big as buckets and the steam rose over the rims in swirls that trailed back toward me as he moved through the room with me on his heels. My stomach growled its demands loudly.

"I didn't realize how hungry I was till you came," I said. "Thank you."

He laid the tray on the table, pushing it toward the center. "I know what it's like to face my father on an empty stomach. Especially on a day like today." He pivoted sharply and gestured toward the chair. "Would you mind if I joined you?"

"There's two mugs," I said, and it sounded unexpectedly terse.

He fidgeted, something so unlike him that I immediately felt guilty. "I'm sorry," I said. "It was a long night."

"I imagine you didn't get much sleep," he said.

I sighed. "The truth is, I did sleep. Quite well." I pulled my chair out and sat, pulling one of the mugs toward me. "That's the problem."

He folded into the chair on his side. He seemed to take up far too much room. "I don't understand."

Wrapping my hands around the mug so that it warmed both my hands, I closed my eyes and inhaled. Just a moment to savor the fragrance. That was all I needed. Not Bloodmist, but then I didn't need that to face the king because it was very likely that I wouldn't be. With a start, I realized I wouldn't even need the drug for any reason. I smiled to myself as I thought of the reason why.

"You're in a good mood," he said, and I opened my eyes to regard him.

"Usually the night before a hunt, I'm all nerves. Going over the plans, walking through any paths I have to take, mentally moving through the fight I think I'll have to take on."

He nodded. "Kind of like creating muscle memory from brain practice," he said. "I get it."

"Right," I murmured, thinking it best to continue as if I was going through with it all, since Stone knew nothing different. "But there is none of that here. I have no idea what the king even looks like. I haven't scoped out the terrain. I haven't tried out the artifacts. I don't even have possession of the bag they're in." I shook my head. "And yet, I slept like a babe with no worries."

I tested the edge of the mug, letting a slurp of coffee touch my lips. Perfect temperature. I nearly sighed and slumped in my chair, but instead, I swallowed a mouthful and watched him over the rim. This wasn't a time to relax. If Stone had brought me breakfast, he must know more than I did.

"If it helps, I slept poorly."

I laughed. "It does help," I said. "Someone should be worried."

I realized with a start that someone should. While I'd slept soundly, the result of Blade's veiled insinuation that Kit was no longer in danger of meeting the king, but instead a demon wearing her likeness, I had no reason to worry about her anymore. But his declaration that he planned to take my place and send me home...After those languid and luscious moments between us that even now made my thighs clench...I suddenly understood how heavy that weight had been.

And would I now lay that weight on his shoulders? Massive, they might be, filled with delicious knots of tension that I longed to hammer through and soften, but he was no Iron King. He might be as vulnerable as I was when it came down to it. The thought of never seeing him again made something crack in my chest.

"You're blushing, Ava," he said. "Is the coffee too hot?"

My eyes flicked up to meet his. I knew just looking at him that he didn't think it was the caffeine making me flush.

He reached across the table to touch my fingers, and, without meaning to, I pulled away. I regretted it the moment I saw the hurt flash across his face. A moment it was there, and then it left as if it had never existed.

"It's been a few days since my body has enjoyed a stimulant," I said, because it wasn't a lie. "I don't doubt that it has no idea what to do with all the energy." I tried to smile, to soften the blow of my withdrawal, but it came too late and his eyes hooded.

Leaning back in the chair, looking like it was made for a doll and not the size of a Fae his size, he said, "Is that all?" he asked, and in his voice, I heard the suspicion.

I leaned my elbows on the table and forced him to meet my eye. "There are many things here in Fae that I won't be sad to leave behind," I said. "But you are not one of them. You're kind, Stone. I wouldn't have made it a day without you."

The whiteness feathering his jaw didn't go away. "Kind," he said. "And kindness isn't what you're looking for."

I stared at him for a long moment, trying to work through the things I should say to him to ease the hurt, but I had nothing. I wasn't good at this. This was Kit's domain. She'd always been the one who knew what to say, how to know when to bring a casserole to someone grieving, where to place a bouquet to cheer someone up. The thought of those small memories brought the ghost of a smile to my lips.

Funny how I could think of all those amazing qualities of hers and not feel a pang of shame.

Blade had done that for me. Not Stone. And yet, I didn't want to hurt the Fae sitting across from me because he was kind. Even Blade believed it. So because I trusted that above all, I got up from my chair.

I had no idea what I planned to do once I stood in front of him, but I knew I had to do something. I didn't want to leave Fae with an enemy behind me. I wanted to go clean and clear.

When I reached him, I fell to my knees with my hands on his thighs. He looked down at me with those crystalline eyes, so unlike Blade's and yet so very Fae, that I knew any other time and place, I might have been able to fall for him. He was in his way, just as magnificent as Blade. Powerful but hurting at the moment. In need of comfort or of being reminded what he was, that he was a gorgeous Fae with power many didn't possess.

He just needed to be reminded of that, I decided. As if I was a child, I laid my chin on my forearms and looked up at him.

"I've not been kind ever. Not in my entire life, Stone," I said. "I've been a bitch. A horrible sister. A terrible daughter. Any kindness shown to me has been met with resistance and often flat out resentment. I'm damaged. Worse than damaged. I've never wanted love. It's always cost me. In my work, it's a liability. It makes me vulnerable. It hurts. It has always hurt."

I shook his legs because he was refusing to look at me. "It's not you, do you hear me?" I said. "I just don't think my brain knows how to process kindness."

He snorted and looked away. "Even here in Fae we've heard that before."

I squeezed his leg, forcing him to turn back to me. "This isn't that."

His eyes glistened as they held mine. "Then what is it, Ava?" he asked. "What if I told you I wasn't what you think? What if I confessed that I'm a bastard. That Blade is nothing compared to the likes of my darkness?"

I patted his leg. "Even in my world, we've heard that too," I said. "In my world, we'd assume you're just saying what you think I want to hear. It's desperate. And that's not you. I've seen you with Mica. The kind of male you describe wouldn't show that kind of concern for another. Hell. Even Blade says you're a good fae."

The words cut off at that because I was afraid I'd divulge more, that if I confessed to hearing just how good a Fae his brother thought he was, that he'd realize we'd been more intimate than that sort of conversation would warrant.

As it was, he didn't go further than what it meant for him, thank God.

"Blade said that?" he asked, and I almost sighed my relief that he didn't press why Blade had decided to say as much.

"He did," I said, but hurried along so he wouldn't ask me anything more.

I plucked a bit of leaf from the hem of his pants. "Listen, Stone. My gut says you're a Fae with a good heart," I said. "And when I bother to listen to it, my instincts never steer me wrong."

His lips twisted as he tore his gaze from mine. The whiteness in his jaw was still there. The muscles clenched and let go as though he wanted to speak but was fighting the urge. I sighed and pushed myself to my feet.

My hand brushed his shoulder, ran the length of his neck to cup his nape for one instant. I felt the tension there, so rigid, I pulled my hand away.

"I never wanted to come here, Stone," I said. "You can't expect more from me than to do your father's bidding. It's a harsh truth, but there it is." My hand trailed over his collarbone. "I care about you, but not that way."

I said it as gently as I could. This wasn't the time to confess to being in love with his brother. There would be time for that when all this was over and the chips had fallen into places where we could pick them up again, try to put things back together. But it also wasn't fair to keep him hoping for something more.

I wasn't sure what would happen now between the dark enforcer and me. Once he sent me home, I didn't know if he'd even be able to follow. He might be stuck in some weird Fae limbo.

The thought of never seeing Blade again sent splinters of pain through my chest.

He exhaled through his nose and brushed at his trousers. Dust and detritus rained down to the floor, and he toed it with his shoe. For the first time, I realized just how dusty his clothes and shoes were. He was usually so immaculate.

"I had hoped for something more, Ava," he said. "But I understand. I do."

He gave me a wan smile that suggested he really didn't understand, but I'd done my best. A day more and it wouldn't matter. I'd be home, and he'd think I'd gone to the harem and then been lost to the king's magic. Maybe I could confess that Blade had chosen to take my place.

Part of me already felt nostalgic about leaving him behind. Even if it was he who had dragged me here by threatening Kit, I understood why he'd had to do it. I knew he'd tried to back that mistake out, and if I could forgive myself, then I could forgive him.

With a tap of his fingers on the table, he pushed back his chair and stood. Neither of us had taken a scrap of toast or egg or even dipped into the custard, and yet his motion signaled time for breakfasting was over.

"I had hoped for a reason to spare you this, Ava," he said. "But you leave me no choice." He sighed heavily. "It's time to meet my father and hear what he has learned."

Chapter 10

The foreboding in Stone's voice echoed in my mind as I dressed and then trekked my way to Terran's chambers. Along the way, we met not a single maid, servant, or guard, and I was beginning to believe something was off in the organization until we stood in front of the ornate doors that led to Terran's antechamber and suites.

There, all assembled and looking distinctly bristly were all the guards I'd expected to see throughout the manse. I counted six burly-looking Fae with boiled leathers and blacksteel swords at their sides.

"What's going on?" I asked, turning to Stone.

His mouth was nothing but a white line. All blood had seemed to abandon them. With dread climbing my spine like a spider, I waited until he opened the door.

Inside, the chambers smelled of fresh ale and wood smoke. The fireplace roared with purple flames, chewing on oak logs.

The faint scent of cat piss wafted on the air as the oak burned with wet bubbles sizzling from the ends.

The chairs were empty. Blade was not here yet, and I wasn't sure if I was relieved or worried. I wandered the room, the sensation of Stone's eyes on my back like a cigarette burn between my shoulders. By the time I neared the broad sideboard where someone had lain out trays of cheese and savory bread, he had come up next to me.

"Father likes a bit of ale in the morning," he said, hoisting a tankard to where a small oak cask lay on its side with the spigot hanging over the edge. "It's not like your earthen beer, but still can pack a punch if you're not used to it. I'd suggest the mead for you. It's lighter on the alcohol scale and tastes delightful with bread and cheese." He smiled fully and genuinely, and I nodded wordlessly.

He shoved the tankard beneath the spigot of the cask and as the golden liquid streamed out, I watched the way his features shifted. Pensive. Focused. He was definitely preoccupied.

When he passed the mug to me, I accepted it with a smile that he returned, but it was almost automatic and not truly genuine.

I imagined he wasn't looking forward to the meeting with his father. He hadn't spoken the entire way to the suite, and so he could be forgiven for the tension in his shoulders and the way he responded to me without true warmth. Whatever news Terran had to deliver, I had a feeling it was bad.

"Do you think it's OK if I take a piece of bread and cheese?" I asked, more to get him talking than because I thought I needed permission.

That seemed to free him from his stupor. He gestured toward a beautifully carved plate of beechwood.

"Please do, Ava. The bread is the same as what I brought to your rooms." He scooped a bit of cheese with a knife onto the plate and held it while I sliced a chunk of bread.

It gave me something to do and I certainly couldn't refuse after I'd asked, but I was getting uncomfortable having just the two of us in the room after the awkward conversation. I kept looking over my shoulder to see if Terran had entered.

Balancing the plate in one hand and the tankard in the other, I stepped out of his way as he poured another mug, this one filled with ale. It smelled divine, I had to admit. Not yeasty or heavy with hops. Just a bright, almost lemony scent. It was quite pleasant and so enticing that I found myself standing on tiptoe, trying to see into Stone's tankard.

"Maybe I should have tried the ale," I said.

He pulled his mug away. "Trust me," he said. "The mead is a better choice for you."

I set my tankard down on the serving table. "No, I think the ale is probably exactly what I need."

He stepped between me and the table, and I eyeballed him until he picked up my tankard and passed it to me without a word.

I accepted it with reluctance. "I'm guessing this is your way of explaining that Terran doesn't like to share."

He shrugged. "You could think that, but it's not quite accurate. I just think the mead is better in your case." He lifted his tankard to his mouth and watched me over the rim.

I didn't see him swallow, but when he pulled away, a bright froth lined his upper lip. He swiped at it with his sleeve. "Too strong for a mortal," he said, and that lemon scent whispered along the air currents, teasing my palette.

My mouth twitched at his words. I might have felt offended that he considered me a lightweight when I'd probably consumed or ingested or shot up more substances than he'd ever thought of doing, but admitting to that would just make me look like the addict I was and I'd rather he not know that of me.

Besides, I'd learned things in the Fae realm could never be counted on to be what they seemed, so I didn't question his comment. And I didn't ask again for a mug of ale.

Instead, I meandered through the room with my plate in hand, refusing to drink the mead now that I'd been presumed to be more suited to what seemed equated to a child's drink.

Just as I'd settled into an overstuffed chair by the fireplace, the hackles on the back of my neck raised and the smell of ozone wafted over the room. I heard Stone scuffle to attention as he swung to face the wall, where I knew Terran would enter.

I looked over my shoulder to see the big bad boss shoulder his way through the door that seamed open, making a grand entrance in a massive bear skin cloak even though it already had to be eighty degrees in the room.

He looked pallid. Circles rimmed his eyes in purple bruises. He walked slower, as if he had to watch his footing. It was so unusual after the strong-arm images I'd seen of him so far, that I stood, laying my plate down on the seat of the chair.

"Stone," he said with an acknowledging nod, and while he looked fatigued, his voice was still strong. "I see you arranged for me to break my fast here instead of the dining hall."

Stone all but bowed as he said, "Indeed, father. I know it was a long night."

Terran huffed out a sigh. "The damn bells rattled my bones long before dawn." He swiveled his gaze to me and scanned me with an expert, if tired looking eye. "I see you brought the assassin. Well done. Saves me sending the guards for her."

I got the sense that he didn't want the guards moved from their spot, and that Stone had the foresight to know that pleased him. Even so, I said nothing, choosing to remain quiet. Gather mode, Gideon used to call it. Shut your mouth. Let the others talk. Find out what you could. Use it against them when the time came.

As Stone edged toward the stack of plates, undoubtedly to pile some sustenance onto one for his father, Terran held up his hand.

"Not till the boy gets here," he said.

Stone inclined his head in a subtle movement. "Of course." His hand retreated to his own plate, where he plucked a piece of bread from the hard crust on its surface. He popped it into his mouth and I thought made a great show of chewing, his eyes on his father the whole time.

Terran turned to me. "I see they've fed you."

Fed me. As though I were a dog or a pet of some sort. I didn't mind. Let him think what he wanted. I had nothing to prove. Not anymore. And since the comment didn't warrant much of a reply, and he didn't seem to need one, he turned from me immediately to Stone again.

"You seem rested," he said. "Did your marrow not hear the resonance of the bells?"

Stone's features stayed schooled into neutrality. "Neither did they the last time," he said. "I fear it's only you who feels them before they ring."

"More's the pity," he said. "One last gift from the king to remind me I am not wholly my own fae."

Interesting, I thought, but I remained just as silent as before. If I was not supposed to hear the comment, I didn't want to show that I had. Terran didn't seem to mind, however. He shot me a look, one of challenge, I thought. Ask me, those eyes said, but I was saved from doing so as the door to the suites opened.

I knew it was Blade before I saw him. Something in my stomach just...pulled toward the door. And there he was.

He filled it as if it had been made to fit just him. My eyes couldn't roam his face enough, couldn't drink in the sight of him fast enough to stave off the longing that pitched itself in my belly like a homeless wanderer tossing a tarp over a branch of wilderness before a rain.

"Blade," Terran said and in his voice, I heard both irritation and disdain. "What are you doing here?"

Blade took his time approaching his father, stopping on his way by at the buffet and picking a piece of cheese from the boards. He stuffed it into his mouth and ran his gaze over me, those eyes suggesting that whatever occupied his mouth, it was not what he had in mind. I tried my hardest not to heat up all over, but failed. I ended up perching on the chair, just so no one would realize my knees had gone weak.

Blade did, though. His grin was proof of that. One languid glance at my throat before he turned to his father again. "While the dark enforcer isn't welcome with your contingent at the gala, I think it prudent he be informed in case something goes awry, don't you?"

"This isn't about strategy, Blade," Terran said, his fists clenched around the collar of his bear skin cloak. "It's about making sure our assassin understands what is at stake."

I was about to protest, but Blade spoke up too fast for me to consider which words would be the best.

"I'm sure the assassin knows," he said.

Terran's gaze swiveled to me. "Does she?" he asked in a musing tone that was an accusation of blame and one he seemed to think I, as the human, bore all the responsibility for. "And just who told you the objects would be useless beyond the veil?"

It took several seconds to sort out the tone from the words, and when I did, I almost spilled my tankard of mead at the meaning. I clenched the mug to my chest with both hands as I turned to look at Blade. "The objects are useless in the harem?"

He gave nothing away in his expression, but I knew by the way he held my eyes that it was true. I pivoted sharply back to Terran. "How long have you known this?"

Terran gathered the cloak tighter. "Since last eve," he said. "Not that it matters to you."

"But it does matter to me," I said, realizing even as the comprehension stole over me, all the true consequences. "It means I'll be expected to assassinate him without the aid of magic."

He shrugged. "You're no further behind than you were when you took the job," he said. "When you agreed, you had no magic to hand. And to be honest, I hadn't held out hope that the cursed objects from Lilah's would be of much use." His shoulders moved restlessly beneath the cloak.

"So that's why you gave in and agreed to let me have access to them."

I thought about the short argument we'd had about having all the means to complete the task available to me, and he'd relented without much struggle. He'd also made sure I wouldn't get my hands on them until I was well on my way to the harem, even if he'd let Stone verse me in their magics. And he drove that point home now with a grin that was nothing more than a sly, subtle movement of his lips.

"Those cursed objects were paid for by the Shadow Court, and they shall remain here until we have the right use for them. It's unfortunate they will be no use to you, but it just hammers home that my original plan to use a mortal assassin was the best choice."

I tried to tell myself it wouldn't matter because Blade had already inferred he was sending me home to meet Kit. Whatever demon took my place might not even travel to the harem by the time Blade removed the king and kept me out of danger. But something niggled at the back of my mind, keeping me from remaining silent.

"I understood it was because you didn't want to risk Fae blood to the king's magic," I said in a derisive voice that had him narrowing his gaze at me. Didn't matter. I wouldn't be here long anyway, so I faced him without fear, but schooled my features into a mask of careful neutrality. Just in case. "Pinning your hopes on a mortal's chance for success never seemed all that strategic to me."

His eyebrow raised along with one finger. "You forget Ferranus will be drained by the time he goes to the harem. As weak as a kitten, needing lots of iron-rich blood to restore his powers."

Right. The blood gifts of all the mortal men and women he had been storing up for the purpose. I hadn't forgotten that. It was the reason I'd visited Kit the night before with the ferryman coin clutched in my pocket. I planned to send her home out of harm's way.

"Even a kitten has claws," I said, not sure why I was pressing the point except that my instincts urged me on. "And in a cage with a bird, it doesn't take a rocket scientist to figure out which will be supper and who will sup."

His throat flushed, and the red rode his skin all the way to his face as his gaze sharpened to barbs.

"I weary of you arguing a point you've already lost with me. If we weren't so close to deliver, I'd have my dark enforcer remind you again what's at stake."

From the corner of my eye, I saw Blade's fists clench. I was sure he emitted a low growl, one that even Terran heard but seemed to misinterpret as a response to my insolence.

"Stand down, Blade," he said, putting a finger to his forehead in the way a pained man might rub an ache from his brow.

My jaw slid to the side as I did my best to bite down on the hateful words that wanted to throw themselves at him. I held my breath. Counted to ten. When he was sure I would hold my tongue, he heaved an irritated, but resigned, sigh.

There was a single stroke across his forehead, leaving a trail of white skin that suggested a great deal of pressure in the movement. It took a long time to wash back into the normal pallor of his skin, and in that time, his head bowed ever so slightly. After a moment, he raised his gaze to scan the assembly before him. And in that instant, all weariness left his face.

"You think I've lived in the shadows of the Iron Court all these centuries and have somehow remained ignorant of our Iron King's ways." He snorted. "While you all offer plan A or B or C all trying to mitigate risk and work around the problem, you forget I *know* Ferranus. I was his bodyguard for three centuries, before he sat the throne, a half century before he took a consort. I know him. I know how he thinks.

"And last night that understanding of our king's nature proved what I've known all along. That he will not take chances with magic if it means his throne or his life. Anything with even a sniff of power, Fae or otherwise, will be siphoned off to the veil and transferred to him, the most powerful Fae in direct line for the throne. He is not so naive to think himself invulnerable to attack. That veil and the harem behind it is foolproof."

"So then we attack prior to his retreat to the harem." Blade's voice. Sure. Decided. Enough so that it drew Terran's gaze.

"Even you, my blade, even you cannot withstand the whole of the king's guard."

I doubted that assessment was accurate after witnessing Blade in action in the catacombs. The memory still sent shivers over my skin, but I said nothing. Be still and know, the bible says, and hunters knew the truth of that adage well enough.

"Full guard, half guard, one guard," Blade quipped in an offhand way. "I'm not afraid."

Terran leaned forward, the cloak spreading out around him like wings. "You might be my dark enforcer, but you will not question me again without reprisal." He glared into Blade's face with such intensity, I grew uncomfortable. Had I been beneath that scrutiny, I wasn't sure I could hold my water. And yet, Blade's demeanor did not shift. He looked just as fierce and sure as he had in the moment before the rebuke.

Terran watched him, seeming to demand his son to relent, while at the same time expecting the opposite. I imagined both brothers had been beneath that gaze plenty enough times to know the drill, but I doubted a hundred times would be enough to quell anxiety.

When not a single muscle in Blade's face obliged, a smoky grin played at the edge of Terran's tired looking mouth.

"I appreciate your loyalty to the oath," he said. "But my spies tell me Ferranus has hired two mercenaries to ensure he enters the veil unharmed. He takes no chances, our king, when his life is at stake. Those mercenaries will not be easily seen or heard."

Stone shifted from one foot to the other. "Do we know who they are? Perhaps we can buy them."

Terran adjusted the weight of the cloak. I was sure the glass eyes of the bear's face gleamed a bit too lively.

"We haven't been able to find that out. Only that there are two and that Ferranus has promised them their heart's desire to ensure he enters unharmed. The mystery of their identities is what makes it too dangerous to attack this side of the veil. It could be anyone. A shape shifter who can drape itself over his shoulders in the robe of flesh, become the eye of Morgana at his throat, a nipple in the belt of suckling teats. Goddess help us, they could be a child at his feet or the current of air that opens the gate." He sighed theatrically. "We've done our best to learn their identities and the best we could uncover was that one of them might be Ruby of the Nocturne."

"Fuck," Stone said, earning a nod from Terran.

"Indeed."

I couldn't hold my tongue. "Ruby?" I asked. "A pretty sounding name for a mercenary you all seem to be scared of."

A soft growl moved through Blade's throat, as though he wasn't pleased to have me think he was scared of this mercenary. Stone's eyes met his for an instant, and even though he addressed the answer to me, I knew something passed between them.

"Ruby Morvannon took the name generations ago when the Fae children of the lighted realms started complaining about seeing rubies in the darkness. It took the deaths of hundreds of Fae to realize the rubies were eyes watching through the shadows. She came out two hundred years ago, when she was banned from the Stygian Darkness. She's a shadow Sidhe. Ruthless and rogue."

"Sounds like you should have hired her instead of a mortal," I quipped.

Another growl from Blade, drawing my eye to him, and while the dark enforcer hadn't given away anything in his demeanor, I knew by the way he'd let Stone do the explaining that the information bothered him. Whoever this Ruby was, he was not pleased.

It was Terran who explained why they'd not hired the mercenary. "Ruby of the Nocturne asks too high a price." His eye swiveled to the door of his suites, and his expression glassed over. "What she might ask of me and be refused she will ask of Ferranus and be awarded."

Interesting. So there was a price Terran wouldn't pay. I wondered what that might be and hoped he'd offer more, but he stood from his seat and started pacing, gathering the cloak ever tighter around his shoulders.

"I will not be indebted to that bitch for anything."

In a few paces he went from the fireplace to the bookshelf and to the buffet sideboard until he finally halted and dropped his gaze to the tankard that was now clutched so tightly in my grip that I knew my knuckles had gone white. Something about his words made my skin crawl with dread.

"Gods, but I'm thirsty," he said, oblivious to the way my heart had started pounding and my hands began to tremble hard enough that I had to sit on them to keep from showing it.

While I struggled to remain collected at his words, he lifted his eyes to peer about the room. "Blast it, where is the boy? I've already waited too long to break my fast."

Stone moved so gracefully at the words that he could have been a pool of mercury leaking downhill. "Here, father, have mine. I'll get another."

He held his tankard out to his father with a neutral expression and, for a moment, I forgot that Terran was in the habit of only eating and drinking after his taster did. Everything normal here, apparently. No reason for the muscles in my spine to suddenly clench around the vertebrae. To keep from losing my cool, I sipped from my own tankard to give myself a chance to think, watching as Terran hesitated but finally accepted the mug from Stone. He sighed, probably irritated with the taster but too thirsty apparently to wait any longer.

He drank deeply as he fell into the largest chair in the room, the one nearest the fire. I supposed if it was safe enough for his son to drink, it was so for him.

"Ah, gods, that's perfect," he said before placing it beside him on a table that appeared as though it existed solely for the moment he wanted to put that tankard down. "I needed that." He crossed one knee over the other as he clutched the cloak tighter and leaned back to survey the whole of the room

"Now," he said, swiveling to look at me, his eyes looking brighter and less rheumy than a moment earlier. "Where were we? Oh, yes. Alerting you to the fact that stepping beyond the veil for any Fae would be a death sentence."

Chapter 11

The meeting went on for another hour, and by the time Terran sent us away, I felt like he'd seared a brand into my soul. Words spoken, details given, but nothing seemed to sink in past those last words, and whatever happened between those moments, I understood the true stakes, and the time I'd snarled my way out of the room, I couldn't say. I was blinded by anger. My lips felt too tight. The skin around my eyes bore grooves that prickled the skin of my scalp.

Stone stayed behind at Terran's request, and I had no idea what the reason was. It was lost on me in the cloud of emotion that swarmed my mind like a chattering plague of locusts.

All I knew was Blade was told to escort me back to my suite, to make sure I dressed appropriately, packed my trousseau, and sat like a petulant student as I was schooled on the basics of meeting a king.

The adrenaline moved fast and furious through my body, dumping too much energy all at once into my thighs. I threaded my way through the manse with the determination of a hunter who knew a vampire was within reach and needed neutralizing.

Blade dogged along behind me very much the way he had the night I'd met him at Lilah's. Patiently tracking my movements without a sound, letting me have my rein the way he would a horse stabled too long. Maybe he was the hunter, and I was the prey who needed neutralizing. I certainly felt like it.

It might have been creepy, except I was so damned mad at him. I was angry at all of them. The whole damn situation. And somewhere inside, I knew that anger came from fear. Because even without being told, I understood what was going to happen once Blade sent me home.

I knew it and I couldn't do a thing about it. Powerless once more.

He let me get to the wing where my suites were before he spoke from behind me, and the softness in his voice when he said my name made me pivot sharply on my heel to face him.

"Ava."

I whirled on him, storming into his path like a storm cloud.

"You knew," I said in a voice almost too soft to be considered angry, and I knew the moment I heard it, that it wasn't anger I felt at all. It was grief and betrayal. "You knew before you told me about the coins what was going to happen if you used them and took my place."

He tried to reach for me, but I swatted his hand away. Tremors started to move through my core, such an unfamiliar sensation under the circumstances that I shook my head, denying it was even happening.

"Death," I said. "Those were your father's last words. A death sentence for a Fae beyond the veil."

My voice didn't sound like my own.

This time when he reached for me, he took my elbow, fighting me to grapple for it, wrangling me like an alligator trying to hold on to a thrashing, terrified dinner, and when he wrestled me into submission, his touch was not unkind. But it was definitely controlling and firm.

"Be still, Alathir," he said in a warning tone.

"Don't fucking call me that," I said, more upset at the catch in my voice that told me I was dangerously close to crying, and I did not cry. I hated weeping women. I would not be one. I sucked in a breath and lifted my chin, aware the whole time that it was trembling. I almost dared him to see it, too. "Not now. Not right now."

"Ava, then," he said and waited to see my reaction to my name instead of the term of endearment. When I gave none, he tried again.

"Ava."

This time more forceful, not a hint of pleading within his eyes as they searched mine. He was all master and commander in that instant, and I stood beneath that penetrating look with all the bravery I might show a rabid vamp because I knew if I didn't muster that kind of determination, he might tug me ever so gently into his arms and I wasn't sure what I would do then. I was afraid I'd melt into his chest and act like a foolish woman.

So I did what I always did. I revolted, pulling away, pushing away, finding myself alone in a spot in the hallway devoid of art or statues or even torchlight. Alone in the darkness because

I was afraid of the light and what it might show. One small word slipped free of me. "Don't."

Don't hurt me. Don't turn away. Don't come near. Don't make me face the next moment, because while I could face a rabid vamp, I could not face the world without him.

His arms dropped to his sides with the heavy, resigned sigh of a man who had worked too hard to give in. With a glance, he took in the entirety of the hall and the staircase that stood as the apex of the wing, leading to Mica's suites, to Terran's, to my own. Then he scoured the hall in the other direction and motioned for me to come out from the shadows.

"Come with me," he said. "Don't make me force you, Ava."

Part of me wanted to be forced. I wanted to fight him. I wanted a reason to strike back. But I nodded mutely and crept out from behind the invisible line I'd drawn. Anger and fear made my joints feel like rusted hinges, but I went. He reached back for me silently, letting his hand hang in the air. Wordless, I slid my palm over his, let his fingers knot into mine and close up over my hand so that his swallowed mine whole.

Then, for one second, the grip on my hand loosened. Giving me the chance to let go again if I needed to. But I needed the contact. I felt more grounded. I lost the urge to retreat back into the corner. The trembling eased.

A breath hitched in my throat mid inhale and I released it before taking the steps that would draw me closer to him. No smile, no frown, no expression at all gave him away. He schooled his features to remain neutral, a giant to a tiny bird in need of cradling.

By the time I edged closer, he tightened his grip again, and I remained docile but silent as he led me down the stairs, and through a darkened hallway where sconces of purple magic revealed stonework walls and massive paintings. The light flickered over a life-sized statue of a bearded man pointing upward to a massive stone that was unattached from anything, held aloft by what had to be magic.

Merlin, no doubt, in the midst of building Stonehenge. His eyes mocked me as they watched our progress down the hall to a set of double doors. I recognized the surroundings immediately. The smells of ancient earth, the sound of condensation trickling down stone.

"We're in the dungeons," I said, and my voice carried for several feet before dissipating into the shadows. The last time I'd been here, Jasmine had been murdered. I'd sat in squalor for days. He'd both given me pain and taken it.

His smile was slow and bitter, even if the words that slid from him weren't. "The dark enforcer is not given luxurious suites in the clouds like the rest of the family. My rooms are not so genteel as yours."

"Your own father forces you to stay here?" I thought of his apartments in the earthen realm. They were luxurious and filled with texture. I suddenly understood why he preferred not to be in Fae.

"I am a creature of darkness," he said. "You know that better than anyone. But are you comfortable here, Ava?"

He didn't say anything more. He was testing me, challenging my resolve. Why else would he bring me here, to this place of horrors? Somewhere the City of Dead lurked in the shadows of magic, waiting to be fed pain and suffering as part of its bargain with the Shadow Court.

I swallowed, but the water in my mouth would not go down.

"Why did you bring me here?"

His face was still back lit, nothing but shadow as he watched me. "I'm not going to hurt you, if that's what you think," he said, and his voice was hoarse and raspy with the cloak of our history in the cellar. His outline was more wolfish in the shadows than man. My breath caught.

"What is this about then?"

He slid his hand up my back to rest between my shoulder blades. "It's about being able to speak without fear of being overheard."

"You hurt me in this place," I said.

"I took the pain," he said. "I healed the wounds as they fell." He shrugged. "It was the best I could do."

His voice was so pained, so earnest that the emotion in it made me sag against the wall, pressing my back into the plaster, my legs no longer able to hold me up as I considered the question.

His body followed mine, molding against me, forcing me to either strain backward into solid wall or forward into solid muscle. He thumbed my cheek, rubbing the liquid he gathered against his index finger.

"Tears, Ponytail?" he asked in a musing voice. "Why?"

My hands burrowed up between us and I tried to shove him away. "I'm not crying."

"You are." He grabbed my wrists and held them in the space between us, small as it might be. He nudged his knee between my legs and I parted for him, letting him close the gap. "Why?" he murmured.

All I could do in reply was bury my forehead into his chest.

There was a long moment when his hand went to the back of my head and cradled it as I fought for control. I clenched my fists against his chest and hammered at it along with the heart that raced beneath my cheek. I was trembling so violently it was making him shake, and at first, I thought he might be laughing beneath his breath.

Right up until the instant he spoke, and I heard the catch in his voice, the emotion strangling the words as they fought their way free.

"Will you come with me?" he asked as his hand slid down my back to warm the hollow above my sacrum. His expression was neutral, but his gaze was so much more earnest than I could have expected. Seeing it nearly melted me. "Will you come inside my rooms? I promise you'll be safe there. Safer than in the realm of kings."

My answer was to spin around and face the door. I took a step and found my legs were like rubber. His palm remained where it was, soothing the ache in the small of my back, both supporting me and giving me free rein to move on my own power. Like a warrior. A fighter. Not the damsel I felt like in that moment.

The sight of the door to his rooms was the only thing that put steel in my step. I needed to get inside. I needed to sit down. To find a way to breathe again because I was going to lose my shit if I didn't find a way to expel the energy razoring over my nerves.

The first thing that struck me as the doors swung open was the heady fragrance of cinnamon that wafted over me in waves that caressed my skin like warm breath. A fire roared to life at our entrance as if bid to do so by an ignition. A large sofa sat in front of it, book ended by two massive and ornately carved tables of ebony wood. The wood of the walls looked scorched beneath several five-foot high paintings of Dante's inferno.

Blade's room. I wondered how many had seen it this way, seen him in his own space. It reminded me nothing of the apartment in the earthen realm, and yet it was very much Blade.

I pivoted, then, facing him, sensing the danger in the air currents, in his eyes as they searched mine. He was afraid, I realized. Not the kind of terror of dying or being harmed, but fear of facing a truth he knew would put him on the defensive. It was a startling realization to think I had more power than the dark enforcer right then.

"You're angry at me," he said as he closed the door behind him.

The knots of muscles in his shoulder looked hard and unyielding. Every inch of his features was the same.

Fury rose inside to prickle my skin like fire ants. Before I realized what I was going to do, I'd launched myself at him, striking him with a closed fist in the stomach. His jaw was far too hard, and I wasn't interested in breaking a knuckle.

And yet his stomach didn't feel much softer. I yanked my hand back, cradling it against my chest. "Bastard," I said and glared at him.

One eyebrow quirked upward. "A sucker punch like that makes you the bastard, not me," he said, running a palm over his belly.

I doubted I'd hurt him one bit, and that made me angrier. I crossed my arms beneath my breasts as I faced him. "You knew. "

"Of course I knew," he said. "I knew everything, as does Stone, and you aren't angry with him."

"Stone didn't offer to exchange my place for his." I was horrified to hear that the words sobbed out of me, and I had to turn away so I could gather myself without him seeing the blur of tears pooling in my eyes and threatening to spill. I did not want him to see me looking weak.

"You're crying," he said in a voice hushed with surprise.

My voice rose in a screech that hurt my ears. "I'm not crying."

Blade closed the distance between us once more. Long before I could take a breath or react to step away. He was so fast. I'd forgotten how fast. In an instant he had me cornered against the wall. He loomed over me, trying and failing to tilt my face up to his so he could force me to meet his eyes. Nothing doing. I wasn't ready for that. I shrugged away, and he gripped me again, this time tighter.

"Is that why you're angry, Ponytail?" he asked, his voice a rasp of emotion. "Because Stone didn't make that offer for you?"

"I'm mad because you made it, you idiot."

"That doesn't make any sense, Ava," he said. "You never wanted to be here, never wanted this burden. I'm taking it from you."

"Why?" I asked. It was one word, but it was all I could manage.

"Why am I sending you home and taking your place?" he answered as his long, powerful legs devoured the distance between us. "Why do you think I wouldn't?"

I backed away as he drew near, too overwhelmed to stay still. "Because you heard what your father said."

"Yes, well," he said in an annoyed tone. "I didn't expect my father to spill the beans about that particular problem, to be truthful. I thought perhaps he'd give you and Stone your last minute orders and be done with it." He huffed a sigh. "All he's done is make things more difficult for me, it seems and I don't understand why."

"You can't go, Blade," I said. "I won't let you." I shoved him away.

He chuckled softly to himself. "Oh, Ponytail. You're good, but you're not that good. And if you did try to stop me, you'd just end up fucking me and we both know it."

His mouth curved up on one end the way I loved the most. "You are a sucker for wrestling," he said, as if I didn't understand what he'd meant. "And while it would be an enjoyable diversion, it wouldn't work in the long run."

My fists clenched at my sides. "I won't use the coin," I said. "You can't force me."

He canted his head at me. Not confused, just...intrigued by the possibility that I wouldn't accept the gift he offered. "You will."

I shook my head. "Your powers will be siphoned by the king. I can't let that happen."

"The veil," he said, correcting me. "It's the veil that does the siphoning. But that's not the point. If a mortal doesn't need magic to kill the king, then surely a strong, magic-less Fae can do the job." His mouth turned hard. "And I'm very good at killing, magic or no."

I shook my head. My mouth felt too tight when I refused.

He canted his head at me. "Give me one good reason I shouldn't take your place."

My arms flapped at my sides. "Because you'll die, you ninny." My voice caught on the words.

"Oh, Ponytail," he said in a heated tone. "That's not something you have to worry about. I'm already dead."

Chapter 12

Blade was dead. The words didn't shock me, not when I'd hunted and given the true death to creatures of all sorts in my lifetime. I understood what he meant when he said it, and it might have distressed me, since anything dead that retained animation and sentience couldn't be more than a monster. Vampires, banshees, zombies, wights, all revenants of some sort. That a being might move and breathe and not be alive was no foreign concept to me.

And yet, I had the feeling he was speaking metaphorically, and that he would do that when there was so much at stake just made me angrier.

"You're being an ass," I said.

His grin matched the mischievous flash in his eyes. "You think I'm lying."

"I know you are."

"My mother was Aiofe. Queen of the Stygian Darkness." One statement said with a flat tone as though that could explain it all and he expected me to know the underbelly of meaning.

But it wasn't the statement as a whole that interested me. It was one word.

"Queen," I said, testing the word on my tongue. "As in some sort of Fae royalty?"

"Not some sort. She *was* royalty. But she wasn't Fae. At least, not wholly Fae. She was a hellhound who shifted to Fae form. Born Sidhe and baptized in the shadow of death the same as I was. We die during that baptism, and legend says we are immortal because we gave our lives to the darkness so it may live, and power our magic, our heartbeat, our breath."

I thought of his connection to the City of the Dead, a portal right here in Terran's cellars, and I understood how he was able to access that sort of power.

"And this is the same Stygian darkness Terran mentioned," I said. "Does he know you're a prince of that realm?"

One long, slow blink. "My mother had only one offspring, so yes. My father knows that truth all too well."

I gawked at him. "So you're her heir. You're...sweet baby Jesus, you could be a king."

The way he kept his expression carefully mastered told me I was right and yet he ran both hands over his hair, scrubbing at his scalp with his nails.

"It's hard to explain, but yes and no. I was a bastard, am a bastard, and even if Aiofe did her best to school me in matters of the court in the vain hope I would inherit her throne, I refused it."

I didn't have to ask why. I knew. It was the same reason he and Stone did most things here in the Shadow Court. That damned Blood Oath to Terran. And yet, the thought that he could be free of it, that he could rule in his own right. I couldn't understand it. He'd have taken that oath long after he would have been offered Aiofe's throne. He shouldn't be bound by it. That could only mean he didn't want to be king.

He dropped his head back, shaking it as he did so. "I have no wish to be a king, Ponytail. I'm not selfless enough, and even in a realm like the Stygian Darkness, the Sidhe expect a ruler to benefit them or that ruler will simply cease to rule."

"But Terran," I pressed. "Surely he'd use that power if he could. Surely he'd want a powerful ally in another court."

He shrugged. "Better to have a powerful minion than a powerful ally, I suppose. But in truth, I don't know why my father tolerated my mother or why he never tried to exploit her powers and influence. I always suspected he was afraid of her. She was terrifying enough. A hellhound shifter who ruled without a consort, and held the Darkness together for more than a thousand years."

"But she's gone," I said, thinking about the way he'd phrased the statement. "Without her, what has happened to the realm if she held it together?"

He waved the question away. "Best not to ask," he said.

This was more than I'd ever heard about his past or his mother and I was transfixed, but there was more at stake at the moment than a casual discussion of his past and a mother who had died long ago.

"And here you are, trying to convince me you are not at risk of dying behind the veil because you're already dead. How stupid do you think I am?"

He grinned sheepishly. "Not stupid, Ava, never that. Just...naive in the way of Fae."

"I'm not naive in the way of monsters, Blade. I might be a shit sister and a horrible daughter, but I'm very good at killing too."

"You don't understand this monster, Ava," he said. "I do. I have the means and the skills. You are finished here in Fae. I won't argue the point."

"And what about Phaedre?" I asked quietly, knowing it was the last chess piece I had to play.

His entire body went rigid. A muscle fluttered in his cheek, and I knew if it wasn't me standing in front of him using that name, I'd be dead already. That was when I knew just how big a secret Phaedre's existence was, and how much he cared for her.

When he spoke, it was in a voice I imagined only the dead by his hand would recognize, even if they would never hear it again. It was so full of threat and violence that I almost balked.

"What do you know about her?" he asked. "Speak plain. We are safe here from prying ears and eyes."

I tried not to react to the undertone of threat that I knew was probably automatic after so many centuries of keeping Phaedre's secret. Instead, I forced myself to step closer to him in a way that was soft and compliant, the way I would a cornered banshee or vampire, disarming them with confusion instead of bluster.

"She's half fae, half goblin," I said, watching his face for a reaction that I didn't get. "She's Ferranus's daughter, and he thinks she's dead."

His chest was heaving more and more with each word and by the time I finished the last sentence, I was frantically trying to convince myself that he was just afraid for her, that he wasn't fighting the urge to hurt me. Because he trusted me. I knew he did. I had his secrets, and he had mine and we were fine. We'd have to be because anything else was unacceptable.

"I know you care about her," I said as I dipped my chin toward where his hands were clenched at his sides, indicating the one nail that always had paint. "I know she's the one who paints your nails. That you have tea parties with her."

Those last words dragged a groan from him. "Once in a dozen years I give in," he said, running his hand over his hair, letting it spill over his ears. "And the one time I do, the hot chick I want to impress catches me sharing pretend crumpets."

His voice was tight and strangled, but at least he was joking. His shoulders released the knots bunching them up toward his ears. His shoulders sagged. A good sign he knew I was on his side before he tossed me a heartbreakingly boyish look.

Relief broke my lips into a smile. "Don't forget the dainty teacup and extended pinkie," I said, feeling the relief in the air currents brush over my skin and easing my breath.

His eyes rolled back. "Gods," he said. "Just what every alpha male wants his mate to see." His eyes flashed as he took me in.

"They do want that," I said in all seriousness. "I don't care what chick it is, she sees a hot alpha male sitting down to a child's tea table and that male is going to get laid. Hard."

His eyes flashed. "I will take you up on that, Ponytail," he said. "But now I need to know how you know all this from a few sneak peeks of a tea party."

"She came to see me in my room. She told me she made your corset."

"I don't wear a corset, Ponytail." His eyebrow climbed upward as he thumped his chest with his fist. "I wear a chest plate but not a corset. But you say she came to you? She told you all those things?" The look of amazement on his face was almost comical if the circumstances weren't so crucial.

I nodded, and he made a thoughtful sound in his throat. "She must trust you," he said with a smile. "No amount of coaxing would get her to show herself to anyone other than me or Mica. And she would never confess to being an Iron heir. She knows the risk all too well."

"So it's true, then," I said, noting his phrasing didn't exclude other heirs. "She's his child."

"She is. And like every one of his children, Ferranus wants her life and her magic."

"And you've been hiding her."

"Only since her mother died."

The note of grief in his voice explained where her mother was, and I didn't have the heart to ask how long that had been. "You mentioned she was an heir. Not *the* heir."

He sighed. "Ferranus has spent centuries rutting about and he has sired many children. High Fae to High Fae, it's not so easy to reproduce pure-blood immortals. We sacrifice progeny for longevity. But it's true that half-breeds abound because the lesser Fae and the other races have shorter lifespans. Magic, even the magic of living, needs its balance. Ferranus has done all he can to ensure he has no heir and the lesser Fae are fine with it so long as they get a chance at their power, even if it's once a century."

"But killing kids," I said in a breath.

"Not just killing, Ponytail," he said. "He... consumes his children. Most times, alive."

I gasped. "But that's...it's monstrous. Surely they would find it repulsive. Surely they would revolt if they knew."

His eyebrow climbed upward. "Indeed, Ponytail. Like I said before. We are not the Spring Court or the Summer Court. We are ruthless."

"So you reminded me before," I said, clenching my fists. I thought of Phaedre and those unnamed, faceless heirs in hiding and all the ones who'd gone before who had not survived the king's lineage and a fire burned in the back of my throat.

"And who fights for those poor children?" I asked without expecting an answer. "Who makes the king pay for them?"

He said nothing and I looked up at him, my eyes hard, my jaw tight. "I'll tell you who," I said and clenched my fists. "It's me."

He started to protest, as I knew he would. I slapped my hand down over his mouth.

"I go," I said. "Killing monsters is what I do. And as God is my witness, that monster king will not live to kill another child."

Chapter 13

I was aware of the risk of making such a vow in Fae, but I meant it. If I'd learned anything in my short life, it was that monsters never rehabilitated. Time was growing short.

"Stone will be looking for me," I said, making to turn around. The matter was settled as far as I was concerned. I'd return to my rooms and dress. I'd pack that damn trousseau and I'd lie in wait for the king and take him out without a second thought. This I could do. This I was good at.

I had my hand on the door handle when Blade spoke from so close behind me, I realized he'd followed me without me even hearing him.

"I can't let you go, Ava," he said. "I told you. I'm sending you home."

I spun on my heel to face him and fished the coin out of my pocket. It lay on my palm with a heavy weight as I held it out to him. "Is this how you thought to send me?" I asked. "Because it seems to be in my possession, not yours."

His eyes narrowed. "Where did you get that?"

I waved his question away by shoving it back in my pocket. "Doesn't matter."

"It does," he said. "Have you used it?"

"If I had, you'd be talking to a demon right now, wouldn't you?"

In a breath, he had me in his grip, burrowing into my pocket, his hands scrabbling inside, almost hurting me with the urgency of his fingers. At first, I fought him out of instinct but gave way just as quickly to yielding even as I cursed and demanded to know what the hell was going on.

The coin sat pinched in his fingers, with as little skin contact as he could manage, when he held it up to me.

"It's not a ferryman coin, Ponytail," he said. "It's the Obsidian Sorrow. It shows the possessor dreams of a past he or she cannot change. Usually some horror from the previous owner. As it passes hands, its power grows. If it is not passed along, the dreams intensify. No one knows if the images are real or remembered or imagined, just that they are more horrific as they go. Legend says if it returns to the one who originally minted it, it will turn all its remembered horrors on him or her."

My mouth felt dry. "Sweet Baby Jesus," I said. "I've been having nightmares. I thought maybe it was something Mica did to me with his magic."

He pocketed the coin, and I started for him. He held me off with a shake of his head. "Mine, now, Alathir," he said. "Whatever horrors you've lived, are mine now, whether they are yours or the past owners."

"Just throw it away," I said. "Or give it to someone."

He grinned. "You mean like an enemy? I like how you think, Ponytail. But it must be passed as in good faith. The new owner must take it of free will."

To think I'd nearly given it to Kit, thinking to send her home. I sighed my relief I'd been sidetracked. A near drowning seemed imminently better than what I might have inflicted upon her.

I was so lost in my thoughts that I didn't hear him speaking until he nudged me. I looked up at him, dazed, until he smiled and brought me back to the same plane.

"What are these nightmares you're having?"

I shook my head. "I wish I knew. But like most dreams, they slip away just as I try to grapple them into language."

"They'll go away now," he said and moved to me in a smooth motion as if his feet were on silent wheels. He embraced me, and the sense of safety in those arms made me close my eyes. I felt his finger beneath my chin, tilting my face upward. I knew he was going to kiss me. I wanted it. I wanted him. At the worst of times, I just wanted to sink into him and disappear.

But his kiss was swift and soft and without passion or heat. I opened my eyes to see he'd pulled away, that he held a coin in his other hand and was about to lay it against my mouth.

I had just enough time to turn away, effectively offering my throat to him instead of my lips, and the coin touched my pulse. I felt a tingle, heard voices, the beeping of car horns. I smelled exhaust and then...then it was gone.

"Dammit, Ava," he said. "We have run out of time. You need to leave."

"You bastard," I said, struggling in his grip as I realized he'd just tried to use the ferryman coin on me without my consent. I fought then, kicking him in the shins and stomping on his instep. It was surprise only and not any pain I caused that made him release me.

"Bastard," I said again, dancing away, out of reach. The coin was still in his hand and he was coming for me once more.

"Don't make me force you, Ava," he said in a low voice one might use for a child who was fighting a dose of horrible cough syrup. "Neither one of us will like that."

"Fuck you," I said, backing up. "I told you I am not taking the easy way out. I'm not leaving you to end up dead in a realm that will drain your magic."

"It hurts that you think so poorly of my abilities, Alathir."

"You'll get over it," I said, flashes of images of him tearing into throats and stomachs flickering through my mind at speeds too fast to grab hold of. "But at least you'll be alive."

That stopped him for a moment. He paused, mid-step, the hand with the coin falling to his side.

"I have no intention of being a martyr to a king," he said.

"I don't think it's a matter of intention," I said. "You heard your father. Ferranus will siphon your magic. Whatever you have, he'll take. I can't let that happen. I'm mortal. I'm a hunter. Killing monsters is what I do. Let me do it."

It took a moment, with him not moving, but I saw the pulse quicken at his throat and I knew he was considering what he wanted to say next. Measuring the words carefully, mastering his physical tells. It was probably more habit than mistrust that made him hesitate, so I waited, knowing eventually he would speak. Slowly, his posture softened and his words came out in measured breaths.

"What if I told you I don't need to go beyond the veil? That I'm already in the best position possible to ensure he dies."

"If that was the case, you'd have done it by now."

His hand seesawed up and down at his side. "Not entirely true. Without Ferranus, who will take the throne, Ava?"

I thought about that and the answer came suddenly and with a jolt. "Your father," I breathed. "That's what this is about. He's planning to step into the power vacuum and take the throne."

Blade's eyebrows lifted in unison, and I knew I was right. "I never thought that far," I said. "I guess it didn't matter to me before what happened here. I was just focused on Kit. But what of his heirs? There must be someone..."

I halted. One look at his face, and the misery etched there, reminded me that there was someone. But she was in no mental shape to take over an entire realm, no matter how sweet she was.

"Surely there's someone better," I said, side-stepping the issue of direct heirs. After all, all through history, new lineages took thrones and ruled. "A new dynasty, maybe."

"I've lived a long time, Ponytail. I've seen few fae with Ferranus's power."

I noted he didn't say there was no one, and I narrowed my gaze at him. I didn't have a pony in this race, really. There was only one thing that should matter to me.

"So what has changed?" I asked. "Why be willing to remove him now?"

His gaze softened as he looked at me. "If you have to ask that, Alathir, then I am going to have to question my prowess as a lover." He grinned, suggesting he wasn't about to do anything of the sort. "And I've not done that since I was a virgin."

I felt the heat rise in my face but held his gaze till he cleared his throat. "At any rate, I just need to be fast enough to make the blow before he steps into the veil."

"In front of the whole of court?" I said. "Where everyone can see and know you for an assassin." I shook my head. "That's ridiculous."

My mind ran to the details Terran had outlined while we'd been in his suites. That the moment after he'd transferred the last of his power to the final gilded token owner, a portal would open using the last residue of his magic. He wouldn't wait. All those blood gifts would step with him into the portal where his waiting harem resided. None of them, but he would come out alive. Some of those consorts had been living in the realm for decades.

"Those Fae who received the power might not care that he's dead, but all those lesser Fae who live in hope of another endowment a century from now will know it has come to an end. We have a saying in the earthen realm, spoken first by one of our presidents, that those who make peaceful revolution impossible will make violent revolution inevitable. They won't stand by and accept the murder of the one Fae who can give them what they want."

"There is no revolution without bloodshed, Ponytail," he said. "They'll get over it."

"You've forgotten about Phaedre," I said quietly.

"I never forget about Phaedre," he said.

"Someone needs to keep her safe."

"She is safe."

I shook my head. "No, she's not. Something happened when she was here. That's what I've been trying to make you understand. Someone knows she's here. Someone knows she's alive besides you and me."

"How do you know this?"

"She said as much. We were just chatting and she sort of froze the way someone does when they hear a noise in the dark. She said then that someone knew about her, that she couldn't stay a second longer. Then she disappeared."

His expression grew dark. "Explain," he said.

I detailed the conversation as best I could, noting everything that might be important, especially the fear on her face. And with every word, his features grew darker.

"You see?" I said. "I can't keep Phaedre safe, but you can. But I can get through the veil and I can make my move as soon as he's through with me. I won't hesitate. I promise you that."

He looked me over and I could see by the way the silver edged his irises that he didn't like the path his thoughts took him to.

"I can do this," I said, pressing on. "I have no intention of being a martyr either. Not now. Not when I have something to live for." I touched his cheek softly, the way I'd seen in movies, the way Claire might touch Jamie, and a tingle ran through my fingers.

I half expected him to soften and yield, but he gripped me by the elbows, hard. The force of it lifted me from my feet and for a moment, that old image of being hanged and kicking out tried to push in and make itself known.

But this was Blade. This was not a threat. This was safety and my body, my mind, my very marrow knew it. The memory, the hurt and pain and grief of it was gone, a feather's weight on the wind. And so I surrendered and found myself clutched against his chest, his face buried in my neck.

Arms, large and powerful, swept around me, holding me there. His heart hammered against mine until the rhythms synchronized.

"It's not easy for me to give you over to the king, Alathir," he murmured against my skin. "But you are a fighter. To rob you of that chance is to insinuate you are less than me, and you are not. You are my equal. My heart. The very spark that draws the eye of my magic."

He lifted his face from my neck and scanned my face, memorizing each feature as if he would never see them again. When he eased me to the floor, he cupped my face in his hands. "But mark me. If I have to come to you in the bowels of hell, I will do so though it burns the flesh from my bones and sears the magic from my blood. Know this. I won't let you die in there."

CHAPTER 14

Returning to my rooms was done in electric silence. Neither of us wanted the moment to arrive and yet it had, and both of us knew we had parts to play that might be bigger than the way we felt for each other. With hands clasped, we approached the door to my suites with the kind of determination that drives a diver to the top of a three-story ladder.

The kiss he stole from me left me breathless. The way he held my eyes as he pulled away, made me strangely sad and yet filled me with hope at the same time. He released me to open the door and then he waited. I stepped inside and closed the door, putting my back against it and dropping my head against the wood. I was sure he stood there for several moments the same as I was doing, because I could hear the brush of his palm over the wood, as though it was my skin beneath his touch. Long and slow and, in my mind, mournful.

A shuddering breath escaped me as my eyes eased closed. Savoring the sensation of his lips on mine for just a moment more before I pushed off the door to begin my preparations.

I showered first, but quickly.

Wrapped in a plush bath sheet, I lifted the top of the trunk that now sat hunched beside the armoire. Inside, several lacy, see-through garments peeked out from beneath a fur-lined cloak. I dug through to discover there wasn't much else inside besides that cloak and gauzy undergarments. But at the very bottom, bunched into a ball of material, I found the pouch of cursed objects and smiled to myself. Whoever had come in to deliver the trunk had known about the pouch. Probably Stone. He'd no doubt slipped in while I'd been in the shower and then let himself back out.

I straightened up, hands on hips, to survey the room. It looked much the same except for the trunk and three books that rested on the hearth. One of them was open, of course, showing a distinctly blue drawing.

Erachne's gown hung on a peg beside the armoire outside of its wrapping. It hung down the plaster in waves of fabric so beautiful my breath hitched. Not so long ago, I'd worn it in front of Blade. I'd known then that he wanted me but I'd put it down to the gown's magic. It hid so many of my flaws, and yet Erachne had said it would bring out the true me for the right mate.

I'd not thought much about it then, but I understood now that his reaction had been one of a mate to his lover. He'd loved my ponytail. He didn't need to see me trussed up like a gilded chocolate. But he didn't disapprove, either. How could he? The gown was gorgeous.

It didn't just hide my flaws, however. The material disguised other things as well. Boots, pants, weapons. Somehow, it was able to alter its size and shape to accommodate whatever lay beneath its material and still look as if I wore nothing beneath.

I dropped the towel to the floor with an eagerness I didn't expect. If I was going to assassinate a king, I'd need him to want me and only me by his side. I needed to look amazing. Pulling on the gown over my skin made me feel both warm and tingly. I couldn't help turning to my reflection and even in the cracked mirror, I looked stunning.

The blackness of my hair took on a sheen that erased the frizz of untended split ends. The arch of my eyebrows softened and the hard eleven lines between them smoothed out.

Instead of the multitude of gorgeous sandals I saw winking at me from the inside of the armoire, I chose to pull on my boots, trusting that the movement of the gown would sweep over and disguise them as well as my karambit.

I shoved them on one after the other and lifted the skirts to peer at myself in the mirror. I dropped the dress, and the boots disappeared beneath the luminous folds. I lifted them again, and they peeked out at me, all scuff and dirt and rubber soles.

A smile twitched my mouth. I moved into a runner's lunge, testing the drape and movement of the gown. The dress moved with me as though it was a second skin. Leaping up, I twisted as though I planned to throw a punch at someone behind me. The material didn't hinder me. I kicked. I spun. I whirled through a dozen fighting movements and fell into a dozen stances. The dress moved with me like a whisper of air and no more.

I planned to take down the king as soon as I could. Preferably within moments of entering the veil. I did not plan to stay longer than that. Get in. Get done. Get gone.

While it seemed Terran and Stone were preparing for a long haul by packing me a trunk with a trousseau, I wasn't in for a long haul.

If I could complete the mission right away, I would need to ditch the dress immediately. Without the corset to glamor me, the dress would be a dead giveaway to any of the king's guards. The last thing I wanted to have to do was rummage through a trunk for clothes.

It would be tricky enough to get back through a disintegrating veil without adding anything extra to the task list.

So I ran to put something underneath, pulling the skirts up as I darted to the armoire. My old yoga pants, tank, and boots sat in a pile on the bottom as though set out for me. A lacy pair of underwear was snuggled into the mouth of one boot. I rolled my eyes at the armoire's choices but pulled everything on beneath the gown, winding the leather straps of the karambit sheath back around my thigh once more.

I pulled the Velcro at both ends tight, tested the feel of it with a leg shake. A quick check in the mirror showed clean lines. Seamless. Invisible. The tank top blended in with my skin and the bodice so perfectly it looked as if I was indeed naked beneath the lightweight fabric.

I could have kissed Erachne in that moment. And when my hair just magically arranged itself into an extravagant up-do made of dozens of tiny braids with sprays of baby's breath and tiny fists of roses along one long curving line, I couldn't hold back the curse of awe.

In all, it had taken me no more than ten minutes to dress, but it looked like some hairstylist and makeup artist had worked on me for hours. I wasn't vain by any stretch, but even I could see just how good I looked. Fit for a king, I thought wryly.

By the time I had dropped the three books into the trunk and buried them beneath a couple of swaths of impossibly sheer material, someone rapped on the door to the suite. I might hope for a quick kill, but I was also pragmatic. And if Stone and Terran thought I needed that trunk, I planned to make it useful.

"Ava," Stone said from his side. "It's time."

I closed the trunk and crossed the room to open the door, and even though my heart belonged to Blade, my breath hitched at the sight of Stone standing there. Only a blind woman could have remained unmoved by the sight of him.

He'd donned a tuxedo so lushly black it seemed spun from shadow. Under different circumstances, my belly might have squirmed with desire.

"You look stunning, Ava," he said in a raspy voice that actually did send a tremor through my belly.

"It's magic," I said, feeling awkward. "Erachne is a sorcer-ess."

"It has nothing to do with her magic," he said, dipping his head as though he needed to hide his expression, but not before I caught sight of the lust in his eyes. "You are stunning in anything. But today, the light seems to hit you just right. You almost look Fae."

A statement he obviously thought was a compliment, so I decided to smile in thanks. He offered his elbow and I hesitated, my gaze trailing back toward the trunk.

"Someone will come for that," he said, waggling his arm. "They'll load it onto the back of the carriage for you. And once we arrive at the castle, someone will unload it and mark it for the harem."

"That easy, huh?" I said, and he grunted.

"Not quite so easy as you think. It has to get past the Fae sorceress and the wards. And then you must be presented and accepted." You'll find the gilded token with your things."

I nodded. There were only one hundred tokens, given by random draw to Fae all over the kingdom. As a human, I understood it was the backup plan to ensure my entry to the ball. I knew they were valuable enough that other Fae killed to acquire them. I suspected the Shadow Court had done most of the killing over the centuries, and I didn't want to think about the poor Fae who might have surrendered his to Stone so I could have it now.

Greater good and all.

With a bracing breath, I took his arm, feeling very much like an old world debutante as we strolled down the hall to the massive staircase. As we descended, a sense of eerie calm fell over me. This was it. This was the day I killed the king. Exhilaration fluttered through my chest, the kind I always got moments before I set out on a hunt. The nagging sense that I'd forgotten something chugging along the back wires of my mind to be picked at as I trod to the battleground. Inevitably I'd realized I'd done all the planning I could, packed all the weapons I'd need. It would come down to my skill in the end or a stroke of luck—good or bad—to decide my fate.

We reached the bottom of the stairwell and I caught sight of Kit's doppelganger arm in arm with Flint, who was equally dashing. It ate at me that he could look so magnificent when he was such a dark bastard.

I wondered if he'd realized it wasn't Kit yet or if the demon in her image had managed to do more than move its arms and legs and found the brain power to speak. I smiled secretly to myself as I imagined it turning on him in the carriage he led her to.

I was still happily lost in the fantasy of that when I realized we'd stopped in front of a carriage drawn by four massive midnight colored horses that would have put Nutkin to shame for their size. Each had a golden mane braided down their necks to drape like tassels of a fringe along powerful necks. Atop the carriage sat an equally massive Fae male dressed in what looked like nutmeg-colored buckskin. His hair was long and shaggy, but the eyes that looked down at me did so almost too familiarly. Despite his clothes—very unexpected for a carriage driver—and his hair, he was magnificent looking, with powerful thighs and broad hands.

"Ava," he said with an incline of his head.

I peered up with a narrowed, thoughtful gaze. That he knew my name was strange, but I didn't have time to give it more thought because someone else said my name, a voice I knew all too well, that sent a shiver down my spine in delicious ways.

Stone's response to Blade's voice was to pull me aside, blocking me from view.

"What are you doing here?" he asked.

"Does it matter, brother?" Blade said.

"It does. You're not supposed to be here."

At Stone's protest, Blade took his place next to the door of the carriage. "Don't worry, Stone," he said, his eyes landing on me with all the lust of a bee for a delicate rose stamped all over his face. "I'm not here to take her from you. I'm merely here to ride with her."

Stone went rigid. "I don't think that's a good idea."

Blade ignored him, reaching for me with one hand and damn if my stomach didn't do a somersault at the way he stood there with the door held open, one hand extended to me like an old world gentleman. He was dressed all in black, but not in a tux. More like the leathers of an assassin. All that was missing was the paraphernalia of an action movie actor.

The smolder in his gaze was enough to burn the dress right off me. The power in his shoulders showed itself as he shook them out to shrug the fabric into all the right places.

He was simply gorgeous.

"You can't do this," Stone said.

Blade tilted his head. "Oh, but I am," he told his brother. "Ride with Flint. I have some last minute details to deliver to our assassin," he said, and then, as if it were a mere add on, said, "Orders from the top. I'll be gone once we arrive, so you can take your place at her side then."

Stone harrumphed quietly but released my hand to Blade's arm. It took several moments of the two of them staring at each other before he stomped off toward Flint's carriage.

I watched him hoist himself inside without using the steps at the side and only when he'd disappeared into its belly did

Blade turn to me, offering me a glittering, heart-stopping smile.

"Your carriage awaits, Cinderella," he said.

I didn't trust my voice. Not with the way he stood there looking so magnificent. I just took his hand and let him guide me into the carriage as though I were a princess. I certainly felt like it, and though it was strange and awkward, the young girl in me who read dozens of fairytales and dreamed of being pretty was so secretly excited I felt my stomach trying in vain to capture the butterflies swarming within.

I climbed in and pulled the skirt awkwardly out from beneath my thighs. He slid in beside me, his gaze running over my throat and down to my cleavage, amply displayed in the tight fitting dress.

"I want to eat you right now," he said in a throaty voice. "I want to lay you out like a peach and bury my nose in your flesh."

The lust in his voice was a heady thing that bid me fan my chest with my hands. I managed to keep from doing that. Barely.

"You've seen me in the dress before," I said.

"I have. But you weren't mine then. I could only fantasize about peeling the material from your skin like the fuzz off a peach." He licked his lips and pushed closer. "Now that you are mine, I can't think of anything else."

It was impossible not to strain for him, to touch his hand. I was aware I was breathing too fast.

"This isn't the time," I said, touching my fingers to my hair.

His gaze followed the trail of my hand and soon, his fingers whispered along mine. The briefest of touches on the very surface of the braids, but one I felt down to my core. "Sweet Jesus," he said in a breath. "It's all I can do not to tear those flowers out of your hair and ram my fists in the tangles."

He inhaled deeply, running his nose along the column of my throat. I felt drunk on his breath. I swayed toward him on the seat.

"You have to stop this," I said. "I'll never make it there in one piece."

His response was to rap the ceiling of the carriage with the heel of his fist, but he did not move away. While the first hand was above his head, the other found its way around my waist.

The carriage jerked into motion and the clopping sound of hooves beat a rapid rhythm to go along with the rolling of the cabin. He kissed me then, long and leisurely, and if I felt drunk before, I was completely inebriated by the time he was done.

"That's no way to get me to keep my clothes on," I said against his mouth.

He eased away to sit like a proper gentleman on the other side of the coach. "I'm glad you're still wearing the necklace."

My fingers went automatically to the stone he'd buried Slavin's tooth in. "You can see it?"

He smiled. "I was testing you."

"Bastard," I said with a grin. "Of course, I'm wearing it. But I decided I didn't want anyone to know it was there except me. My secret."

"And mine," he said in a husky voice, then he sat for long moments in a silence that began to make me nervous.

"What is it?" I said, finally, unable to keep myself from asking any longer.

"I need your blood," he said.

"My blood?"

"Yes. And you need mine." He leaned forward, his gaze hard as flint. "We can't leave anything to chance, Ponytail. That token will be a beacon for any Fae who decides you're easy pickings. Stone is good but he's not me. If something goes wrong, I need to be able to track you."

Immediately, I began searching the cabin for something to prick my finger and remembered the karambit. If I was careful, I might be able to score a small hole in my finger without gashing my entire hand. I had a habit of keeping the thing so sharp the barest of pressures would slice open skin like hot metal on butter.

As I pulled it free of its sheath, he gently pushed my hand away. "Not that way, Ava," he said.

"I know what I'm doing."

"It's not that. It's...well, it's got to be more intimate. Remember how angry you were at me in my apartment when I forced you to cut me?"

My mouth twitched at the memory. I didn't need to answer because he knew I remembered it. "Tracking someone in the earthen realm is easy. Smell works much the same on me as it does for a bloodhound. I trailed you from the clothes you left at the witch's house. But tracking someone realm to realm gets trickier. Blood was necessary then. Your emotion gave it power to linger."

"So you want me to get pissed at you?" I leaned toward him too, letting my hands rest on his knees. "Or is it that you want something stronger?" I waggled my eyebrows suggestively.

He sighed. "I wish it could be like that," he said. "But the strongest power comes from death's blood."

CHAPTER 15

The mere title death's blood made me shiver. "You want to kill me to track me?" I asked, my voice filled with sarcasm. "Seems a bit much, doesn't it?"

"I only said death's blood was the most powerful, Ponytail," he drawled. "Obviously I'm not going to use your dying blood to track you." He looked out the window of the carriage and I enjoyed the view of his side profile for a moment before I realized what his answer meant.

"So," I said. "Fear then."

He nodded and turned back to me. "It's not going to be easy to scare you, Ponytail, since you know I wouldn't hurt you. So to do that, I can't be anywhere near you."

"I don't understand."

He picked at the seam flattened out against his knee. "Because if I'm here when it happens, I would likely murder the one who is helping me." He flashed me a grin that didn't quite meet his eyes, suggesting he was being truthful, and that he did not enjoy the decision he'd made. That alone made the hair on the back of my neck stand up.

The long look he gave me seemed as much for him as me. He wasn't certain about his decision, as far as I could see. I swallowed down a mouthful of anxiety.

"What are you planning?"

"Wait," he said, holding up one finger. "We need to be out of the city first."

One of my eyebrows lifted. I wanted more, but he was being stubbornly quiet. By the time the carriage began rolling and rocking in earnest as it beat a path that indicated it had left the cobblestones of the city behind and had set out on the rolling roads of the plains and woods between the town and the castle, I had begun to despair of just what he might do to instill fear in me.

"Well," I said, impatient.

He braced himself on the seat opposite me, and after a long, measured look, raised his fist over his head. The muscles in his shoulder and neck flexed as he rapped the ceiling three times in hard, quick succession.

As he did so, he said, "Get ready."

"Get ready? What the hell for?"

Reaching for the carriage handle, he took a moment to look at me over his shoulder. "Do you remember what I told you about Nutkin?"

My brow furrowed in bewilderment. "Nutkin?" I asked, desperately trying to puzzle out what he was going on about. "What does he have to do with anything?"

His gaze dropped to the floor of the carriage. Guilty? Ashamed? "He's not always in horse form, Ponytail. Sometimes he shifts into a man. A very large man." His boot nudged up against mine, parting my feet suggestively.

The horror of what he was inferring began to dawn on me as I recalled the conversation. "You said he enjoys taking mortal women," I said in a tight voice.

"I did," he said. "What I didn't tell you is that he hasn't had a mortal woman in a hundred years. He has not shifted into a man in all that time."

"You wouldn't."

"You see," he said, glancing up at me with a hard light in his eyes. "You're entirely right, and that's the problem. I wouldn't. But I have to, and so you understand why I can't be here then when he climbs down from the driver's seat."

My eyes widened painfully as he threw open the door as I tried to grapple with the thought that the man who loved me so fiercely, my mate if he was to be believed, was about to surrender me to another man. And not just surrender...but with the full expectation that said man planned to pillage me in the medieval sense of the word.

He had to be insane or joking. There was no way he would stand by and let that happen, and he had to know I understood that to my very core. There was no way he'd arrange for it, and even if he did, he had to know I'd not quail like a damsel, but would fight back.

If he thought the threat of that sort of violence would fill my blood with fear, he didn't know me well enough.

It wasn't going to happen. I knew it wasn't. And yet, as the carriage came to a sudden stop, Blade leaped from the coach, leaving me blinking in shocked befuddlement after him. The tails of his jacket flapped noisily at his back, catching the air currents with a snap. A thudding sound indicated he'd landed in the grass by the road.

And even as I told myself this was a ridiculous situation, that there was nothing to be afraid of, my mouth went dry. Whatever protest sang through my entire body, turned to adrenaline as I heard the soft muttering come from above. A roll of the carriage as a great weight moved and lifted off.

My whole body went electric with awareness. I peered out the open door. Boots dangled from above, toes pointed in. Blade was nowhere to be seen.

Well, fuck and damn and all the horrors I could inflict. He had actually planned this and was bootstrapping his damn ass out of the vicinity to facilitate the deed.

Bastard. He wasn't going to get fear blood, he was going to get straight-out rage blood.

My body came alive then. Adrenaline pumped through me in a sudden squeeze as I slid the karambit from its sheath long before those boots swung inside. A laugh bubbled through me, the effects of a good dumping of hormone combined with the days of inactivity and useless worry.

I made a swipe for the calf muscles as smoothly as sweeping my arm to pull for a seatbelt. Nutkin was far too quick for the maneuver, and I expected it even if I didn't expect him to kick downward. The result was a perfect presentation of my forearm to his booted heel. It connected with my forearm instead of the chin.

The strike hit a nerve that rang like a cracked bell down my arm to my fist.

The karambit fell from my grip. My arm dropped, paralyzed, to my side.

He swung into the cabin with such ease then, that I couldn't imagine him in any other form except man.

His leathers were faded and worn but supple looking, as though he'd crafted his garments from his own equine skin., and he moved in them the same way. A lush braid of thick chestnut hair was clubbed back in leather laces intertwined in the braid.

His familiar eyes flashed at me as I scrabbled to position myself to fight in the tight space or find a way to fling myself out the carriage door.

"I've been wanting to do this ever since you ground your sweet ass into my back," he said in a husky voice.

"Strange," I said, angling myself so I could get some thrust to the punch I planned to throw. "I wouldn't think a man would dream about taking an ass-kicking, but it takes all kinds, I suppose."

He canted his head at me. "But Blade told me you were mine for the taking. That he wouldn't interfere."

A dry laugh rasped through my throat. "If you think it's just Blade you have to worry about after the wendigos," I said. "Then you deserve to have your ball sack kicked out through your arse."

At that, I brought my knee up through the slit in the skirts so I could reverse donkey kick him in the groin. He moved the way Blade and Stone did. Fast. Adroitly. With a warrior's discipline. We skirmished for far too long after that. He was powerful, the way a race horse might be powerful, with muscles that obeyed his every movement no matter what tangle I put in his limbs as I grappled in and out of his reach.

At one point, I managed to yank my skirts free in a swish of material that allowed me to lunge for the karambit. It came to my grip like a magnet, snuggling into my fist like a lover.

"Enough talk," he said from behind me in a grunt that suggested I'd struck him hard enough to hurt him but not stop him. I was about to change that. I'd slice him taint to teeth and give it no more thought than if I was cutting through a piece of cheese.

And yet I hesitated. This was Nutkin. I'd fought alongside him. He'd trampled his share of the wendigos right along with Blade and I.

My instincts told me this wasn't going to happen, and so I paused. Like an untrained woman accustomed to feeling safe, the cardinal mistake that most women make, of trusting that primitive energy.

I didn't roll over in time. The moment I hesitated to bring the blade up, he came down on my back, dropping me to the seat with my chest pressed flat enough that I could barely take in a breath.

Whatever air was in my lungs wheezed out of me. He was as heavy as a horse. Dead weight of a horse, to be correct.

I couldn't breathe. There was no room between my boobs and the seat to raise my lungs. No air moved beneath my nose. Seconds would be all he needed to lift my skirts and yank down my pants. I had no air to fight him. My entire body began to sag into the seat. Heart pounding, wasting precious oxygen, I twisted my head, hoping to free my face, find some air for the moment he raised his hips to position me.

And yet...

He did nothing. Just lay atop me with all that weight pressing me deeper into the cushion. His arms splayed out at his sides, covering my shoulders. Legs that felt like logs of timber weighted down my thighs.

Moving beneath him was like trying to wriggle free from beneath a mountain.

That was when I realized he was dead.

Dead on top of me, pinning me to the seat in such a way that I'd smother or be pressed to death as surely as the witch in Salem begging for more weight. Blade gone. No telling when he'd be back.

My lungs already felt like they were on fire. Tears stung my eyes. I was alone here with no way to fight myself free. I might as well be buried alive.

At the thought, panic came like a lightning strike.

I couldn't scream, couldn't move, couldn't squeeze out a tear.

But I tried. I rocked and rolled and twisted and kicked out as though I were wrestling an alligator and its mouth was poised to close down on my belly. I flapped with my arms, trying desperately to find something in the coach to grab hold of, to leverage myself, and yank myself free. There was no dignity in the way I flailed about, and all I could think was that this was a hell of a way for a hunter to die.

Because I was dying.

CHAPTER 16

I fought to live for nothing. There was no escape, and all I was doing was wasting what little oxygen I had.

But I still fought. I wouldn't go down gently. I'd grab for the air, clasp whatever I could with my nails. I'd curse that last razoring pain of breathless exertion as the shadows took my vision.

And yet...just as darkness wavered over my vision, the butt of my hand struck something that yielded. Fabric, I thought, and flesh beneath that. I thought for a moment that it was such a shame to come so close to rescue only to be denied. I could already feel myself disengaging from my body. Bubbles like champagne burst behind my eyelids. They popped beneath my skin. I was going. It wasn't such a hard thing, dying. It didn't hurt, at least.

As if death had heard my thoughts, it struck back. Something hot and stinging sunk down into my wrist and I felt a suction that made me feel as though my entire soul was being drawn through a straw. Before I had time to process the sensation, Nutkin's weight just...disappeared. I barely felt hands cupping my head. Pressure exerted itself against my lips, but I couldn't feel what caused it. The swishing of a cloak or a curtain made a rustling sound against my ear. Words? I wasn't sure.

The pressure against my mouth finally passed through the numbness as air leaked into my lungs. A sigh, a curse, both of relief danced in the surrounding air.

"Take me," someone said. Blade, I thought. "Just a swallow. That's all you need."

Cinnamon, I thought. He was force-feeding me cinnamon drops that melted on my tongue and turned to honey as it slid down my throat.

I blinked. Lifted my head. Nutkin was on the floor. Blade hovered over me and when he saw my eyelids flutter, he scooped me into his arms.

"That's it, Ponytail," he said. "Breathe. You're alright. We're alright." His body shuddered against mine.

At first I melded my body to his, relief swimming through me. Then I remembered what he'd done to me. I yanked away, glaring up into his face, determined to growl at him.

But he looked stricken. His had a far-away, panicked look in them.

"You almost died," he said, gaze wide, face a sickly custard color.

"You were going to let him rape me," I muttered, still wanting to scold him, but the words were hollow, all the heart gone out of them at the way he held himself. Like a scared rabbit.

He shifted in the seat, glancing at Nutkin as he lay unconscious on the floor.

"I was never going to allow that, Ponytail," he said and raked his hand through his hair. It trembled, I noticed. "I thought you'd get one look at that massive horse cock of his and scream."

"Scream?" I echoed, the dullness in my voice a testament to how in shock I still was.

He nodded. "Yes. I've witnessed mortal women seeing it for the first time. It's pretty...impressive."

My mouth dropped open for a moment as the full effect of his words landed, then I waved away the image. "Please," I said. "I don't even want to know how you managed to be in the same place as Nutkin as he revealed his naked self to some poor wench." Feeling was starting to flood back through my limbs. I tried to scoot off his lap and out of his embrace, but he held me tighter.

I narrowed my eyes at him, wordlessly warning him.

"I can't let you go, Ava," he said. "My body won't let me. At least not until you understand."

"I understand."

"No, you don't." He ran the backs of his thumb over my cheek, and I steeled myself against his touch. I was mad at him. I had every reason to be.

"The veil needs powerful magic," he said.

"So, you told me."

"I did. I know. But you don't really understand. I knew you would realize I'd never hurt you. There was no way to get you to feel fear, not real fear. I wasn't even sure you would be afraid to die. You've faced death dozens of times." His eyes warmed as they regarded me, the wrinkles at the corners smoothing out. "I couldn't think of a proper way to scare you when you've already faced so much. You're a hellcat, Alathir. And they don't back down."

"So you decided to have someone rape me."

He groaned. "Not like that. You still don't get it. I was never going to let that happen. I thought I'd just wait until he showed himself to you and you would be afraid, and I'd swoop in to stop it all."

I blinked. "Like I'm sort of damsel in distress and you're the white knight?"

He had the grace to drop his gaze, ashamed. "Is it so bad to want to be the hero sometimes?"

My mouth twitched as I tried not to give in. "I'm trying not to scratch your eyes out right now."

His eyes closed, as if he thought I would actually do it. That softened me. I hated the way he'd got what he needed, but in the end, I did understand. But understanding didn't mean he was off the hook.

"I understand the need to be a hero," I said softly. "Hell, I've done some horrific things myself in the name of it. But this..."

He opened his eyes to catch mine and his gaze was fierce. "I nearly get you killed and you're mad at me for arranging a peep show?"

The look on his face could have fried an egg, it was so heated. "I'm no chivalrous knight to balk at taking a woman's virtue. I'm a monster, Ava. You knew that when you bedded me. I'd cross any line to keep you safe."

His speech left me wordless because I knew exactly what he'd do for me. I'd seen it in the catacombs. I'd lay under his determined care later when I'd had to struggle through withdrawal. In his monster's way, he loved me. He would do whatever he had to for me, and I knew it. I knew it because I knew the lengths people like us would go to in order to protect those we loved.

There was an almost shameful warmth that stole around my heart and belly, thinking that I was on the other side of that sort of commitment. I'd never been loved that way before. I didn't know what to say.

Instead, I nudged Nutkin with my boot as he lay in an awkward position between the seats. "Did you kill him?"

"I must confess. The hound in me wanted to," he said, puffing out his chest just a little. "But my Fae self remembered he's a friend. Once I got myself under control, I just choked him out a little with a touch of magic. He should be awake soon."

He looked down thoughtfully at Nutkin as he spoke, and almost as if the Fae heard him, he roused. He took his vengeance out verbally on Blade for several moments before Blade apologized with a half grin playing at the corner of his mouth. It took the comment that Blade had arranged for a real mortal woman to meet him at the gala. One accustomed to the vagaries of Fae males in all their forms.

That brought a spectral smile to Nutkin's face that I found a bit too creepy, so I was glad when he climbed back on to the driver's bench. Blade closed the door after him and sat with me, silent, the rest of the way. I didn't speak either. I spent what time I had fixing my hair and straightening the gown, that miraculously didn't tear or rip anywhere.

A heaviness cloistered the air in the coach the nearer we drew to the castle. I watched the trees and scenery through the small window as it blurred by in a cloud of dust and dying light until paths filtering in towards us broadened to roads. Sporadic groups of fae came in clusters and crowds then. All rode, walked, or flew in ever-growing knots of humming, buzzing, chattering life that soon drowned out the sound of the horse's hooves as Nutkin drove the carriage on.

As we ambled along, the rolling countryside changed to something more rural, with thatched buildings turning into taller wooden structures with three stories. Trees became more scarce as broader paths filtered into the main road we traveled. Dogs and goats and chickens gave way to rats and cats, and finally, we entered the city gates. A strong odor of manure and rotten meat clung to the air.

The castle itself loomed up over the city walls. Chatter and noise became a din that reached into the carriage with scraping nails. The window held all my attention as I took it all in. Blade remained silent. If he realized I was storing it all away, the streets, the various taverns and rooming houses, he said nothing.

Nutkin pushed the horses forward without a whip but lots of gentle encouragement, and they sped up at his suggestion when we threaded our way onto a curving road that led upward toward the castle.

We pulled up to the castle behind a larger carriage, one built of black onyx with gold filigree and drivers wearing scarlet dust jackets.

From the window, I could just make out several large men shouldering their way from the cab to cluster around each other. Dressed in suits of all sorts of earthen shades that looked as soft as moss and as rich as soil, those men looked more civilized than the last time I'd seen them.

"Stone and Flint," I said in a tight voice, knowing that the woman alighting from the carriage behind them was not my sister.

"I hope she eats his face," I said through gritted teeth, and Blade craned his neck to see out his window. "You mean Flint, I suppose," he said as his brother reached behind to help the changeling from the carriage.

"That thing is too docile," I said, noting the delicate way the thing wearing my sister's face picked her way down the blacksteel steps to the ground. Her skirts looked dirty at the hem and as she lifted them, a flash of crimson stocking showed through.

"The nascent demon will be for a few hours yet," he mused aloud. "But if you think Flint will let it get near enough to his face to take a bite, you'd be underestimating him." This said with an almost proud air that made me look at him. I'd not seen the two together as much as he and Stone, and I was surprised to discover it was entirely possible that Blade liked his brother.

And something else struck me. "He knows," I said in amazement. "Flint knows it's not Kit." The truth surprised me.

Blade ran his hand over my arm in reassurance. "He won't betray us unless he has to."

"But why?" I asked.

"If you have to ask that, Ponytail," he said. "Then you've been fighting monsters far too long. You've lost your understanding of romance."

His shoulders rolled in his suit as he reached for my shoulders. "Here is where I leave you, Alathir." His eyes flashed, and he leaned forward to kiss my right shoulder. His breath moved over my skin where it was bare of material and my breath caught in my throat. "The Shadow Court's dark enforcer is not a sight most Fae want to see when they greet their king after a century. I'm the thing they like to keep in the shadows. Like your human bogey man, just...more terrifying."

At that, his lips dipped to the hollow in my throat and swept a moth's light kiss against the light pulse there. I almost felt the wings ignite at the heat it generated in my body.

He pulled something from his pocket. I recognized the corsage from the cache of cursed objects I'd taken from Lilah's mansion.

He must have taken it from the pouch at some point. It looked as delicate as it had the first time I'd seen it, and while I expected it to have wilted by now, it looked as fresh cut as any other flower.

That alone was creepy. I almost shivered as he pinned it on my bodice.

In an instant, the corsage came to life. Stretching its stem down to root with the vine tattoo the gown made of my scars, and it became almost a part of the glamor except for the way it elongated into a cluster of ghostly petals that closed into a tight bud, keeping its poisonous pollen clutched tightly within its harboring petals.

"The bud will open at your wish," he said. "It's sentient in a way." His fingers brushed along the fabric, warming the curve of my breast in a way that made my throat ache. "You have only to brush your fingers along the stem, like you were stroking my—"

"I get it," I said, and he grinned. "It will be inert in the ballroom, of course," he said. "But it is pretty and every woman should receive flowers from their lover."

"How very fitting of my lover to gift me a killer rose," I said, my eye going to the window where Stone stood in his black tuxedo. The thickness of his neck showed just above the collar in a clean line of skin that suggested he'd shaved. Each cord of muscle moved like a python beneath his skin each time he shook someone's hand. I noted he craned his neck, looking for someone.

Me, I realized. He was looking for me. I inhaled deeply, pulling in the kind of courage a warrior might take from the air of the battleground, letting it steel my spine, steady my hand. And yet, when my fingers curled around the handle of the carriage, my hand trembled.

Blade's palm touched down on my wrist and I turned to him one last time to gather his features to my mind for recall when I needed it.

He pulled me toward him with both hands, cupping them around my face so that I was drawn upward as my eyes gazed into his.

"You are fierce, Alathir," he murmured in a hushed voice. "You are a warrior. You don't need me to protect you. But know this. If something goes wrong behind the veil, I will come to you. If it's across the wastelands of the frozen fire, into the shadows of death, or beneath the trench of liquid fire, I will find you. And if there is no out for either of us, I'll live my days with you in the nothingness of air until I am no more."

I swayed a bit at the declaration as it reached into my core and massaged a tight knot into smooth, velvety tissue. I was still gathering words for a reply when he reached past me to open the door.

Stone was there, hunching over to find my hand.

A blink. That was all I had time for before I was tugged from the carriage and the door was shutting. I stood in the dying light, willing myself not to turn around and look into the carriage. I didn't want to see the coach pull out with him inside, leaving me at the court and all that awaited me inside.

"You'll see him again," Stone said in a voice that was not quite bitter. "You won't die this night, Ava Ashe. As my life is bound to the Shadow Court, I'll make sure you see him again."

I nodded wordlessly, accepting the vow without acknowledging it verbally, because I wasn't sure what sort of magic I might incur if I did.

He patted my hand as it rested in his. "Are you ready?" he asked and the way he said it, sounded as if he thought I was going to meet my death.

And by the way the back of my neck prickled, I had the feeling he might be right.

Chapter 17

Dying took patience. So did hunting. Cold killing couldn't be much different, except that it was intentional. That was what I kept telling myself as Stone escorted me to a carriage that had just pulled up as Blade and Nutkin pulled away.

The area was filled with fairy lights glittering and winking in and out in the early gleam as we drew up to the front of the massive palace facade. Stretching upwards five stories in white stone that gleamed in a tranquil, almost effervescent light that cascaded down from a light source too high to see in its turrets, the castle was an impressive bit of architecture. But except for that stony facade, the area surrounding the castle, from the gates to the walls to the courtyard, was filled with fragrant shrubs and gardens that emitted myriad fragrances. Within the foliage, smaller lights winked in and out like cat eyes. And over our heads like a silk parachute, a canopy hung by invisible strings, showering the courtyard with glittering light.

"Magnificent, isn't it?" Stone asked quietly.

I exhaled a long breath. "It is," I admitted.

"It's much grander inside yet. This is a big deal for the realm," he said. "No matter what happens, Ava, I'm glad to experience this with you."

Turning to him, I smiled wanly. I knew he meant it, but I couldn't return the sentiment. Something felt off, and whether it was knowing Blade was out of my reach or just that I was worried I would never see him again, I just couldn't offer Stone more than that half smile.

But the response seemed to be enough, because he slipped his arm around my midriff and guided me toward the onyx carriage, to where his father and Flint, and my changeling sister waited.

Queues of fae, both high, low and base, chattered excitedly around me in languages that could have been English or anything else. Some words, I understood, others sounded like noise or low-pitched echo location. I'd not realized how varied the Fae were in shape and form until I saw them all clustered around in lineups or arriving by horse or foot or carriage.

Not all were fully humanoid, and some had tails, wings, and horns. I was sure I caught sight of tentacles here and there, but I remained silent, taking it all in. Short and round, hairy and smooth, winged or clawed, all sorts were out tonight for the start of the Days of Endowment. The high Fae were easy to pick out compared to the rest, even if the lower Fae had exquisite almond shapes to their eyes and slight angles to the tips of their ears. High Fae, I noticed, had a sheen to their skin that was much more evident when in proximity to the lesser Fae.

And those high Fae, those like the mafioso that I approached, lined up in a different spot than those they considered less in rank. I passed them with my head high and my eyes on Stone. If I hadn't been listening to everything and trying to sort through important noises, I wouldn't have heard the mutterings of even the lesser Fae discussing the peculiar fetish their king had for mortal women and just how many he might need to sate his appetite.

It occurred to me that they didn't realize it wasn't about satisfying an appetite for lust and sex, and my lips pressed together as I kept my attention rapt on our destination. I couldn't risk any trouble at this point, and whatever they had to say, it didn't matter to me.

All that mattered was the task ahead of me.

I caught sight of Terran alighting from his carriage just as a portly Fae female dressed in a garish yellow dress far too tight for her frame shoved me with a glittery cane. I stumbled, losing sight of him as I clutched at Stone's arm reflexively.

Stone's body was as good as a boulder, and he didn't fail to support me. His arm tightened as he cast a glare the female's way.

"Take care," he growled. "This mortal is a blood gift for the king."

"It's a walking, talking sex toy is what it is," she said with a sniff. "Disgusting. We shouldn't have to endure these things out in the open."

"And since when have the Fae been so genteel?" he asked, letting go of me to bully toward her.

She raised her cane at him. "There was a time," she said. "In the days of the Old King. Just because you of the Shadow

Court don't remember those ages, does not mean it didn't exist."

He softened immediately and surprised me by placing one hand on hers and lowering the cane to the ground. "It must have been a very long time ago," he said gently. "And that means you deserve your respect old one."

I might have made a comment about what she really deserved, but I was already too engrossed in the way Terran minced into a circle of his men, all the while trying not to look like they were his men. I noticed several of the Fae I'd met at his dinner watching him too keenly from various spots in the courtyard, as if they had taken up strategic places.

Things felt very Bloody Sunday, all of a sudden, and yet Stone was guiding me toward his father as though nothing was out of the ordinary. He ignored the men stationed throughout the crowd, and drew near enough to his father that I could see the red rimming Terran's eyelids. He looked tired as his attention settled on me.

He scanned those bloodshot eyes over me, taking in the gown, the way Stone held onto my waist, and sighing as though he had to make do.

Terran squared off with me, his expression hard and business-like. The man standing beside him, pretending not to be noticed as part of Terran's entourage made a swirling motion with his hand, low, beside his hips and a shudder of energy moved over my skin. Magic, I knew, but I wasn't sure it was welcome, because Terran sent him a subtle nod before settling that gaze on me.

"How good are you at killing, exactly?"

It was such an odd question to ask at that point that the words slid free before I could think them through. "I have a treasure box filled with trophies in my office that will have a wendigo tooth added to it when I return home."

He considered that, his eyes narrowing, and I realized he'd had one of his men cast some sort of silence spell over us so we could speak freely. I had the feeling it would be the last bit of magic we could afford to use, and I was proved right when he said, "All weapons past this point, concealed or overt, save those of the King's Guard will be spelled to turn upon the wearer."

He pointed to a wooden sign with a notice burned into it. WEAPONS IN THE BALLROOM ARE THINGS OF INTENTION AND WILL BE TURNED UPON THE BEARER.

"What does that mean?" I asked.

Stone was the one who answered, and he did it while casually looking around and nodding at others as though he was merely making conversation. "It means that if you intend to use a weapon, whether it's an apple or a knife, the weapon will turn on you."

In other words, no chance of killing the king or anyone else. I nodded at the trunk two Fae were hefting from Terran's carriage, followed by Kit's trousseau chest. "So the pouch of cursed objects—"

"Useless," Stone said. "All of it." He jerked his chin toward my skirts, where the karambit was sheathed beneath the material.

I glanced at the sign again. "He's confident he only has to worry about the ballroom, it seems. That's something."

"Every little something is valuable," he said. "I have faith in you."

Terran snorted beneath his breath as he side-glanced at me, but the effort it took to do so seemed to bow him over. "It's not faith we need, idiot," he said. "Now, be still. The magic is waning."

He swallowed hard, as if it hurt. Over his shoulder, I could make out three of the Fae he'd introduced to me peering at him from angled glances. Scanning over Stone's shoulder, I made four more, all watching Terran just as keenly. It was only Stone who seemed to be oblivious to his father's state of health. Even Flint seemed more preoccupied with the Kit doppelganger than his father. I supposed they didn't want to raise any sort of suspicion.

"Shall we go, Ava?" Stone said, withdrawing his hand from my waist and holding out his elbow.

I took it the way I expected a lady might because I wasn't sure what else to do. I'd had only a few lessons on court etiquette, but watching others, it seemed the most apropos. Looking around, it seemed the portly Fae woman was right. There was some gentility left in the Fae world.

As we threaded our way through the crowds with me trying not to gawk at some of the lesser Fae, I bumped into someone's shoulder.

She turned on me and ran a silver gaze over my gown. "Erachne," she breathed. "You're wearing Erachne." Her voice was so filled with wonder and surprise that I looked down at my cleavage, sure my boob had popped out.

It hadn't, of course, but the pitch and level of her voice gained the attention of several other Fae women, who cut through me with their gazes as though I was soft butter.

"That dress is meant for a high Fae," she said, inclining her head to Stone, whose shoulders squared out at the comment even though she seemed not to notice. "What is a mortal woman doing wearing it?"

Stone's grip on my elbow grew tighter as he felt me go rigid. "She is a gift for our king," he said, "not that it's any of your business. But a king should have the best. And Erachne is the best, is she not?"

She sucked at the back of her teeth. "Too good for the likes of a ragged human."

I seethed silently beside Stone, telling myself there were more important things than the comments of a Fae who had no idea what was going on behind the throne. To my surprise, Stone's voice went deadly quiet.

"You know who I am, right?" he asked her in a low voice. "I could have your offspring tortured and killed for nine generations to come. If I say this mortal woman is a worthy gift for our new king and that she is fit for an Erachne Allure gown, then it is so."

I sucked back a breath as the woman paled, no small feat for the already milky complexion she wore like a piece of fine silk ribbon. "I'm sorry," she said, her hand going to her throat. "I didn't realize you were Shadow Court."

Stone didn't relax one bit at her apology. "If I were just Shadow Court muscle, you'd be dead right now. Real death. With much pain. But I'm not just muscle." He waited a beat for the female to realize how much power he held, with so much threat in the current of air between them that for the first time, I truly saw the resemblance to Blade as brothers.

Astounded I might be at the undercurrent of violence in his tone, I also remembered the flat, unwavering hardness of him when we'd first met. He was Shadow Court, for sure. Mafia. Violent. I'd let that information slide away over the weeks, when it was still there all the time, just not overtly noticeable.

The Fae woman blinked rapidly before dropping her gaze and inclining her head ever so subtly toward me. A waver of energy, not unlike a horizontal hold on an old cathode ray television set, moved over the air, and I guessed some sort of magic was being accessed. I just wasn't sure who initiated it.

"I apologize," she murmured. "You look stunning. The king will love you."

Stone grunted, and I looked sideways at him. A muscle in his jaw still held onto tension, and the hard edge of his profile didn't move from hers. I tugged at his arm. He resisted for a moment, then relaxed, tossing me a smile that didn't reach his eyes.

"The line has moved," I said, thinking a verbal nudge might help.

"Indeed it has," he said, casting another look her way, one that chilled me to the bone. "But I'm tired of waiting."

The set of his shoulders and the tone of his voice reminded me acutely of what he was, and I mentally noted not to discount him again as a soft touch. He was Shadow Court Fae through and through, even if he did act more gentle towards me.

I let him guide me to the front of the line, where it stopped at the massively tall castle gates. Looking back, the queue of

Fae regarded us with surly expressions, but no one argued. Terran and his small retinue of guards stood aloof from the queue, watching us. He might have worn a proud expression if he didn't also look so stooped and tired.

A few feet away, Flint stood holding onto Kit's changeling by the hand as if he was afraid she'd break away and attack everyone. It all felt so surreal that I had to blink several times to refocus myself.

We had lurked there for several moments, with Stone seeming to expect to be noticed and let past through the gates. Whether we were being ignored by the willowy Fae servant dressed in a crushed green velvet gown, I couldn't tell, but Stone seemed to think it was an affront. He cleared his throat noisily.

In response, the line behind us backed up. The gorgeous page looked us up and down before catching Stone's eye. Whatever she saw in his gaze made her gesture us through so broadly, she ended up with her back to the wall. We swept past her to an imposing foyer, where the grout of the stones was embedded with crystals that caught the light and reflected it back so that the entire room looked like it had been bathed in silver.

Inside, I discovered we were not the first to arrive. The ball was already filled to near capacity with every manner of fae I could imagine, and some far past imagination, all dressed in their finest attire.

Intricate carvings spiraled around a dozen or more wooden columns, and marble statues stood in places against the walls where lush tapestries didn't cover the stone. The ceiling, lit with what looked like stars since I recognized several constellations in miniature, seemed both wide open to the heavens and topped with a dome at the same time.

The majesty of the room was enough to instill awe even without the broad fireplace on the far side of the room, centered beneath arched columns. But the fireplace was magnificent in itself. With a great maw of a firebox stuffed with logs that didn't get consumed, it threw off a royal purple light that cast a glow over the faces of the high Fae within a hundred feet, turning them a strange pallor. Skin glistened in the light of a hundred torches in addition to those embedded crystals.

The mantel above the hearth writhed with shadow and light as if it were alive. The greenery that swathed it seemed to grow an inch for every one of my heartbeats until it covered the top half of the fireplace face and stretched along the columns. I was sure I recognized vinyalia leaves amidst the foliage and ran a hand over my arm in reflex.

"It's amazing," I said in a breath, turning in space and taking it all in. It went beyond anything I could have imagined. The only ordinary part of the decor was the rushes strewn with herbs that hugged the walls and corners. I noticed a large heap of kindling cradled in one of the beddings of moss that softened the hard edges of a far corner.

"He's there," said Stone, nudging me with his elbow and drawing my eye away from the room itself toward a large Fae male seated in the middle of a dais. The platform spun just slowly enough that the king could be in full view of his subjects the entire time while he was able to see each of them.

I had the sense it wasn't just done for effect, but so that the reedy looking Fae to his left could see every inch of the room as the platform spun. Her ears had sharply pointed tips that nestled against multicolored tawny hair piled high on her head in a thick, samurai type bun.

She was breathtaking, this fae. Slim but athletically built, much as I was, with a larger bosom than befit an athlete. Her build suggested any exertions she saw fit to undertake were more of a warrior's sparring and not that of an endurance athlete's grueling schedule. I doubted she trained every day, and yet I didn't doubt her proficiency. Because despite the roundness of her bosom, there was no softness in her.

Where she stood, a mist of obsidian darkness swirled and fidgeted around her like the dust cloud around the Peanuts Pigpen, and each time it moved over her, she changed shape. Not in the way Blade shifted into a hellhound, but as if she had a hard time holding one form.

At times, she resembled a hawk, at times an owl, but mostly, I saw that hard-edged jaw and sharp gaze of a Fae woman. And at the odd time the darkness cloaked her from sight, those eyes peered out like jewels from a velvet cushion.

No matter what shape that elusive form took, one characteristic remained. Whether she was darkness, human in form, or bird of prey, the set of iridescent wings remained folded over her ribs like a pair of massive hands holding her in place.

"Ruby," Stone said in a bitter voice that tore my gaze from the Fae mercenary to look at him.

The muscles in his jaw were white with tension. It was in that moment that I knew the truth.

"You know her," I said.

His head swiveled toward me and for a moment, I saw death in his eyes. He didn't just know her. He hated her.

CHAPTER 18

I edged closer to Stone. "How bad is it?" I asked.

He angled his body so that he was in profile to the king and his mercenary. A shake of his head indicated he didn't want to discuss it, so I peered back toward the dais. Ruby stood no more than a foot away from Ferranus and while there was enough room on his other side for the second mercenary, it was the king's guard who took up the remaining space. So, whoever the other mercenary was, he was not visible.

With no other opponent to look out for, I focused my attention on the king and the black cat draped over his lap. I squinted at the feline, thinking it looked at me with more than the typical arrogance and disdain of most cats deigning to notice a human in its presence.

The throne, though, that drew my eye from the malice-laden glare of the cat. It had been carved from black ivory and was encrusted with precious gems that sparkled in the soft light. Seated, he appeared uncomfortable. The crown seemed to weigh heavily on his head, a skull bathed in locks so black they swallowed the light as they draped down his collar to the cascading velvet robe that pooled onto the floor at his feet.

At the crown's base, thick bands of iron wrapped the circumference and gave way to pointed spires that gleamed with a black metal shaped into twisted branches. Its center held a large gemstone that I didn't recognize, but it cast a blood-red glow over his face, making him seem to be hewn from red marble.

"There's cold iron in his crown," I said, noting that in itself, it could be a weapon.

"Not just cold iron," Stone said. "But a sacred gem some say carries the blood of the ancient king."

I was about to ask what would make such a gem so sacred, but from somewhere behind us, music began to play. A crush of fae moved to the dance floor as one, as if they'd been waiting for a signal. The scent of lilacs and vanilla carried over the air as they moved.

"We should dance," Stone said, taking my hand and spinning me toward the front of the dance floor, just in front of the king. "The presentations will be later but it's best if we act natural."

I was no slouch at cutting a rug, but my moves were all club style. I could shake and shimmy and twerk with the best of them on nights I felt like letting loose. Here, I had no idea what the steps or protocol were for the intricate, formal moves the Fae were performing. They seemed very much like the horrors of a Jane Austen based movie.

I was all left feet and baby toes, and I trod on Stone's shoes more times than I cared to admit. With one more hard stomp on his left foot, I winced even if he didn't.

"I'm a mess," I said.

He looked down at me. "I have to confess; I'm used to the delicate features of a fae's footwear. To anyone else, your sturdy combat boots might look like soft sandals courtesy of Erachne's magic, but she did nothing to disguise the sensation of cement blocks dropping onto my toes."

My eyes rolled back in mortification. "Oh, God," I said. "This is my worst nightmare."

He pulled me closer to his chest as he looked down at me. "I might wish you'd find being in my arms a bit less horrific."

I tilted my face to look into his eyes. "I didn't mean that, and you know it."

"I do," he said, but his words were empty and bland, like he'd put up an armor around them.

The swirls of colors and sometimes monstrous faces dancing around me made me dizzy. A searing sort of burn ran up my spine and halted mid back, right where my heart would be. I gasped in surprise and the next time Stone spun me, I caught sight of the king.

"He's looking at us," I whispered. His gaze had been the source of that awful burning.

But he wasn't just looking at Stone and I. His eyes were on me, drilling into mine in an overly familiar way. I didn't have to guess if the king would accept me as a blood gift. Everything I saw in his face indicated I would be exactly what he wanted.

Stone's hand pressed tighter into the small of my back, and I noted the king's eye narrowed and hardened possessively. I got the distinct impression he didn't just think I belonged to him, but that he'd already claimed me.

Everything inside me balked at the thought of being presented to another being as a gift. But I told myself it was part of the hunt, a prelude to the battle. Victory seldom came without sacrifice, and I was about to let myself become collateral damage.

Stone paused, causing my foot to stomp down on his once again, and I flinched at the flash of discomfort in his eyes even though he made no outward show of pain. I thought he let go a small sigh when he gripped my elbow and guided me toward the dais, where the king's eyes on me felt very much like a lasso made of flame.

There was no holding that gaze, no matter how many monsters I'd faced or stared down or put six feet under. The sense of naked possession and desire was too fierce.

My eyes trailed to the floor and remained pinned to the edge of my gown as we halted in front of the dais. I couldn't let my frustration and anger at the whole situation show on my face. I didn't dare do more than run my palm over my thigh, just to feel for the karambit hidden beneath my skirts. Its hard surface did more to calm my heartbeat than several deep breaths.

Stone twirled me out of view and brushed his lips against my ear. "He's watching us."

I almost twisted my ankle as my feet stopped moving while Stone kept going. Then, suddenly, he halted, pulling away from me, but taking my hand. "Wait," I said. "What are you doing?"

"That's enough. We just need to get his attention."

I tried not to look like I was fighting him off as he led me back off the dance floor. Relieved as I might be to stop the infernal dancing, I was too confused to comply immediately.

"You're a horrible femme fatale, Ava," he complained as he tucked both of my hands in his. It was awkward going, but effective in stopping me from struggling. "The presentations come after the Endowments, and that might take days. We need to create a bit of mystery around you in the meantime."

I almost stumbled over my own feet as I sought to walk beside him with both hands being held. "Let me go," I said. "I'm fine. I get it."

"Do you?" he asked without slowing down or letting me go. "Ferranus has had lovers in the thousands over the centuries."

We had brushed and shouldered our way past dozens of glaring, staring, annoyed dancers by then, and I'd had enough of being Fae-handled. I halted, digging my boots into the floor.

He stopped short, yanking on my arms at the force that strained between us. I held my own, stubbornly yanking backwards enough that he was forced to angle his body toward me.

"You said I was beautiful enough to catch his eye." It wasn't ego urging me on. I was making a point.

"I did," he said. "And I meant it. See how you just got his attention?" He let go of my hands, though, and slipped one arm over the small of my back. I side-eyed his arm before lifting my gaze to his face, still angry.

"Then why are we retreating?"

The fingers splayed over my waist twitched. Not a lot. But enough that I felt it.

"Not here," he said.

I nodded and jerked my chin toward a heavy-looking tapestry hanging from ceiling to floor. Broad and heavy, it reminded me of one akin to the one Hamlet had stabbed Polonius through.

"There. Everyone will just think you're leading me out of sight for a little necking."

His features shone with lust for a moment and I realized I'd just put a lot of images into his mind. Without waiting for him, I headed toward it.

The tapestry was indeed large and heavy, and lucky for me, there was a gap between it and the stone of about a foot. With barely a glance, I side-stepped behind it and let go a long breath. The scent of dust and mold wafted over me. My feet pushed at damp, heavy rushes that smelled of urine. I wasn't the only one to use this handy spot, apparently.

With enough room to stand sideways, I shuffled over to leave space for him to slip behind.

His shoulder met mine, and he let it linger as he spoke. "A momentary notice isn't enough, Ava," he said. "You remember your history?"

"I remember sucking on a joint outside my history class's window," I said. "And history is long, so what in the god damn specific timeframe are you referring to?"

His hand reached for mine and I swatted him away. "Anne Boleyn teased and tempted Henry for years until she gave in."

"So she was a cock tease. And he was an idiot. What does that have to do with me?"

He ran his hand down my thigh a little too intimately, and it took a moment before I realized he was searching for my karambit.

He patted it when he found it nestled on the inside of my thigh.

"By the time she let him have her, he was rabid for her. He started a new religion just so he could screw her. Our king will have dozens if not hundreds of gifts in the veil to choose from. He needs to be rabid for you. He needs to want to come to your bed first."

First. Meaning while he was the most vulnerable. Before he'd had a drop of any other blood to gain an iota of strength. First, meaning I had that moment and that moment alone to kill him.

"So you're thinking I need to be seen not just when presented, but lots of times so that he remembers my face and seeks me out before any other."

"Exactly."

I let my breath go slowly, purposefully. "And what of the mercenary?"

"What of her? Beyond the veil, she'll be nothing. Her threat will remain on this side."

"And the other one?"

I felt him lay back against the stone of the wall. "I have no idea who it is."

That wasn't encouraging. As far as we knew, someone could be standing right next to the king, invisible, and we'd not know. That someone might have any sort of magic.

Ferranus might even have planned to pull both mercenaries in with him and chow down on their magic before starting in on his blood gifts.

My jaw slid to the side as I considered all the possibilities, none of which seemed hopeful without knowing all the information. Damn, I hated being so uninformed.

"Don't you think we need to find out who that second is," I said. "I need to know their magics, their power, what they look like." I was dying to step out from behind the tapestry to look again at the dais, but he was in the way. "Maybe you could do a little intel."

"Agreed," he said, but he didn't move.

I nudged him with my elbow and he sighed. "It will be more difficult to ask questions with you at my side." He kicked at the bottom of the tapestry.

"Then let me wander. I can do some as well."

He shook his head. "Not a great idea."

I nearly groaned out loud. "Then I'll wait here."

I can't just leave you unattended," he said. "Not in a room filled with fae."

"I'm a big girl," I said, my eyebrows raising at the insinuation that I couldn't take care of myself when he was about to sic me on the biggest and baddest of the creatures within the realm, and because I didn't dare say it out loud.

"You're right." He leaned down and hooked his finger beneath my chin, turning my head toward his. In the gloom behind the fabric, I thought he might kiss me and I held my breath, not sure what I would do if he did.

But he tilted his forehead to mine instead, touching down on it so lightly I barely felt it. "Whatever happens, Ava," he said. "Whatever you see and whatever you hear in this ballroom...know that I care about you. More than you realize."

My breath caught, leaving me speechless as he swept out from behind the tapestry. I saw him adjust his waistcoat and then stride purposefully toward a group of his father's thugs. I recognized the Fae with the carved wooden pipe from the dinner party on my first night in the manse. Eldric, I think his name was.

My gaze scanned the room, looking for Flint and Kit as I wondered if the demon had gained any more sentience and if Flint was struggling to keep it contained. I almost hoped the damn thing had chomped his face off, but that wouldn't be helpful. Not yet anyway. As I surveyed the ballroom, a tall Fae female with slender antlers and a gauzy dress that did nothing to hide the flickering tail beneath her skirts strolled by and in her wake the room seemed to change.

In the short time I'd been behind the tapestry, the gala had become a seething mass of bodies. Perspiration was ripe in the air, but that pungent fragrance buried itself beneath the stronger scent of perfume and wood smoke. A deeper, more resonant one underpinned all those scents. Pheromones, I thought, since I wasn't able to give the aroma a name.

If I looked too closely, I could just make out naked limbs rolling about in the rushes in the further corners, and several more, hasty glances about the room revealed just how many of those shadowed places cloistered men and women of all orders dancing with each other in naked abandon.

I dropped my head back, letting it rest on the wall behind me. I hated standing there, doing nothing as I waited for someone else to do the leg work. In the earthen realm, I'd have all this information. I wouldn't have begun the hunt without having all the details wrapped up. Lilah the witch had been the exception. I'd been mad and hurt and taken a ridiculous chance.

Some part of me thought it was kismet, if such a thing existed. Without having done that job, I'd not have met Blade. I'd be still clinging to the horrors of my past. I'd be the same unhappy hopeless addict I'd always been.

Blade. The thought of him made my stomach hurt. The ache for him was so acute I felt it in the back of my throat, and the images of all those cavorting Fae did nothing to assuage it.

I wondered where he was. If he was upset that he was left out of the ball like a male Cinderella. The Days might have begun, but the Endowments were many hours away. The presentations further than that. It might be hours or days before things started to get moving and I was already anxious.

To pass the time, I watched the crowds grow larger, the Fae more lascivious and rowdy. It was shaping up to be one hell of a party. If I studied the forms carefully, I could dissect Stone from the throngs, going one way and the next. I followed him for long moments, bored enough that my mind went automatically to counting the males he spoke to.

Most of them at first were easily recognizable as his father's thugs, Fae of a lesser order than Stone and Blade, but higher than the base Fae who I'd come to recognize were more animal than sentient beings.

I noted that the longer Stone took to go about in search of that intelligence, the less recognizable the Fae he spoke to became. A flicker of my gaze through the crowds showed he'd gone past some of the more obvious of his father's soldiers and to some that he hunched with like a football huddle.

I counted ninety-nine in all, excluding him before I grew tired of the game and decided I was tired of waiting. I was going out there.

Just as I decided to step out from behind the tapestry, someone muscled their way behind it, stomping on my foot and all but shoving me to the floor.

CHAPTER 19

"Hey," I complained.

Two bright green eyes lit the darkness as they swiveled up toward me. "Sorry," the owner of them said in a hushed voice. "But I need to get away from her."

Before I could complain or question, a large, furry hand clamped down over my mouth. I tasted goat and funk and I gagged as I fought off the grip.

My fist aimed for where I thought the throat was, but it sailed straight through empty air. Dust or fur or hair injected itself into my nostrils with my next breath, and I sneezed into his hand.

"Shh," he demanded. Because it was a he, I realized. A short, very funky smelling he. "You're going to get me caught."

His grip was strong for sure, and I realized he was much shorter than me. Knowing that made all the difference. I kneed him right in the groin.

He let go my mouth and yelped in pain, then cut the sound off so quickly I suspected he'd bitten his tongue.

"What in the actual fuck?" I said, as his hands started to roam my body.

I pushed him away with enough force that he should have gone sailing into the bright lights of the gala, but instead, I only managed to push myself deeper into the shadows behind the tapestry.

"You're mortal," he said in a curious voice, and those hands found my breasts as though they'd been a target for the heat-seeking missile of his fingers. He gave my nipple a tweak and in fury, my palm shot out, expecting to take him in the nose.

What they struck wasn't a nose at all. It was bone. Or cartilage. I wasn't sure. I pulled my hand back in surprise, cradling my fist against my chest.

"Who are you?" I asked. "And what the fuck was that?"

He chortled. "I'm guessing by the way you recoil at my horns that you haven't laid your delicate fingers on a faun's second best feature," he said, and a small glow lit the darkness, a soft yellow light coming from his palm.

It was enough light to see that the man palming my boobs was not even full man. He was half goat on the bottom, and judging by the size of the erection, he had the same lusty disposition.

"You're one of the king's figs," he said in a near squeal. "I saw you outside. A soldier from the Shadow Court brought you." He eyeballed my chest like he wanted to run his hands over my breast again.

"Don't even think it," I said, glowering at him as I laid my hand over my chest.

He smiled. "I wouldn't dream of assaulting one of the king's figs," he said. "But since you haven't confirmed that's what you are, I might well expect that you could be anyone's."

He eyed me up and down, measuring me in a way that made me want to gag. "It's been a while since I've taken anything but a nymph to my bed and I do love the challenge of a human woman. Are you brought to the Days as entertainment for the masses? If so, I'd dearly love to be the first to attend you."

He was so earnest and forthright that despite the smell and his crassness, I found myself chuckling. "And just how many mortal women have you found that enjoy bedding a half goat?" I asked.

His chest puffed out. "I'm a man where it matters," he said. "But if you desire to see a whole human male, I'm happy to oblige you."

As if to prove it possible, he suddenly appeared to be a gorgeous brown-haired lumberjack complete with stubble and plaid shirt. I thought of the few thirst traps I'd got caught in on social media and wondered if he'd somehow plowed through my fantasies to find that particular image.

"Glamor," I said, dismissing him.

"If a bit of glamor makes it easier for you, then what does it matter?" he said and then inched closer. "I assure you, I have all the necessary parts to make a human woman swoon." He gestured to his erection, which peeked out again from a nest of black fur and above a set of hairy goat legs. "I might even argue it's a much better endowment than some will see this night."

I chuckled at the innuendo. "As well-endowed as you might be, I think I better pass. For the good of the realm."

He grumbled to himself beneath his breath, as though I couldn't hear him before he brightened up and clutched my arm.

"At least, help me get away from her," he said with a shudder. "I've had her too many times already and I'm bored, but she's..." he flung his arms out helplessly. "Well, she's addicted to me."

As if to prove his point, the tapestry got yanked back, throwing a blast of light into the small space. The faun let go a shriek of surprise that was strangely feminine for all the size of his masculine chest and throat.

"There you are," said a woman with long green hair swept over one bare shoulder. Silver paint adorned the fingernails that clutched the edge of the tapestry. Her chocolate brown eyes, framed by inch long lashes, seemed lit from within, the same as the faun she sought.

She wore a dress made of leaves that cupped and shaped her body like they grew from her skin. Gorgeous, I thought, and far above this funky smelling creature's reach.

The tapestry lay over her back as she peered behind into the depths of the space.

The demand in her voice totally negated her allure. "What are you doing with that human?"

His shoulders slumped and he gestured to me. "This is one of the king's gifts," he said. "A nice ripe fig if you ask me."

"Ava," I said, not liking the way I'd been introduced as a 'this' and not a she.

The dismissive way she glanced at me made me want to throat punch something.

"You didn't touch her, did you?" she asked. "Because if you have, you'll need to wash before we do any more cavorting tonight."

Any more? Gods, maybe that was the funky stink coming off him in waves. I had to work not to imagine the beastly fae entwined with the gorgeous creature before me and shivered at the effort.

The little creature pinched the bridge of his nose. "I told you I'm off human women," he said. "I haven't touched one in a century." He made a big show of shuddering in revulsion, and my head ticked back in offense until he shot me a conspiratorial wink.

Her gaze narrowed, and those magnificently long lashes fluttered. With another disdainful glance at me, she grabbed the faun's arm and yanked him from behind the tapestry.

"Come," she said once she had him completely free of cover. "I've arranged for a few water nymphs to join us." She stroked his already large member into an even more raging erection. "You don't even need to work to get them wet." She winked.

He tossed a look at me over his shoulder. "Until we meet again, King's Gift," he murmured. "I have a nest of nymphs awaiting my service and as you heard, they are already drenched in a pool of desire for me."

He sketched a formal bow with a glint in his eye that made me like him all the more. I found myself bowing slightly with the same sort of conspiratorial grin. Then he let her lead him away, his erection bouncing obscenely.

I stood there for a long moment, trying to decide if I should stay out of sight before deciding I'd had enough of hiding.

With a sigh, I slipped out from behind the tapestry, shielding my eyes against the light. One sweep of the room revealed the king had stood from his chair and was scanning the room with an implacable expression. The cat rubbed itself against the throne's base, arching its back before it curled onto the floor, its paws folded beneath its body. I was sure it was studying me.

It was such an intense scrutiny that I didn't realize someone had come close to me until they touched me on the shoulder.

I spun, just barely finding the time to check the snap of my elbow backwards when I heard a familiar voice, one that still put a chill in my bones despite the healing Blade had done for me.

I spun around so fast, I wasn't sure my boots hadn't left a skid mark on the floor.

"Heuil," I said.

The little half-trow nodded, a harried movement that made me think he was in a great hurry to move on past. "I thought it was you, mistress." He shot a glance over his shoulder and inched closer.

Emotion, both buried and budding up into my throat, cut off my speech. He seemed to notice and cast his eyes downward shyly. "I'm glad to see you survived."

I swallowed hard. "I did," I managed to say. "Thanks to you."

"And I because of you," he said, skirting another look over his shoulder nervously before pinning those eyes back to my face. "Were you cavorting with Pan behind there?" he asked, gesturing to the tapestry. He said it in an off-hand way that had the makings of too casual a comment.

"Bold question for so young a male," I said, even as I was surprised to discover the randy faun had been the god of the wild and fertile nature of primal things. "Why are you so concerned about who I'm here with?"

Heuil's lips thinned in embarrassment as he chewed them between his pointed teeth. "Not so young as all that. I have a full century beneath my boots." He edged closer. "Bold it might be, but I have to ask it," he said, even more boldly gripping me by the elbow. "Please tell me it is Pan who brought you here."

I pulled my elbow gently from his grip. "If I was, I'm sure I wouldn't be standing here talking to you. I'd be...busy." It was a teasing comment, one meant to defuse the strange tension in the air that I sensed was building out of some confusion or concern on his part. I hoped it would be enough to crack the shell.

He shot me a half-smile that suggested he found humor in the comment, but shame as well. No doubt he was remembering the circumstances of my confinement deep in the bowels of the catacombs. He'd freed me only when he thought he was going to be sacrificed along with me to the deviance of the auctions. But even if that was the impetus of his kindness, I was still grateful. It had bought me time. By the time he'd run for safety he'd met Blade in the tunnels and directed him to where I could be found.

I was genuinely glad he was safe and alive.

I fished into my bodice to extract the gilded token. I stared down at it for a long while, wondering just what kinds of powers I'd been bestowing if it found the wrong hands and was presented to the king for reimbursement. Then I shrugged. This little Fae had done me a solid. I owed him.

"Please take this," I said. "I want you to have it. I don't even know why they gave it to me. I'm not even Fae."

After I'd pushed the token into his hands and curled his fingers down over it, he stared down at his fists for a long time. I thought I heard him sniffing.

He didn't look up. "This is a lifetime of magic," he said in a soft voice.

"Not a lifetime as I understand it. But perhaps you can find some joy in a year of magic."

The silence drew out between us like a hum. He shuffled his feet from side to side. When I glanced down, I caught sight of teardrops staining his suede boots. They were scuffed at the toes and brushed until they were nearly bare of velvety pile, but I thought they were his best.

"I've never been given such a gift," he said.

My throat tightened at the emotion in his voice. I found it difficult to speak around it but I forced myself to. "I owe you my life," I said. "This is nowhere near ample repayment."

In a flurry of movement, he stuffed the token into his pants, digging around as though he was searching for some interior pocket, before he pulled his tunic down over his hips.

"What do you think it will be?" I asked as he cast a look over his shoulder again. Apparently, he was ill at ease in such a glamorous affair, but he was no worse off, no more shoddily dressed than hundreds of other fae, and it didn't seem to bother them.

"Eh?" he asked, his hands wringing in front of his waist.

"Your magics?" I said. "What do you think they'll be when they are bestowed?"

He swallowed, and his gaze darted past my face and over my shoulder. "I don't know, mistress," he said. "I've lived a lifetime without magic and I wouldn't dare even dream about what such a gift would be."

"Surely you've wanted to have something?" I said. "The power to grow things, to change shape, to..." I shrugged. "I don't know," I said. "But surely there is some magic you'd love to own."

He marshaled the courage to face me straight on.

"I hope it's flying," he said with a timid movement of his mouth that might have been a smile if it had bloomed all the way. "I've always envied the winged ones."

I didn't know how magic worked, but I didn't see any evidence of wings in the ballroom. Still, I smiled encouragingly and patted him on the back of the arm. "I'm sure it will be grand no matter what it is."

He shuffled his feet together nervously. "Mistress," he said. "Might I ask you again about your escort?"

My eyes narrowed as suspicion dogged my spine. "Why is it so important to you?"

He lowered his voice and leaned ever so slightly toward me. "Has he abandoned you?" he asked. "Your escort, I mean. Has he brought you here and left you alone?"

I smiled as I realized he was trying to be chivalrous. "Not abandoned. Just...busy. You needn't worry about me, Heuil.

I'm fine." I patted his shoulder. "I have a companion. He's just busy elsewhere for the moment."

A look of determined decision swept over his features. "Leave now, then," he said. "While you still can."

This in an uncharacteristically commanding tone. I had the horrible thought that he was afraid for me. And I couldn't imagine why unless he was trying to tell me that the two fae from the catacombs who had escaped Blade's vengeance were here. That I was in danger.

The hairs raised on the back of my neck as I imagined them, and I knew it wouldn't be me in danger if I caught sight of them.

I grabbed his elbow and drew him, struggling, out of range of the dancers and couples and flitting Fae who kept jostling us. I stepped behind the tapestry, pulling him with me so that the sounds of the ball were muffled, the light just a bit gloomier.

"What's going on?" I demanded.

I was all spit and fury in that instant, ready to throw it all to the wind for a chance to put to death those who might still live who had carried out that atrocity.

"Are you trying to say I'm in danger, because if you are, it's they who should be running, not me."

He nodded, his eyes wide and bright.

"Fuck," I said, my eyes scanning the crowds until he tapped my shoulder. His fingers felt warm and harsh on my bare skin, like sandpaper heated from use. "Tell me where, Heuil. I'll end them here and now."

"Not my comrades, mistress," he said. "The one who hired us. *He* is here. He is the one you should be afraid of."

He is here. A simple sentence, but it weakened my knees so that I sagged against the tapestry. Not just the man responsible, but the one who had hired Heuil's gang to abduct me.

It boggled my mind that there was someone in the realm who would pay money to have me abducted. I couldn't fathom who would bother, who would even care or know I was here.

Unless it was Flint. My eyes narrowed as they searched him out on the dance floor, holding onto Kit's demon in too tight a grip on her hand. Apparently, the demon hadn't come into its own yet and was content to be handled, but the time would come when it wouldn't.

I wouldn't feel sorry for Flint then.

But even if it wasn't him who had hired that rotten gang of bastards to take me to the catacombs and sell me to the highest bidder, that someone was here. Right in reach. And I would kill him. I would slice him sac to scalp and I would dance in his fucking blood. I'd hang his balls in my trophy room and watch them shrivel to raisins. I'd make a damn macaroni and raisin necklace of them.

I felt my jaw go tense and had to strain through gritted teeth to ask, "Where?"

The fear on his face was palpable. I watched his Adam's Apple plunge down his throat.

"Tell me where, Heuil," I said in a low, threatening voice.

"I saw you arrive in your carriage," he said softly. "I wasn't sure it was you at first, because well, because it didn't make sense that you were here when I knew you had been saved. But then I recognized the Fae who hired us, and I had to be sure it was you. To warn you."

My mouth went dry. Had he seen Blade and me together in the carriage before I met Stone? Was he telling me that the dark enforcer had been the bastard who sent me to that horror? Was that how he'd managed to find me in the catacombs? My stomach lurched at my stupidity.

I thought of the huskiness of Blade's voice as he told me I was his mate. I felt his hands cupping my face as he declared he'd walk over coals to find me.

No. It wasn't Blade. It couldn't be.

I struggled to ask the words because I was terrified of what I might hear in answer. "Who did you see, Heuil?" I asked. "Was it the Fae who you met in the tunnels of the catacombs, the one you sent to look for me?"

He shook his head, looking thoroughly miserable. "You don't know, do you?" he whispered. "You don't know that he hired us." His hands sped up as he twisted them in and out of each other.

"Tell me."

"The big Fae. The one who pushed to the head of the line. The one you were dancing with."

Sweet Baby Jesus. It was a good thing I was wearing the sturdy boots and not thready sandals on my feet because the realization had me swaying. I had to grab for Heuil's arm to steady myself.

"Stone," I said out loud. Stone was the one who had betrayed me. Again.

Chapter 20

I knew two things in that moment when everything else tunneled down to a pinprick of light where the only thing I saw was the half-trow's eyes. One was that I was going to kill Stone. The other was that I had to get Heuil somewhere safe before Stone saw us together and put the whole entire rescue and my discovery of his part in my abduction together.

I couldn't repay Heuil for that information with more danger.

"You need to hide," I said, clutching at his arm." You need to get your magic endowment and get the hell out of Dodge."

He rocked back on his heels. "Dodge?" he said. "I don't understand."

An exasperated sigh fled my lungs, not so much at the innocence of his questions, but my own foolishness. I'd trusted Stone, and now once again, I had to deal with his treachery. And now I had to convince this little Fae to run for his life because if Stone saw us together there was no telling what he'd do to either of us.

"You need to flee the kingdom." I shoved him hard enough that he stumbled as he pin-wheeled out from behind the tapestry. "You can't hide here with me," I said. "He'll find you."

Scanning the room in desperation, my eyes landed on the pit of raunch and lust where Pan was drawing a crowd with his nymphs. "There," I said, mindful not to point but to draw him out from behind my back and point him in the direction best able to see the crowds gathering.

Even the king's eye had roamed to the activities going on in the nest of rushes and boughs. "No one will even bother to look at anyone in the crowds there, they'll be so interested in what's going on."

From where we stood, it looked as though Pan was enjoying three nymphs at once. With both hands on full breasts and his cock deep inside a bent over nymph being held aloft in the arms of two others like a fireman's carry, they had pulled quite a crowd of spectators.

Heuil took one look at the goings on and blushed all the way to his fingers. "Oh sweet Aifoe, I couldn't."

"You have to." I shoved him. "Now go. And for God's sake, wear a hood when you get your magic so no one can see you. Don't take it off until you are well away from this castle."

"But I can't leave you here." His expression was panicked. "I can't leave you to him."

I leaned close, letting him see everything my eyes had to say that I couldn't. "Trust me," I said. "He is more in danger of my wrath than I am of his."

He looked at me with panicked eyes. "He is very powerful," he said. "He has many allies."

I snorted. "I know exactly who his allies are. Now go."

I whipped him sharply around to face the corner and shoved him. He took tentative steps at first, then he hung his head, looking both ways the way a child might do before crossing the street, then he brushed between two chatting Fae and disappeared into the crowds.

I didn't wait to see if he made his way to the orgy. I spun on my heels with fists clenched at my sides.

Stone was going to die.

The last I'd seen the bastard, he'd been near a door on the other side of the ballroom.

Ever more creatures were edging into the room, and the grand double doors of the ballroom seemed a league away as the room expanded to encompass the massive amount of Fae, growing larger still like a lung inhaling. I could almost see it swell and let go as it adjusted.

Across the room, Flint was herding the Kit lookalike into the midst of a cluster of Terran's thugs. No doubt he wanted to keep the demon out of the way in case it raged forth. I wasn't certain, but it didn't look like that was about to happen any time soon.

Terran stood off to the side, looking wholly miserable in his tailored suit. A knot of thugs surrounded him, scowling in expressions that seemed a default setting. Gaggles of fae in every sort of dress, size, shape, and height moved like waves on a rippling ocean tide.

But there was no Stone.

Finding him by sight alone would be impossible in the throngs on a constant move. The weight of my anger demanded I get out from behind the tapestry instead of lurking there like a dolt until he deigned to return for me with information on the second mercenary. It was easy enough to see that creature—whoever or whatever it was—had yet to arrive.

Ruby of the Nocturnes stood with such a bored expression that even from my distance I could see that the few feet between her and the king's right hand were there for show, a temptation almost, for a would-be attacker.

The left hand of the king looked painfully exposed to attack. Had it been me advising Ferranus, I'd have suggested putting a decoy there, at the very least. Even if it was just for show.

Except I wasn't advising the king, I was planning to be that attacker, and I highly doubted that spot was as exposed as it looked. Like Ruby phased in and out, mists of shadow curling and uncurling over her form, it might well be possible that the other side held a fae invisible to the naked eye. Tempting attack, daring the challenge.

I thought of Stone's comment that I needed to build the tension and the mystique, and I almost pushed closer to the dais to give the king a good look, but realized Stone apparently had other motives. Might be best if I studied the king from afar before I teased him with glimpses of a hot seductress wearing yoga pants and combat boots beneath her delightfully risqué gown.

With that in mind, I slithered my way between a trio of females with long green hair cascading down bare backs to meet the apex of backless gowns that barely covered their asses and trailed along their thighs like tentacles of material. They raked me with nasty glares, but I pushed on, ignoring them as best I could so I could situate myself in a spot where I could see the dais clearly but not necessarily in full view of the king himself.

I used those green-haired fae as cover to peer around them. The cat had stood, baring her sharp little teeth in a yawn. The king's gaze dipped to it and lifted. Searching. Locked on something in the eddying waves of fae below the dais.

For a moment, I thought Ferranus met my gaze. Something snapped in the air. Then it sailed over me like a bad wind. The trio of females shivered visibly. They jerked sideways as if something had shoved them out of the way.

For a moment, I had the feeling that something had happened outside my sphere of perception and I looked askance at the females . They acted as though nothing out of the ordinary had occurred.

So. Nothing. I was just being hyper vigilant, I guessed.

I was about to shrug off the sensation, but then something did catch my notice. A noise. From behind me.

I froze, my entire body straining to reclaim the memory of the sound. Doubting at first that I knew what it was, but then knowing...like a fisherman knows the tug on his line is something alive and not a bit of flotsam catching the hook.

My whole body cried out in reply to that sound. Instinct borne of repetition and hundreds of hours of hunting and training, a habitual reaction, the way a mother responds to the cry of a baby even if it isn't hers.

Because I knew that sound like I knew no other. Even if the fae around me could ignore it as white noise, I knew someone had screamed—a muffled, human note of distress—but a scream just the same.

Instinct peeled out from behind any thought of vengeance like a formula one car and raced it to the finish line.

I turned on my heel to seek out the cause so automatically that at first, I expected to see the source right in front of me. But there was nothing. Just a sea of fae. All colors of the rainbow met my gaze in costumes that glittered over top skin that glowed. White teeth, sharp and blunt alike, flashed at me in laughter. But nothing out of the ordinary. Just a bunch of fae oblivious to the noise, enjoying their revelry.

For a moment, I doubted myself.

Then I saw her. She was surrounded by three males, this thin young woman. A bloom of roses in her cheeks floated on the surface of her milk-bath complexion. Slim of build and narrow-hipped, she didn't have the droop in her cheeks that indicated she'd passed much more than twenty. She looked closer to fourteen.

That fact that she was dressed in a long velvet gown as red as blood, made me think the color was intentional, and the way she was being ignored by all those around her except the three burly Fae who held onto her...that told me she was human.

Knowing she was so young made me furious. I thought of Phaedre and all the king's children he'd put to death. I thought of Jasmine and her revelation that she'd been in Fae for years. I thought of the future that poor girl might have ahead of her if she was forced to stay here... and I abandoned my search for Stone and my bid for vengeance. So too, the examination of the king and his absent mercenary.

The poor thing fought them with all she had while everyone around them acted as though nothing was going on. My anger at Stone went sharp as a pin and narrowed into something long and piercing. Even as I watched, pushing my way through clusters of fae who pushed me back the way concert-goers do to keep their spots, those who held the girl began to drag her toward a narrow door between two marble statues.

It took a second to recognize the vines covering the door.

I didn't know where they planned to take her, but if vinyalia was involved, I knew whatever they planned when they arrived, it wasn't to plait her long auburn hair.

I pushed through knot after knot of fae in all shapes and sizes until I cleared the laughter and tinkling music.

My dress moved like a whisper across the floor, the stomping of my boots unheard in the ruckus of the chamber. Bless Erachne. Her gown moved easily, allowing me to get within striking distance of the Fae trying to shove her through the door.

I was about to shout at them when the door opened and they shoved the girl through into the shadows beyond.

There wasn't much I wouldn't do to help a young woman, or anyone being victimized or hunted by creatures afoul of the nature of things. But I hesitated. Just for a second. This wasn't my business. I was here to assassinate the king because that bastard had killed scores of innocent children. Babies.

My hesitation cost her the seconds she needed for me to cross the threshold before the vinyalia began to close over the opening. The gloom of the corridor beyond the door married with the bright green of the vines and the black tarlike quality of the stems.

These weren't the same genus as the ones in Terran's underground cells. Some sort of cousin or evolutionary child, that might not even be poison.

I had to go through, and yet...

I held my breath, closed my eyes, uncertain. I cursed myself for hesitating when I would never have waited in the earthen realm. I would act. I would make them pay--

Then another shriek pierced the air, a banshee wail of a sound that apparently gave no one else a care. Fuck these fae and their disdain for humanity.

My breath let go all at once as I seized on a stem, praying the black woodiness might be the lesser evil.

My skin burned as though I'd laid my palm flat against a searing griddle.

But I couldn't let go. Everything I was and had become through pain and shame was in that girl. I wasn't going to just abandon her. I gritted my teeth. I yanked on the stems. I held my own.

And I broke through to the other side into a dark hallway with a length of vinyalia coiled around my wrist.

With a thud, the door hauled itself closed behind me, nudging me inside and stinging me in the ass with one of the barbs caught on the handle.

Even if I thought my sharp, surprised intake of breath was nearly silent, I must have made enough sound to catch the ear of the male at the end of the queue shouldering their way through the darkness.

He spun around, his face intermittently lit by a sputtering, guttering torch in his hand. Just where he acquired it in the few seconds, I didn't care. I whirled, coming around with my arms high, slipping the vine over his neck and twisting until it circled his throat.

I braced my feet against his torso, pushing him against the wall as I crossed the ends over his neck. Throwing my bodyweight back, I used gravity to tighten the garrotte.

It stung like razors slicing into my skin. Holding on through the pain as blood burbled to the surface of his skin, took more effort than I thought I could keep up. Where the vines touched, the wound blistered. His breath came in gurgles as I leaned back, using the leverage to sap the rest of his breath. I thought I was winning. He was sagging against me, growing heavier as he lost his battle to stand.

That was the instant everything shifted. Pressure built up around my throat. The more weight I put into the garrote, the greater the pressure. Pain razored into my palms as I dug in. Tight bands circled my throat, constricting harder each time I renewed my efforts.

My breath gagged out of me, then stopped altogether.

For an instant—just one—I dangled from a rafter in an abandoned school gymnasium. Twenty inches off the floor, my feet danced in the air in a wicked, gut-broiling frenzy. My hands clawed at the hemp rope strangling me of my air. Eyes strained, bugging out in a panic.

As I fought for breath in the castle corridor, my fingers tearing at the leaves and the stems, the vines slid from my hands to circle my throat. My fingers clawed at the woody vines as darkness crept into the sides of my vision. I thought

I smelled my own blood mingling with the earthy fragrance and acrid venom of the leaves.

My eyes rolled back. I lost purchase of the floor and my feet slid toward the fallen fae, fighting for some grip to keep me standing because if I lost touch with the floor, I would not survive and I knew it.

Some part of my lizard brain whispered to me. Maybe it was Blade's voice, maybe my own, but this time...this time, control wasn't in someone else's hands. It was mine. All mine.

The necklace with Slavin's tooth grew warm against my neck. Maybe I just imagined it, but I felt Blade with me. I felt his ferocity moving through me, reminding me that I wasn't a pathetic teen anymore. I was Ava Ashe. I was a hunter. A killer.

And a killer used what she had available as a weapon. I was doing exactly what a killer would do. In the absence of a weapon to fight the vines, I used my hands.

And that was the moment realization washed in. I was using a weapon. In the castle where weapons turned on the wielder.

It took an effort of sheer will to let go of the vine that clung to my throat like the scar I still wore from that earlier near-death.

It took all my courage.

But I forced myself to let go.

By the time the pressure on my throat eased and the vines fell away from my neck, I was breathing in squeaking, whistling breaths. But I was breathing.

I fell to my hands and knees, sagging in relief. The smell of dust and newly disturbed earth clawed a path through my nostrils. I sucked in several long breaths, my shoulders arching as my head hung there between them.

From hands and knees, I eyeballed the fae crouched on the floor against the wall beside me. He blinked at me in shock.

"Violence is banned," I whispered through a hoarse throat, and he nodded, still gawking at me with shot-wide eyes.

"Where are they taking her?" I demanded. I didn't think he'd care that my voice sounded like it had been razed with sand paper.

He pointed down the hallway...half a dozen yards, maybe less, there was no sign of his comrades or the girl, but there was a deeper darkness.

And there, cut through the gloom by only the barest winking of torchlight, a set of steps descended to some place beneath the first floor of the castle.

I thought I smelled stale water and excrement rising from the well of shadow and wafting back at us on currents of disturbed air.

A noise behind me drew my gaze back to the door. It had cracked open to show three identical females peering in through the door. Each had pink hair and lashes so long they brushed the fringe of bangs that fell in curtains around their faces.

Keen eyes blinked rapidly, changing the color of their eyes in unison from one shade to the next, a prism of rainbow in three curious stares, lit by some internal glow that made them all the more mesmerizing.

At catching my eye, however, they startled backward, fanning themselves and chattering excitely to each other. I imagined I looked a fright of blood and rash from the vines.

Maybe they just didn't expect to see a human staring back at them.

Whatever it was, other fae, curious about whatever had their attention enough to cluster around behind them, began to filter away, uninterested. Maybe they couldn't see past the trio to the fae slumped against the wall in the dark or make out the way he was struggling to stand on legs bowed by exhaustion.

The trio sniffed their disappointment at seeing a mortal woman trying to drag in labored breaths as she tried to haul herself to her feet. They muttered something about nothing worth watching and then they were gone.

I pulled my gaze back to the male who still crouched there, looking shell-shocked and nervous.

"Whatever you do comes back to you," I said, waving at him to leave. "If you value your life, then leave. Let your companions suffer whatever fate they have in mind for that girl."

"You don't understand," he said, eyes wide, hands shaking as he pushed against the wall to get up. He scrambled to his feet and shoved through the crack in the door, looking back at me over his shoulder. "It's not her but we who are in danger."

And then he was gone, leaving me to decide if forging on was the smart thing to do or just my default setting.

CHAPTER 21

The dungeons smelled of rat shit and blood so strongly that there was no doubt where the stairwell led. Despite the set of glistening white stone steps that lured my gaze down into shadows that swallowed up the treads bit by bit, I knew what lay beyond was not so pure.

It wasn't just the fae's comment that the males were the ones in danger drawing me toward it like a curious cat. It was because I couldn't be certain that the spell cast over the castle to turn their own violence against them would still work beneath ground. And if it did, what would happen to her if she was left alone in that darkness. Her age would make those traumas stick for a lifetime. Maybe change the course of who she was and who she would be.

I couldn't stand the thought that she might end up in some sort of arrested development, trying to soothe her pains with sex and drugs and gods knew what else.

Not like that. Not like me.

So, I descended those ghostly stairs as it funneled into a passageway made of arched stone pillars that glowed enough to light the earthen floor beneath my step.

Barely suppressed screams leaked back at me from ahead, speeding my pace beneath vaulted ceilings and upon packed soil that smelled of wood and insect carcasses. At times, the stench was enough to make me hold my breath. It was easy to lose track of time as I hurried. I thought of the library on the Shadow Trail and the long passageway Blade and I had taken to get to the greys.

This felt different. Like the air was taking nips out of my skin and sipping at the blood that welled in tiny pools. But she didn't stop screaming, so I didn't stop running.

It seemed to take forever and no time at all before I halted at another copper door with yet another vine covered handle. Patterns of all kinds, shapes and lines, had been hammered into the surface beneath the foliage. The vines had begun to creep from the frame, where they'd been planted to cover the handle and the surface. Bright new, minty green leaves unfurled as I watched.

If I hesitated, those vines would completely cover the door. My hands and arms already burned enough that I was hesitant to plow them through to search for the latch. And yet...I had to keep going. That girl was on the other side and I knew from experience what could wait in the dark underbelly of Fae.

We are the ones in danger. The words whispered back at me in a rasp. Was it a ruse meant to keep me from plunging into the darkness, instill fear in me?

It was already too late to turn back the moment I pushed through the first webbing of vinyalia. But I did pause at this copper door. Leaned in. Shuttering my eyes to hear things that might go unnoticed with a full raft of senses interfering with them, I tried to listen for the threat of danger without touching the foliage.

A tiny leaf unfurled in front of me, like a dog sniffing a new treat. It opened wide, sprouting tiny needles of thorns at its base that strained toward me with a sort of liquid droplet at the tips.

The needles were very sharp and numerous and growing in number as I stood there being cautious. Any longer and the door would be covered.

I let my breath go slowly, uncertainty needling my skin as surely as those thorns.

Mindful of using violence again lest it turn against me, I ran the backs of my fingers cautiously over the leaves. A gentle touch and no more. I waited. My entire body felt like a lung on half-inhale.

I thought I heard a hushed sort of sigh moving along the woody parts of the vine. They shuddered, and then...

They fell away.

I stared at the door for a long moment, not sure what had just happened, just certain beyond any shadow of doubt that those vines had not been touched like that in centuries. Maybe never.

Gripping the latch with as much care, listening with all five senses, I levered it downward.

The door swung open to reveal a chamber filled with dozens of blacksteel cells and a light so bright I had to shift my gaze to those behind those bars and vines to shield my eyes. I prayed my vision would adjust quickly because that swift aversion of my gaze told me all the cells were full. And that whatever had gathered itself into the darkness beyond was not human. Maybe not even fae. Whatever it was, power surged from it in waves that moved my hair. Heat suffused my cheeks as though a hot flash had prickled over my skin.

Beyond that first blush of power, a waiting, thrumming thing, it did nothing more. It waited, like I did, to see who would make the first move and what move that would be.

My eyes roamed the cages to each side, making sure danger didn't lurk there. Only terrified faces looked back at me and when I caught their eyes, they shifted their gazes to the darkness ahead of me.

Something waited for me in those shadows and I had the feeling it had been waiting for a long time. It wasn't just the fae I'd followed. Not just the girl they'd carried along with them.

It was something...more.

Precious seconds might be wasted as I waited for my eyes to adjust enough to see beyond and into the gloom, but I had no choice. I had to trust the hairs on the back of my neck to alert me to sudden danger, the tiny hairs in the middle of my ears to warn me of attack.

Three fae and one mortal girl had entered this chamber ahead of me. They had to be here somewhere. I had to know if they had brought the girl to this doom in the shadows.

I edged closer, the hum of tension in the room delivering to me half a dozen pieces of information: the chamber had gone immediately silent upon my entry, but the prisoners were there, clutching the bars, watching me. The light that blinded me disguised a darkness beyond it that was much deeper than could be measured from where I stood.

Spinning in a circle, I panned the space. My gown brushed the flagstones like a broom, gathering dust that rose in a swirl around me. No one had trod these floors in decades. I saw only one set of footprints in the dust—my own—and they led to the swirl of patterns I made in the dirt as I pivoted and turned.

I knew one thing. This wasn't on castle grounds. It might not even be in the same realm. It certainly wasn't the king's harem, because if it was, Ferranus had done little to protect his lovers than supply a copper door protected by only venomous vines.

This had to be something else. Somewhere else.

My eyes began to adjust. More details showed themselves to me as my surroundings wavered and shifted. The dungeon-like quality of the passageway grew more cavernous behind me. A steady, rhythmic dripping of fluid from some far off water source sounded like a heartbeat. A sheen of mercury slithered along gunnels in front of the cells. I could see, finally, into the cell nearest me.

A man wearing a ratty coat reminiscent of the old South from the civil war stared back at me with sunken eyes. He grinned, showing me blackened teeth.

"Sweet baby Jesus," I muttered.

"Not that god," came a feminine voice from the shadows.

I whirled around to face her. She looked much the same as she had in the ballroom. Willowy, young. Long, lush red hair. This much closer than I'd seen her in the ballroom, the milk and rose cheeks held dimples that framed her full mouth like quotation marks.

"Who are you?" I asked as my hand trailed to my karambit.

Out of the castle, out of the protective magic, I told myself.

"Some would be afraid to demand such an answer of me."

She didn't sound young. Not in the least. It had been a ruse, after all. Just not the sort I'd thought.

Her hip cocked to the side as she swept a graceful gesture over the front of her body. "You came to the aid of this girl?"

I eyeballed her suspiciously, understanding dawning. "It's glamor," I said. "You thought I'd see a mortal girl in trouble and rush to her aid."

Her hand seesawed in front of her chest, a very human movement but it was disjointed and jerky, like she was still practicing. "I had to know what you would do."

"You lured me here," I said, feeling braver when my fingers brushed the hard weight of my blade beneath my skirts. "Where are we?"

"Kumara," she said, as though I should know what and where that was. When I didn't react, she cocked her head to the side like a broken doll. "It is where we wait."

Dread and foreboding crawled up my spine like a swarm of fire ants. And yet the comment begged one more question. I swallowed hard. Lifted my chin.

"And what are you waiting for?"

That smile moved only half of her mouth, as though she couldn't lift both edges at the same time. "For now, we are waiting to see what you are made of."

"Sticks and snails and puppy dog tails," I ground out, feeling duped and angry at myself, and more so when she chuckled and stepped back into the light and probably the shadows behind that, and left me alone in the passage with the prisoners and their deathly quiet.

Something crackled through the air, like sheets in the wind. In the next instant, a whoop went up from somewhere in the shadows. Not one of joy but of grit and determination. A war cry.

I spun to face it.

A second later, the three fae who until this point had been invisible, all rushed me at once.

Muscle memory took over long before they made it to me. I dodged, spun. The dress moved like water around me. I swept a roundhouse kick, hoping to connect with something, but not fully expecting it either.

And yet it did. I felt the strike of bone on the bottom of my boot, ricocheting up my shin. The fae whose leg I'd struck went down with a snort of air from his lungs.

I was on him in a second.

The creatures behind the bars made a hell of a noise then. A terrible din of banging, slamming, and shouting, not all in languages I understood. The other two fell on my back as I pummeled the one beneath me.

I felt them pulling at me as though they were loath to hurt me and just wanted their comrade safe from the barrage of punches I was landing on his face.

Then it all shifted. A loud clanging sound ricocheted through the air. It reverberated and echoed for too long before it died.

The two holding me, the one beneath me, all three froze. I saw panic in the eyes of the face below me.

"What the fuck?" I muttered.

"Run," he said.

In a heartbeat, those yanking on me fell away, leaving me free to strike at their partner at will, but some instinct stayed my hand.

I rolled off him instead. He scrambled to his feet, lunging back toward the entrance of the passageway long before he gained solid footing. He pin-wheeled for several long strides before he caught up with his comrades. Their soles beat a hard path in the direction we'd come. Toward the stairs and the first copper door beyond that. To the ball-room.

It took me several seconds to stand. Confusion swept over me in rags of tattered thought.

That was all I had, those few seconds.

Next came a rush of stink and air and energy. It throttled its way toward me. Every hair on my skin strained for air, pulling in information to send along my nerve endings.

I pivoted sharply, the dress moving smoothly with me to keep from tangling in my legs. It was a perfect movement. Not just graceful, but the kind of execution Gideon always harped at me to practice.

I was fluid as water. A ballet of movement. The thing that struck me first went down hard beneath a half-turned donkey kick. I rounded my back just in time to flip the next one. I almost laughed as another grappled my arm and I swung it, hurtling into a gang of more lumbering creatures.

One sleek turn and one sharp pivot, and my karambit was in my grip so easily, no awkward pause put space between one movement and another.

I sliced expertly at first. My mental count ticked up with each swipe. One body. Two. The vague awareness that fluid was spraying, that I had to mind my step so I wouldn't slip, that I shouldn't lick my lips. Just keep striking out. Just keep inching backwards toward the stairwell, out of the passage. Strike. Cut. Count.

I made it to five before the throng of creatures flooded over me. Then I could do nothing but hack and slash at anything that moved.

And just like that, I was fighting for my life.

Every creature who had been in the cells swept over me like a wave. I only had time to realize they weren't human. Not anymore, if they ever were. They tore at me with teeth and nails and—heaven help me—claws.

Nerves and adrenaline became my only allies. I blindly felt for the corsage but my arms were suddenly pinned against the crush of bodies. The karambit stuck in something solid and I didn't have the lee-way to pull it out.

If there was pain as they attacked me, I didn't feel it. And yet I knew I should feel pain. I'd long lost the ability to fight back. They struck at will.

Shock, I thought. I was in shock. Reason fled in the face of the onslaught and I struck out blindly when I could because there was no space for calculated movement. I counted two more opponents fallen to my strikes, and a quick glance showed them writhing in agony or completely immobile.

I stumbled over too many arms and legs, rolling like they were logs in a river.

And then...blessedly, there was a break in the melee.

The passage way to the stairs glowed like white light. The scuffled footprints of the fae who had escaped, showing me the way home like breadcrumbs.

I threw myself at the break. Laughed like a mad woman when I realized I was free. I raced like the fae had, sprawling, pinwheeling, as I gained my footing and stole several yards of freedom.

My breath was in tatters. As I ran, they clawed at me. What was left of the gown was as ragged as the wheezing coming from my lungs.

Someone was crying in soft sobs and it took the sensation of fluid dripping from my chin to realize it was me.

By the time I reached the rune-covered door, I was too numb to consider being gentle with the vines. I yanked at the latch, tearing through the foliage. They scratched me, razoring yet more slices into my skin.

I blinked at the sight of my hand beneath the greenery, shock-numb and clinical in my examination. Lashed with crimson lines of blood, the sight made me realize the creatures had done a lot of damage.

My legs swamped beneath me. I swayed on my feet.

"Not yet," I muttered. "Not fucking yet."

I wasn't sure if the things were following any longer, but I wasn't taking the chance. With my lungs hauling in air in short, spastic breaths, I shoved at the door. Stinging nettles of pain bit into my shoulder, my hip, my ribcage. I shoved all the harder.

And when it burst open, I ran, crookedly and half-hunched, toward the stairwell.

All that was left was to drag myself up the stairs. Time ceased to exist. Pain was nothing. All there was, was a gritty determination to get back inside the sanctity of the ballroom.

When I reached the top stair, an hour, a day, a month later, the fae were gone. No evidence that anyone but me had even entered. And yet...

The door was open a crack. I was almost there. A sob fled my lungs on its last bit of air.

I managed to get my arm through it as I staggered finally. My body was too spent, too shocked to take one more step.

And I knew I was going to die there.

CHAPTER 22

I'd been beaten in Fae before, but this time there would be no dark enforcer to heal my wounds or take the blows away from me. My karambit was gone. I was half-naked. I had nothing but my feet and hands and head to defend myself.

I lay on my side of the ballroom door, thinking about how close I had come to dying.

Not that being alive was much better. Now that the adrenaline dump of energy had dissipated, I felt every ache, burn, and pain. Doing an inventory of injuries made me anxious, so I didn't. I just lay there with my hand sticking through the door, hoping someone would notice because my calls for help were no more than whispers.

There was no telling how much time had elapsed between my collapse and the feel of someone's fingers stroking my palm, but it woke me.

I shook awake just as the door to the ballroom yanked open. Heuil stood there, peering into the darkness with large, unblinking eyes.

"Help," I croaked out.

He was on his knees in an instant, so I knew he recognized me. I couldn't say I was relieved by the look of worry I saw on his face. He said nothing as he hoisted me into his arms. I was too limp, too heavy for him to manage alone, and my legs dragged beneath me like a hanged woman's.

He carried me anyway, letting my feet drag. As my head hung onto my bare chest, I could see the blackened marks I grooved into a trail as we went. No one aided him, though I caught sight of several curious glances as he made his way to the great broad doors of the ballroom and begged to be let out. A knowing glance from the guards as they snickered and pushed open the door.

Relieved of the protective spell of the ballroom, true pain lanced through me then. Blackness feathered my vision, and I drifted away from consciousness on splintered pieces of driftwood.

I bobbed to the top of consciousness various times during the journey and each time I was bid awake by a stream of hot sick tearing up through my gullet. Vomit released itself onto the flagstone beneath our feet, leaving a wretched trail to follow us to a dank little room.

And yet the little trow did not falter.

I was pretty sure I was hyperventilating. I only felt the tremors of my body when my skin met his. At one point, I realized he'd somehow managed to hoist me all the way into his arms. He was breathing hard. Stumbling as much as he was walking.

My head sagged backward, all ability to hold it up gone. The view of Heuil's chin held me rapt for long moments as I watched the muscles in his jaw clench and let go with exertion.

"Not long now," he said, looking down as though he knew I was awake. His nostrils flared. There was fear in his eyes.

I shivered again, and his brow furrowed. "You're in shock," he said in a tight voice.

At that, he halted and stood immobile for several seconds before he spun around in a dizzyingly drunken circle.

"You," he barked over my head at someone in a voice I barely recognized as the little half trow's. It held such command, he could have been the dark enforcer.

"Give me your cloak," he said. "Hurry."

A flurry of activity sounded beside us as I felt his arm move, jostling me. Then a scratchy piece of wool got tossed over me and my body shuddered at the touch. It smelled of perfume and old sweat, but it was heavy and heavenly just the same.

Shadows crept into the corners of my vision. The ceiling and his face started to blur.

"Ava," he barked at me. "Stay awake."

I blinked stupidly, trying to figure out why Blade's voice was coming out of Heuil's mouth. I tried to reach up to touch his face, but my arms were as heavy as a tree trunk. A wan smile crept over my mouth at the sight of Blade's eyes. Such a relief. He would fix me. He would make it all better.

"Stay awake," he said, and I willed my eyelids to remain open because an order from the dark enforcer was an order that couldn't be disobeyed.

But my eyes fought their own battles, and they did so much harder than my will.

"Ava," he said again, this time softer. "You will look at me. And you will keep looking at me until I tell you to shut your eyes and rest."

When I didn't respond and refused to do as he demanded, his eyes narrowed to slits. "Do you hear me?"

Because of the rasp of huskiness in his voice that suggested he would jostle me in his arms until I answered, I blinked. It was all I could do. Everything else felt far too painful, and what might not be outright painful was just too impossible.

"Your nose is broken," he said in a ragged voice, and this time it sounded more like Heuil. I didn't want to look at him and see his face instead of Blade's. I wanted Blade.

"You have several cracked ribs. Gods know what else."

I swallowed and even that hurt.

Tears stung the backs of my eyelids and my cheeks felt wet.

"Hold on," the half trow rasped. "Just a little longer. I'll find a healer."

I wasn't sure how long he carried me, but I knew he had met the end of his strength when he let go a sigh of relief so loud it roused me from a dream where the smell of roasting chicken teased my senses and bid me sit at a long wooden table.

I opened my eyes to see past his flaring nostrils to a ceiling made of rougher, more natural things than in the ballroom. Plaster and rough-hewn lumber, I thought. And the walls as they sailed by had a stucco feeling as well.

I smelled wood smoke to go with the roasting chicken. The savory fragrance of herbs lifted to the air around me, intermingled with that of manure and hay.

The kitchens. I recognized the dried rosemary and thyme hanging from pegs in the wooden rafters.

Radiant heat pumped through the room like a blast from a furnace. The bustle of activity became a roar of noise that made me wince. I wanted to bury myself beneath the blanket. A gasp came from several people at once, and the sound made him stop short.

"I need a healer," he said.

A thick-waisted woman with harshly pointed ears bustled over. "Our healer is at the gala," she said.

Heuil made a sound deep in his throat that I swore he pulled from the depths of his soul. "Call for him, then. Now. Please."

I didn't miss the look she sent him before her gaze dropped to my form beneath the blanket.

"Call for him," he said again. "She's dying."

Chapter 23

I was never afraid of dying. It was a risk that came along with the job of monster hunting. But the thought of dying right then, when I knew I had unfinished business. It bothered me a lot.

Babes were dying in their cradles. Phaedre was in danger. Stone needed to be punished. Blade needed to be loved and longed for.

Dying was not for this moment. It was for another day.

"Put me down, Heuil," I said in a voice that didn't sound like my own.

He swayed on his feet with such magnitude, I thought I would fall from his arms, but he did not put me down.

"She needs help," he said.

The female glared down at me with her hands on her hips. "She's mortal," she said.

"I know that," he said. "She needs help."

The woman pursed her lips thoughtfully. "He's the king's healer," she said. "You're not going to get him to come back here when it's the first gala in a century. He bought enough magic to glamor himself an entire high fae body."

The cloak slipped just enough to show enough of my skin to make a sailor blush, but the fae woman didn't so much as blink. "She is all but naked and bleeding in my kitchen," she said. "Do you realize just how disgusting that is?"

"Far less disgusting, I should think, than the dark enforcer spraying your blood all over the walls," he said in a measured voice.

She went white. "The dark enforcer?"

He nodded. "He rescued her from the Catacombs of Dread. He will come for her here." His voice was soft. "You don't want to know what he did to those who injured her."

Her blink was long and slow before she snapped the cloak from atop me with a thwack that sounded like a gunshot. Then she shoved her arms between his, helping him hold onto me. Together, they tried to muscle me onto the table, but it was still filled with dishes and bowls and food. They propped me against it, pinned between the wood and their bodies as Heuil swept the table clean.

The din of breaking pottery and whirling bowls on flagstones was a momentary distraction before she let go of me long enough to spread the cloak over the table.

That was when the agony intensified. Neither was strong enough to wrangle me onto the surface, and it took a lot of awkward maneuvering that made me groan and moan and yes, whimper like a child. I tried to help them to make it easier and less painful, but moving took effort. Where I didn't hurt, my joints felt gummed up.

At last, I lay flat on the table's surface. She tsked over what met her gaze like a mother hen. Through swollen eyes that were burning so badly with the need to close that the sheer effort was making me sweat, I saw her face go white.

She glanced up at Heuil, and whatever he saw in her face made him stiffen.

"I need help," she said, then cast a bunch of sentences over her shoulder in a language that had no earthly equivalent.

A flurry of activity swept through the room, then. The sound of plates and glasses and pots being shoved, moved, and dropped echoed all around.

Then, I felt myself being poked and prodded. The room swam for a second as my brain tried to work through the blur of pain. The hard surface of a wooden table dug into my shoulders before the woman barked a command at someone else over her shoulder.

"Tea. herbs. Now," she said.

My arms hung over the side in an awkward angle. Heuil collected first one, then the other, and tenderly laid them next to my sides, tucking my thumbs slightly beneath my waist. It was sheer will that kept me from crying out.

She shoved him aside with her hip. "Give me space," she said in a chiding tone. "You're in the way. Don't hover. And for the gods' sake go find someone to help. My magics can only go so far."

She loomed over me, peeling open my eyelids with her thumbs, leveraging her palms against the hollows of my cheeks. I flinched, and I was pretty sure I went comatose for several seconds because next I knew, a cool cloth hung over my forehead, dripping some noxious fluid into my hairline.

One turn of my head toward a sound beside me and everything swam again. A voice, I thought. I had to close my eyes to cling to the knowledge that I wasn't spinning like a top on the table. Only when the world stopped whirling like a dervish was I able to take a deliberate breath.

"I don't have the healing magic," came a voice from beside me. "But I am of the woods. I know herbs. I can ease the pain until a healer comes."

I blinked and tried to find her face. It took a moment for the blur of beige and green to transform into a face with black eyes and a knot of hair so thick even the kerchief covering it couldn't tame it.

A groan escaped me when I meant to speak.

She smiled at me. "You're alright," she said. "Not dying as he suspected. Just very, very badly broken." Her glance swept toward my legs. "Although I do believe setting those bones will make you want to die."

"Did your man do this to you?" she said, and laid her palm on my forearm in probably the only place it wouldn't hurt. "Tell me, child. Don't lie. I know you mortals lie. But don't you dare lie about this. I can sense these things."

"Stone," I mumbled, this time pleased the words actually came out.

"What's that?" she said, her brows knit together. "Is that his name?"

I tried to shake my head, but it hurt too much. "Stone," I said again because I was certain that whoever was in the basement had lured me there because Stone had bid it. No one else would have cared. And he'd already tried to have me killed once. Whatever his motivation was, I knew it was him.

"It was Stone."

Her jaw ticked to the side, thoughtful. She let go a pensive hum before tossing another command over her shoulder, this time in English. "Toss out the dram of bitter-butter, Pliny and get some coffee instead," she said. "I need you here, and we don't want some bairn drinking your joy-juice and end up having its wee stomach pumped before the night is over."

She looked back at me. "I needed to know," she said. "I wasn't about to work herb magic on you just so a lover could take you away again and repeat his atrocity."

She said it like she'd seen it happen before, and I didn't doubt it. Here in Fae, humans didn't have any rights.

I wanted to say something, to let her know I was still there, still present and accounted for, but no words came. She watched my face with sympathy as she took the cloth from my forehead and squeezed it out into a bowl beside me.

Liquid sluiced noisily next to my ear before she plunged the cloth in again and plucked it, still dripping, from the bowl.

She laid it on my cheek this time, dabbing gently. "This is for swelling," she said. "No sense telling you the name of the herb. It won't sound but like a bunch of syllables to you. But it's very good. I can already see how pretty you are, so it's started working."

I wanted to turn away from the compassion in that voice, but she held my head with the cloth and a gentle pressure for several more moments. Mercifully, I felt the swelling subside. Like magic.

"There," she said in a voice that was very reminiscent of a dentist poking about for a cavity and finding a nice white tooth beneath a bit of tartar.

I swallowed, feeling a freeness of muscle that had been nothing but constricted tissue before. With a flourish, she peeled away the cloth and dunked it noisily into the bowl. Water bled down my face and soaked into my hair.

"I feel much better," I said and tried to get to my elbows. With a start, I yelped and fell back down onto the table.

She put her hand on my forehead, holding me down. "Your arms aren't broken," she said. "Mercifully, just badly bruised bones. We're working on that."

I rolled my head to face her. She was soaked from neck to waist. Perspiration beaded her forehead and clung to the tendrils of hair peeking out from beneath her kerchief. Beyond her, several more sets of eyes and similarly drenched tunics came into view.

"Yes," she said. "These are mine." She cast a look over her shoulder. "Five forest bairns, given to me by the wood gods. All have the same herb magic as I do. It wasn't me alone who helped, you understand. I wasn't enough. Not for your injuries." She shook her head sadly.

"Thank you," I said.

Her smile came easily, but it was tinged with sadness. "I'm ashamed to say I didn't try to help right away."

"I understand," I said. And I did. She didn't know me. One thing I'd learned in Fae was that magic took energy no matter how small. To expend it, meant you took something from yourself.

"My hesitation was an unspeakable affront to the gods of the woods and herbs." She sighed. "But they have not punished me for my lack of compassion, and so I am grateful for your forgiveness."

I had the feeling it had more to do with the threat of the dark enforcer, but I kept quiet. What did it matter why she'd helped?

One of the five standing behind her came forward with a long, white sheet draped over his arm. She took it from him without a word and shook it over me. In her hands, it snapped as though a strong wind had tried to tear it from a clothesline.

"I'm sorry to leave your injuries to such open-eyed invitation but it was necessary to bring the swelling down. Your bones will knit with the right magic." She shook her head, indicating her remorse. "I don't have that healing power, but your abrasions have closed at least and begun to heal."

I nodded. What she was saying was that while she'd taken the pain and some of the swelling, cleaned the wounds, she could do no more. And what was left was not pretty.

More than that, I supposed I shouldn't have hoped for, but as my tears burned my eyes, I realized I had hoped for more. To my own shame.

"Rest now," she said. "When the trow returns, I'll be sure he is given salve to spread over the few injuries that are still swollen." She waved her hand over her head and a long arm with painted nails snaked toward her palm to plant a jar in her grip.

With a swift motion, she dropped the jar beside my head on the table. "But this is for you. This..." she murmured. "This has something different." Her gaze narrowed as she leaned in close enough for me to see the flecks of brown in her eyes. They looked like rings in a tree. "This powder will paralyze him," she said. "He won't be able to move for several minutes." Those black eyes sizzled with barely disguised fury, and I wondered how much experience she had with abusive males. "If you need time to run," she said meaningfully. "This powder will give it to you. Not a lot of time, but enough to get a good head start. Place it in your palm and blow. Easy as that."

Apparently, she remembered my comment about Stone, and I didn't bother to correct her. It was enough to eye the jar as it hunkered beside me and consider what paralyzing Stone might mean. Stop him in his tracks so I could slit his throat or empty his belly onto his feet?

I shook my head. When I took the bastard down, I wanted the moment to be clean and righteous. I wanted to take my time showing him the kind of woman he'd double-crossed and I wanted him to feel every strike.

With a heavy hand, I pushed the jar away. "It might be best I leave," I said. "I have places to go. Things to do."

She snorted. "Looks to me like the best you'll be able to accomplish is a fat nap."

I tried to lift my head. "Have the Endowments started?" I asked, doing my best to keep her in focus. Damn the woman she kept phasing in and out. "I'm to be presented to the king."

Outright laughter at that, but not unkind. A blur of movement met my gaze that suggested she was shaking her head. I couldn't blame her for thinking I was out of the running, but she didn't know me. She didn't know how determined I was.

I caught at her sleeve. "My dress," I said.

She gave me a lingering look of sympathy. "Gone, child. Torn to shreds when you came and not much left to save if we wanted to get to your injuries quickly."

Erachne's gown was gone. Destroyed. I wanted to weep at the thought.

"Do you have something I can wear?" I asked. "I need to get back. They'll be waiting for me, and I'm just putting you in danger by staying here."

She eyed me curiously, as though she was considering arguing with me, but then I almost saw her recall Heuil's comment about the dark enforcer and she finally waved her hand over her head. The gesture drew the attention of those same five young men lurking around the various shelves and wood piles. "Yes, well," she said. "As it is, I do have work to do, and you *are* in the way."

Her brood hustled over to me like ants from the corners of the room, looking very much like they had every intention of hoisting me from the table, sheet and all. Brusque and business-like, every single one of them reached for a corner of the cloak beneath me, and I thought they might just dump me on the floor.

I must have made a sound of protest because the kitchen fae laid her hand on my shoulder. "Hush, child. They're just going to help you up."

They looked about as strong as the spine of a dove feather. There was no doubt in my mind that they'd be in so much of a hurry to do their mother's bidding that they'd end up spilling me onto the floor, cloak and all.

Not going to happen. Before they could draw near enough to put a finger on the cloak or on me, I draped a leg over the edge of the table.

"Hold on there, young pups," I said, lifting a finger to hold them off. "I can get up on my own steam."

My knee ached as my toes searched for the floor. My arms felt like someone had poured lead into the crevices where bone met bone, but I worked at it. I had to.

Hanging a leg over did nothing to dissuade their approach, rather it seemed to hasten it, so I slid my backside sideways as fast as I could manage.

"Not that you all don't have the best intentions" I said. "But you look like between you all, you might be able to carry a feather pillow for a few yards and that's it."

For a heart-stopping moment, I felt victory's cold circle of golden ring within reach. My leg hung over, my palm propped me up. I was dizzy and awash in a rush to get moving, but I had managed to move on my own steam even if it was just a few inches.

But that was it. I didn't have what it took to keep myself from dumping onto the floor. The boys let me fall. By the time I struck the flagstones on my side and got blasted with another jolt of pain, they all stood over me. The kitchen fae clucked her disappointment in tones that sounded very much like, I told you so.

Pain scissored into my shoulder blades and I sucked in a loud breath that exited with an equally large curse. Apparently, one of my legs was broken and the other in bad shape. I couldn't bring myself to look at them, for fear I'd made things worse.

Curled into a ball was the best I could do as the pain spasmed through me and abated repeatedly. I let it come, thankful I could feel it. Feeling it told me I was alive.

The kitchen fae let me shudder through the pain before she reached to pat me on the shoulder. Kindly. With a mother's touch that made me bite my lip to keep it from trembling. Then, just as I was beginning to think she was all care and comfort, she heaved me over onto my back.

I bit back a cry and a curse. Black shadows bled into the edges of my vision.

"Are all mortals as foolish as you?" she asked.

A fresh wave of cold sweat accompanied the pain this time as I stared up at her. "Stubborn is what you're seeing here," I said, correcting her when I found the energy to speak. "Stubborn and stupid. And no, I don't think there is any other mortal as foolish."

With a wince, I tried to roll onto my side because I was feeling very much like a bug about to be squashed, and despite the kindness of the cook and her brood, I didn't relish feeling vulnerable in front of anyone.

A strong core and a hard head gave me leverage to move without using much of my legs. It took some doing, with a lot of sweat, and a hell of a lot of cursing just to get onto my shoulder. I wanted desperately to get to my knees but the movements had cost me. It was all just one humungous agony.

My head dug into the floor. Perspiration dripped from my nose as I watched the six of them watching me with raised eyebrows and crossed arms.

My eyes had a peculiar and telling sting to them that sent a wave of humiliation over my spine.

By the time the room came back into focus and I was staring at perfectly clean grooves in the wooden floor, feeling a fair bit victorious at not crying out, everything in the room had gone deathly quiet.

At first, I thought I simply couldn't hear anything since the ringing in my ears was so loud, but once the dizziness swam away, taking with it the most of the tinnitus, I swallowed down a lump of dread.

All of them were looking past me. And all of them looked terrified.

CHAPTER 24

Alarm bells rang out in place of the tinnitus as I realized we weren't alone. That something deadly this way came. I panned my gaze sideways. A sweep of the room revealed the cook and her brood standing a few feet away, huddled together, their eyes on someone beside me.

My mouth went dry. I wasn't just an insect on the floor in my state. I was an overturned turtle, a mouse out in the open field.

My eyes closed of their own accord as I understood just how terrified the expressions were on their faces. Only one thing could be that scary, I decided.

"Blade," I said, hating the hope in my voice because if it was him, I didn't want him to see me like this.

"Not the dark enforcer," said a softly feminine voice that sounded like it was as dusty as the floor, filled with cobwebs and gossamer. "But that doesn't mean someone who cares for you didn't seek me out and send me to you."

I knew the voice. I just couldn't recall from where.

"Let me help you, child," she said.

As if I were a feather being plucked from the floor, several fuzzy pads grappled beneath me and lifted. As my head lolled to the side, I caught sight of a gargantuan spider.

I started without thinking, pulling back in surprise. Eyes the color of tiny black stones blinked back at me, eight of them working independently.

There should have been some sort of fear creeping through me at the sight of the creature, but instead, a sensation of warmth swept over me. Comfort. Ease. I was safe. At least that was what my gut told me.

Even though the lesser Fae serving the cook all looked as though someone had put spiders down their collars, I knew this creature would not harm me.

I didn't even wince when mandibles descended to my wrist and bit down. A sting. Nothing more than that. And then heat flooded me, rising from my arm to my chest and then swamping over me in a luscious breath.

"I'm sorry," I said, thinking of that beautiful gown. "They ruined it."

"Hush," Erachne murmured. "It's of no consequence to me."

The kitchen fae started from her corner the way a person does when they are about to stomp down on some bug they found crawling toward a basket of cheese. She had her wooden spoon raised like a sword in front of her. If she intended to crush Erachne like a bug, it wasn't going to go well for her. I almost called out to her but she cut me off before I could warn her.

"Get out of my kitchen," she said, aiming the spoon at Erachne. "I know how you spin your cloth. Be gone."

One of Erachne's eyes rolled toward her. When she replied, it was in such a cool tone, I knew the spider-fae had faced more fearsome beings than a kitchen fae with a spoon.

"If you know such a thing," she said. "Then you wouldn't tempt me to spin this warrior another dress to cover her nakedness. Now *you* be gone. We have much work to do."

The kitchen fae and all her sons backed off so quickly I could hear them falling over each other. I couldn't make out their shapes in the corners of the room, but I certainly felt them huddling there.

All I knew in the moment was that those velvet pads of Erachne's legs? Hands? I didn't want to name the things as they cradled me against the softest fuzz of a bosom, that she lifted me as if I was weightless from the floor. I felt myself being carried, but there was no pain.

"The Bestowal of Magics is about to begin," she said to me. "Time will stand still in the ballroom while this happens."

I could barely nod. If they were about to start, then the presentations of the blood gifts would, too. I tried to move, not thinking, just knowing I had to get back to there. Phaedre's life depended on it. So many lives depended on it. Little lives. Innocent ones.

As if I weighed no more than a fly, Erachne laid me on the table again and I heard a grunt from the corner. The kitchen fae offering a final complaint, I supposed. Erachne's eyes remained on me, a disconcerting flurry of blinks as whatever passed for eyelids ran over her eyes.

With one of her legs, she pulled a gossamer string from over her shoulder and stretched it over my torso. I felt my weight lift and lower, the sensation of sticky threads laying over my skin.

I started then. Had I misinterpreted her purpose? Was she planning to cocoon me like a fly for later. I tried to swat her legs away, but there were too many of them now. Too much thread moving over my body at rates of speed that astounded me.

"Be still," she said. "My quarry have much better flavor than the taste of mortal men." Two eyes rolled toward the fae in the corner, bare figures of grey matter now as they tightened together in a knot of fabric and skin. At her words, one of them made a chirp of fear. Erachne chuckled to herself before those eyes landed on me again. "I've given you something for the pain. You'll be safe as you heal."

Protests worked their way up my throat, but she hushed me yet again.

"Stop moving, my child. I'll shroud you here and plant you like a little seed somewhere safe. Time will stand still in the ballroom, but it will pass as regular for you outside the chamber. That will give you time to heal. Whatever task you have that you feel is so important you would try to stand on sprained ankles, will wait for you."

The threads had covered me by then, and all I could see of her was a gauzy grayness with burning eyes.

"Shame about the dress," she said. "But Lilah is not the only fae sorceress who can bend time and space to her will. And where I plan to hide you is going to need all my magic."

Lilah. The name on Erachne's lips surprised me. I wasn't sure I wanted to know how this creature knew the woman I'd neutralized back in the earthen realm, thinking her merely a black magic witch. The witch was dead. I guessed Erachne hadn't heard the news.

Except....Gideon used to tell me there were no coincidences. Only consequences. I'd watched the light go out of Lilah's eyes. I'd stolen a blue stone from her hand. It was true I'd fled without salting her bones, but Hell...I'd had a hellhound and a nasty fae on my tail.

Again...except. Those fae, one of them Blade and the other Flint, had gone there on Terran's orders. Had they been there not just to claim the cursed objects, but to hire Lilah to counter the spell the king had ordered put on the ballroom?

I peered up at Erachne, not wanting to believe where my mind was taking me. If she could bend time and space, was she the sorceress who cast the spellwork on the ballroom?

Whatever the truth, I knew I could trust her. At least, I hoped I could because it was already too late to fight her off. But the thought that I might be able to use her to undo the spell was the last thing that went through my mind before the numbness in my body reached my consciousness.

I was barely aware that the threads had grown so thick around me that I couldn't see the Erachne's eyes anymore. Even her mouth and fangs looked like a vague shape without the razor sharpness. I just knew I was tired. So tired.

I closed my eyes for a moment. That was all. Next I knew I was stepping up to a broad set of copper doors inlaid with several symbols. At first, I recoiled, the cell memory of the moment beyond another rune-covered door firing through my synapses.

But then, as if I was dreaming, I found an almost clinical detachment. I could examine the blacksteel that formed a great handle in a horizontal bar without fear. My fingers curled around it, giving it a test pull.

At my touch, the doors opened inward, not out, and a shiver ran down my spine.

A throne room, I thought. Large and ancient, where the creatures inside wore primitive dress but their skin glowed with a luminescence that reminded me of phytoplankton swimming in a quiet midnight sea. The air was thick with an otherworldly energy, and the dim light of dozens of torches cast an ethereal glow on the intricate tapestries that adorned the walls.

Rows of fae stood watching me enter. They waited silently as I took my first steps, forming a gauntlet toward the dais where three very tall, very powerful-looking Fae sat on gilded thrones. The confusion about why the chamber had changed, why the fae were no longer dressed in sumptuous garments faded as I realized this was the moment I'd been brought to Fae for. Whatever elegance and grandeur had come before, whatever glamor had been laid on the castle, that was over.

The Endowments had been completed. Now it was time for the Blood Gifts presentation and the king's withdrawal to the harem.

I was either that or the last because the chamber seemed so taut with tension and expectancy that it electrified my skin in static bursts. Panning the room, I searched for Stone.

Like before, I couldn't find him. Unlike before, this throne room looked nothing like the gala I'd attended just hours before.

Looking up, I noted that the ceiling soared above us, adorned with an elaborate mosaic depicting scenes that would be reminiscent of the Sistine Chapel's frescoes except with nymphs and fae and mythical creatures. The paint on the plaster seemed to pulse with life as the torchlight reached for it with soft fingers.

A sound at the front of the room drew my attention again toward the dais, toward the three figures sitting in state in majestic silence. Each throne was a masterpiece, carved from the bones of ancient trees and adorned with glistening gemstones. But it was the figures sitting upon them that caught my attention.

Even as I regarded them, my mind struggled with what I was seeing. I expected the king to look as he had when I'd danced with Stone, trying to get his attention. He didn't. He was more ancient looking. Wizened and stooped even as he sat far back in the seat, his eyes possessed a keenness given to much younger males. Old he might be, but his mind was sharp, his eyesight keen. Nothing would get by his notice.

My first hazy thought was that the king had lost his glamor, that he'd peeled away the magic of the room and the fae within to show it all as it was. But then, I noticed that the mercenaries on each side of him had thrones as well instead of the places they'd taken at his side, standing at attention.

Ruby of the Nocturnes didn't swirl and evaporate like mist, either, but sat in her seat looking sickly pale with silver hair and purple eyes. The previously empty position on the king's left was now occupied by a broad-shouldered male.

And I knew immediately that these creatures were not hired guns. These creatures were royalty. If I squinted, I might even think the male was Ferranus, except he looked far too young.

In the instant I knew that, I also knew I'd seen them before. In glimpses of half-remembered dreams. In a blast of energy from a young fae's magic.

I was still filtering through the information when a noise from behind me made me pivot sharply. I gasped as someone walked right into me as though I wasn't there. A chill cascaded over me from head to toe and I felt like I was being plucked apart by a thousand ants.

Then, as if it hadn't happened, the male kept going, rushing toward the dais in such a hurry that I turned on my heel to see what the fuss was about.

I thought I'd pass out when I saw pieces of myself floating like a swarm of insects flinging themselves off his back and humming their way toward me once again. The moment they touched me, I swayed on my feet, taking the impact as though it were a blow.

He'd run through me, I realized, and that was when I understood I wasn't actually in the throne room, but in some long gone past, a ghost, like the one of Christmas past or future. A shade no one could see.

Erachne's magic, I realized. Shaping time and space like she'd said it would. Hiding me in some small place, she'd said. Perhaps a bit of cell memory or a wrinkle in time.

As disconcerting as it was to realize I was there and not here, I was rapt by the movement of the male who'd bled through me. I was sure I recognized the shape of his shoulders, the tilt of his head as he bowed then knelt in front of the king. If only he would turn around, I would know if I'd met him.

He didn't. He rushed on, oblivious of me as he hung his head. When he spoke, I recognized the timber but I couldn't make out any words. I strained for better acuity but it was no use. His pause held the bloat of tension about to burst. In a covert movement, he swung his head ever so slightly toward the male on the king's left.

I needed to know what was going on. Why I was being shown this if I wasn't party to the events. What I needed was a better viewpoint.

I had only to think I'd like to see it closer to find myself moved to a better position.

I stood on the dais between the king and the male, looking down at a very youthful-looking Terran.

The shock of seeing him there was nothing to the realization that he was dressed in the King's Guard uniform. The badge on his chest was pinned there by what looked like dragon's eyes, two large rubies with emerald lids, decidedly serpentine but without the slit pupils.

They knew each other, I realized. More than that, the way Terran's gaze slid to Ferranus's so covertly, they were intimate in some way. Lovers, maybe. Or companions. I wasn't sure. But I was certain that the two of them shared some secret communication. Something the old king wouldn't approve of.

Even as I wondered what that could be, and why Erachne's magic had brought me here, the doors to the throne room burst open behind me.

Everyone in the room fled to the walls at the sight of an Amazon sized female who swept into the room. Her hair was blood red with highlights that resembled the yellow golds of a flame's belly. She wore thick burgundy leather. Two sets of ears, resembling a doberman's, snickered close together as perky, attentive pairs peeked through the loose-flowing locks at the top of her head.

Her face was fierce, yet magnificent. I didn't think I'd ever seen a creature so lovely and terrifying at the same time.

"Aiofe," the old king said as she strode toward the dais, her thick-soled thigh high black leather boots pounding the tiles like a drum as she moved. "What honor do I have to welcome my half-sister to the Iron Court?"

"You know why I'm here, brother," she said, coming up beside Terran so close, her thigh brushed his cheek. He went rigid at the touch, and I was sure she'd done it on purpose. "You owe me. I want what I was promised."

The old king's face gave nothing away, but his knuckles whitened as they curled tighter around the armrests.

"I owe you nothing," he said in a cool voice. A tone that made that gorgeous face of Aiofe's turn hard. A single breath, that's what she took, and it barely moved her chest, yet I saw the inhalation. I felt it as it drew the air like a funnel from the room.

Something fierce and primal stole over her face. It took a moment for me to realize I knew the look, the posture. Her glamor was dissolving, and she knew it. Her hand reached out for Terran's shoulder, clutching it so hard I swore he winced.

And just when I thought I'd see what lay beneath all that magic, everything froze.

As though this was an important moment. As though Erachne's magic had plucked the instant out of time and let me stand within it. As though this was a video and this last second was the final scene before the film ran out.

Curious, I gazed around at the players, my mind reeling until it occurred to me that I could move easily and unnoticed around the entire tableau.

Whatever was going on here, I needed to see it. I moved with purpose, crouching down so I could see up into Terran's face. I looked back over my shoulder at the direction of his gaze as it held Ferranus's eye. Yes. Some sort of communication, and both of them were worried.

If I looked at the old king, he just looked angry in his freeze-frame capture. He regarded Aiofe with disgust and disdain. But I noted he'd leaned away from the female sitting on the throne to his right, and something about the way every inch of his body seemed to be working to draw attention away from her and to him suggested he was protecting her.

I turned my attention for the first time to her. For a fae, she looked frail.

And the moment my gaze searched for her face, everything spun and warped and bowed in and out with such speed, I lost my balance. I lurched sideways, hands out, fingers splayed in reflex to catch myself as I fell to the tiled floor.

But it wasn't a tiled floor anymore. It was a void of nothingness where mists swirled and pained screams lifted in the air so loudly I stopped up my ears with my palms.

Wincing, I swayed on my knees, praying for the sound to stop, and when it did, it was replaced with the cries of infants. Dozens of them. All wailing. All at once. The feminine core of me tensed up and flooded with the kind of energy all mothers must feel at the sound of a crying babe.

I wanted it to stop. I wanted to stop it. I wanted to help, to soothe, to rock and calm. Anything to halt that horrible keening, so badly that when the mists disappeared, I didn't question the sound of running water until I felt it seep up to my thighs. Cold and thick. Like amniotic fluid spilled in a basin of porcelain.

With a blink, I took in my new landscape. An old-fashioned telephone booth with sea water rising high and fast. So fast it was already up to my armpits and I could barely lift my arms to slam against the walls, hoping to bend the accordion doors to my blows.

Still the water came. Still, the doors, the wall, wouldn't bend. It all rushed in so fast that I could barely keep my chin above the tide. I smelled sulfur and cloves and the faintest trace of cinnamon before it all disappeared—so suddenly that it left me staggering on my feet in the throne room again.

A flash of image. Aiofe's face was so close to mine, I could see the flecks of black in her ruby-colored eyes.

I jerked back, jolted.

"It's time," she drawled in a quiet voice. "Get up or die."

Chapter 25

There are some things worse than the thought of dying. Finding yourself dropped out of nowhere and landing naked at the feet of a powerful and vindictive enemy just might be one of them.

I had no idea where I was for a full moment as I lay on my back, blinking up at the unfamiliar canopy of stars and mist above me even as my peripheral vision suggested I was inside somewhere. Swashes of color and light moved around me. Muttering in languages of all sorts.

Dazed, it took longer than it should have to notice the movement to my right. I turned in what seemed like slow motion to see familiar eyes looking down into my face. Terran, I finally realized.

But it wasn't the young Terran I'd just seen bowing low before an ancient-looking king. This was the more mature version, the one I recognized as the leader of the Shadow

Court, whose face held hard lines now softened by an uneasy illness.

I knew where I was then. In the grand ballroom. Naked as a newborn, slick with fluid. With hundreds of Fae clustered around me. The king staring at me as he stroked the arched back of a black cat as it sat on his lap. Terran at my side, still kneeling the way he'd been when the vision had ended.

I started, instinct bidding me to scrabble backward, to dig my bare heels into the cold stone of the ballroom floor, but I couldn't move. My gaze was pinned to a dusty-looking cotton ball sticking out from beneath Terran's collar.

Squinting at it, I thought I could make out threads of cobwebs trailing down his back. When he scraped his hand toward me and clutched at my arm, I tore my gaze from the threads and stared at him.

"The Endowments are about to begin," he hissed at me from the side of his mouth. "Where the hell is Stone?"

About to begin? But that was what Erachne had said as she'd collected me from the kitchens and shrouded me with her gossamer. Had she bent time so sharply that not a moment had passed between that moment and this? I felt like I was nestled in the middle of a wrinkle in time, peeling apart like a stretch mark on skin.

A quick inventory of my body told me I didn't have any aches anywhere. Movement was easy and fluid. Nothing broken. Breath came and went through my nostrils and throat as though I'd never cracked a bit of cartilage in my nose.

Confusion roiled around me, and I clung to Terran's presence the way a drowning woman might clasp a life preserver because his was the only familiar voice I knew. It grounded me enough that I was able to flip over onto my knees, crouching so that my legs covered most of my breasts.

It took an effort not to look around at my surroundings. The tension coiled in my belly warned me that this was not the time to scrutinize things too overtly. I had to trust that where I was, things were moving at speed, but moving the way they were supposed to.

Terran's hand behind my biceps steadied me, and while I had no warm and fuzzy feelings for the bastard, I was grateful for that touch because the reeling from the shift in terrain and surroundings was making me dizzy.

The pressure on my arm grew rougher. He dug his fingers into the flesh of my arm.

"Kneel," he rasped. "For the gods's sake get on your knees."

I did as he bid without hesitation, bowing low as one of my knees took my weight. Shadows and colors flickered at the side of my vision, tempting me to gawk at them, but I kept my head bowed. I had no wish to look at the king again. Something about that cat made my neck prickle.

And when Terran gathered me closer to his side, I leaned in, grateful for the bit of fabric that swept over my breasts as if he'd bid it happen.

I cast a sidelong glance at where a frantic bit of movement caught my attention. Heuil. Head bare of the hood I'd begged him to wear so Stone wouldn't notice him and decide to get rid of him.

I cut my eyes in his direction, trying to warn him, but he either didn't notice or didn't care. Instead, he held up his token out in front of his chest so I could see it. He smiled brightly, too brightly, I thought. Several Fae knotted in clusters around him. Someone jostled him and his smile faltered.

"Your Grace," Terran said, recovering himself as he gathered me to his side. "My sons have gifts for your pleasure and while I'd hoped for my son, Stone, to present you with this most unique one officially so the whole of the realm could know how the Shadow Court feels about its sovereign, it appears as though he has left the task to me."

Stone. The name ignited a blind rage as I recalled Heuil's warning that he'd arranged for Slavin to kidnap me. I still hadn't seen him since that moment, and whatever happened in the next few moments, it was probably a good thing that he wasn't here. I wasn't sure I could hold myself back from attacking him.

The memory caught me up so strongly that it took precious moments from me as I fought to gather my wits, to shift perspective, all while trying to look as if I wasn't drugged out of my gourd as I faced the king and that mercenary.

I was aware that my chest heaved with anger. That clusters of Fae had gathered, curious about the naked mortal woman who had apparently dropped out of the ether at Terran's side. I was acutely aware of Terran's fatigue as he stood beside me.

At least, I was sure that was what everyone else thought. I was now pretty sure Erachne had tucked me into the folds of his cloak somehow.

"Terran of the Sentinels," Ferranus said in a scalding tone. "You honor me with a gift, and yet I wonder at its delivery when magic such as this might be construed as dangerous on this day and in this place." His lips thinned, and Terran made the smallest of movements. The way a priest might ward off evil.

I thought he was trying to adjust his cloak and that it was too heavy. Why he'd decided to wear such an awkward garment over his stately suit was a mystery I decided wasn't worth unravelling.

"The only magic a king might be concerned about on this day and in this place would be if it was ill-intentioned," Terran said. "Surely, if I had hoped to commit harm, your sorceress's spells would turn the gift against me."

Ferranus made a sound low in his throat that might be taken as displeasure. The cat rose from his lap and leaped to the floor. It stretched, claws extending and scraping along the tiles of the dais floor as it raked its paws back to its chest. Ferranus flicked his gaze toward it but his words were for Terran, and anyone in earshot would know it.

"Most who address me would take care not to sound so arrogant in their correction of my words," he said. "As always you presume too much on my kindness"

I almost snorted at the notion of Ferranus's kindness. And I could almost hear Terran's thoughts as he struggled to find some explanation for my sudden appearance at his side. A single glance at him showed he looked far more haggard than he had before we'd come. His lips had a gray pallor to them. His hands shook at his side.

"You say you have two gifts for me," Ferranus said in a wheedling voice. "And yet there is only one beside you. And at a most inconvenient moment when the long-suffering fae of the realm expect to end their long-anticipated wait for their own gifts. Explain why you chose to usurp this moment from your fellow fae."

"I have no explanation," Terran said. "As I told you, both were to be presented by my sons. I had no intention of robbing their glory or the patience of my fellow fae."

If he was expecting the king to be indulgent, his tone did nothing to pacify Ferranus. I didn't have to look up to know he was displeased at the insolence in Terran's voice.

"Your intention and your actions are, as always, of warring appearances, Terran of the Sentinels."

Whatever was in their past, apparently, it was the only thing keeping Ferranus from reducing Terran to a pile of ash. I certainly couldn't imagine any other reason why the king didn't take him more to task.

"I am not Terran of the Sentinels any longer, your Iron Grace," Terran said in just as tight a voice that somehow managed to come out as chagrined even if his voice was hard and firm. "As you well know and refuse to concede these long centuries."

I half-expected the moment when Ferranus's temper to boil over, but if he planned to do more than glare at Terran—and I was quite sure he was—a familiar voice piped up from somewhere behind us.

"I'm afraid I'm to blame for the sudden and ill-timed appearance of the blood gift, your Iron Grace," Erachne said, scuttling forward until she was abreast of Terran.

I could feel Terran lean away from her and closer toward me. It was clear he was repulsed and surprised but he said nothing. I kept my eyes on the floor, my mind racing with the things that could go wrong in the next moments.

"As I had made a gown for the lovely human that got ruined, I felt pity for her." I heard her little feet sweeping the floor and Terran edged ever closer. "I thought perhaps a magnificent entrance might better catch your eye since she is woefully ill-prepared for such a moment of importance."

A long pause stretched tight enough to snap back if released too soon. My eyes closed as I prayed...prayed this wouldn't turn rancid. If my heart was hammering loud enough to hear it in my ears, I was sure Terran could too. He certainly tensed up beside me.

"There is no ban on simple magic, is there, my king?" she asked so sweetly she could have eaten honey for breakfast. "And if your sorceress has be-spelled the chamber so powerfully that you should have no fear of attack, then there should be no worry."

At that, the cat hissed and it drew my gaze so sharply, I forgot to keep looking down.

Luckily, no one noticed. Ferranus's gaze was directed to the black blur on the other side of Terran.

"Indeed," he hummed, while the cat arched its back. This said, though, in a voice that was prim and disapproving instead of conciliatory.

Erachne's feet made rustling noises on the floor that made me want to wince as I thought of those furred limbs and how they'd felt on my body. But I didn't think she did so because she was afraid of the king. Just posturing, as he seemed to require.

"If you wish for me to test the validity of the spell, Your Iron Grace," she said in a voice no less smooth and sickly sweet as before. "Then I will be happy to serve at my own peril."

The king glanced down at the cat. It didn't look up, but kept its black gaze directed toward Erachne.

After too long a pause, he finally leaned back. "That won't be necessary. I have no need of spells to keep me safe, you understand. The spell is to protect my subjects from harm while they revel in the Days without worry for ill-spellings."

"You are wise, my king," Erachne said.

I didn't dare look her way. She'd been truthful, but not forthcoming. Quite a feat, I thought, and one that might have saved Terran's life, as Ferranus leaned all the way back in his chair and adjusted his cloak.

"A blood gift is a very valuable thing," he said in a hushed voice. "I've received many of them over the centuries, but none secreted to me nude beneath their leader's cloak like a second-hand Cleopatra to her Caesar."

He smiled broadly at that, a practiced thing that some might believe, but there was no partnering light in his eyes to show a hint of mirth.

"It has been more than five centuries since the commander of the Host of Iron-Bone Sentinels brought me a gift." I was surprised to hear a lisp in his voice. It was too strong, too commanding to show any sort of weakness, and yet I guessed it wasn't an affectation. He'd probably been glamoring his voice and had dropped the magic. I thought that might be a good sign.

And yet, impossibly, I felt Terran stiffen by my side at the king's words. I swept a glance his way and noted the look of stubbornness on his face.

"I am no longer one of the Host of Iron-Bone Sentinels, let alone their commander." While his tone was polite and respectful, his body was rigid, his arm over my shoulder, too forceful. "And it has been more than six centuries since I've been to court."

The outright correction of the king in the company of his entire court seemed so purposeful, I had to wonder if he didn't have a death wish.

The scolding met its mark. A shadow passed over Ferranus's eyes, but he blinked and it was gone. It seemed he would choose to ignore the tone in Terran's voice, but I didn't think it would go unpunished at some point.

My gaze went to Ruby. She was leaning in, her head tilted as she eyed me right back. I dropped my gaze, not out of fear but because I didn't want her to see the challenge in my eyes. I swallowed, cringing inside at the way the tension in the air seemed focused on me and the Fae at my side.

Ferranus heaved a sigh. "I never accepted that resignation," he said. "And I see you are trying to force my hand in front of this court to do so now. Very well. I concede your resignation and the dissolution of the Host." He shrugged his shoulders. "Now. I would dearly love to see this gift, considering the excitement of its arrival."

He waited. The entire assembly nearest the dais went silent. I waited on my knees, feeling like a piece of spoiled meat. No one moved, even though it sounded to me like the king had ordered me to be presented. When he slapped his hands down on the arms of the throne, it became clear why no one had so much as blinked.

"And yet, the endowments cannot wait. Our good fae have traveled far and wide to be here." He swept a lingering glance over the entire chamber. "We cannot rob them of an honor they have waited a century to be awarded."

I thought I heard Terran curse. Maybe it was me. Because I knew right then, I could be left kneeling, naked, for days.

A long moment of tension drew itself along the currents of air. Terran didn't back down. I was impressed as he stood with steel in his spine as he stared down the king. Whatever had been between them centuries past, the king did not scold him, and Terran did not seem afraid.

"Forgive my impertinence, Your Radiance," he said as he sketched a bow that made him sway on his feet. "I would be acknowledged for such a fine offering even if I'm not thanked for it."

Oh, the balls on him. Even if he did hide the wavering of his body by leaning on me, he had bulls' balls. Brass and big and loud as they clanged together.

I knew I shouldn't look at him, but I couldn't help myself. This was out of the ordinary. And not because he was challenging a king in the midst of his court, but because the Terran I'd met would never show weakness and certainly not to the mortal he'd extorted into doing his dirty work.

A rustle of fabric from the dais drew my gaze away from Terran, and I stole a look up through the fringes of my hair.

As impossible as it seemed, the king rose from his throne so gracefully he might have had invisible wings lifting him from the seat. And the moment he stalked to the edge of the platform, I knew.

He was coming to decide if I was worth inspecting.

Chapter 26

"Very well, Terran," he said. "I'll inspect your gift. But only because I am curious to see this Cleopatra up close."

At that, a cheer went up from the crowds from the front to the back, and I imagined most had no idea why they were even cheering. By the time he strode to the edge of the dais, the sound of his perfectly cobbled boots was lost on the waves of sound.

He stepped down from the platform. The female mercenary straightened as she grew more alert, on edge, as if she really thought he was in danger mere feet from her in a room where magical threat was spelled to reverse itself. I watched her almost as closely as I watched Ferranus, and as he peeled off his white kidskin gloves and tucked them into the sash at his waist, my eyes were on the thin, curved dagger on his belt.

"You have always been impatient, Terran," he said, dropping the put-on sense of formality as he drew near, and yet stumbling over Terran's name as though he'd forgotten it for a moment. He'd lowered his voice to a threat. "And your impertinence has not softened in all these centuries."

"It is not impertinence to request a gift such as this be acknowledged in front of the realm."

His eyes flashed in warning. "Don't let your ego get in the way of your courtly manners, old friend. Most of Fae is already too drunk on wine to care."

He shifted his attention to me, dismissing Terran outright. His finger touched down on my chin, a moth that might have beaten its wings against a fire.

I found myself rising as if that one finger had found some purchase beneath my chin and was lifting me, weightless, to a stand.

He tilted my face upward, demanding I meet his gaze.

The Iron King stood a mere inch taller than me. More magnificent looking up close than he was even at a distance, I was sure he'd lured more than mortal women to his bed.

His head canted slightly to the side as that glittering gaze roamed my face until it found a home on my throat and the pulse hammering away beneath my skin.

"Exquisite," he said in a rasp of smoke and heat that made the ember in my core flare brightly. It was as though a fire had been smoldering there for weeks, begging to be given a final spark.

Terran didn't move as he stood beside me other than to still my hand with his as it trembled at the king's touch. I was sure my blood was calling out to the magic in his, and I understood right then just why Terran was loathe to risk any of his own soldiers to this fae's magic. Even as a mortal I felt the pulse of it run through me and flush my skin.

I was acutely aware of Terran's words from days or weeks before, that his natal magics could pull the iron straight out of my blood like a magnet.

The king's eyes ran over each inch it could see of me, lingering here and there in places I wouldn't have expected. The curve of my thigh where it turned toward my knee. My wrists. The swell of my belly where my navel created a miniature cup.

A jolt of energy ran through me, not unlike the one I'd suffered when Mica had infused me with images, except this was more controlled. A prodding very much like someone rapping lightly on a bedroom door.

Unlike the time with Mica, my brain resisted, and I wasn't sure if it had been so insulted before that it remembered the assault and barricaded itself against it, or if Ferranus's magics were more muted than Mica's. Whichever was the case, I was relieved the reaction wasn't so powerful. I understood right then just how dangerous Mica could be with his lack of control over such a powerful magic.

Ferranus looked at me with a tilted head, as though he was waiting for my reaction. I gave none except the rash of goose flesh that ran over my skin as everything within me fought the images back.

A smile. Not large. Just a curve of his lips that suggested he had been testing me with his touch and was pleased to see I'd held my own.

"Perhaps I was too hasty," he intoned, his head angling in the other direction, his eyes flitting over my face and down my throat. "The heart within pounds like a lioness's and the course of the river's blood is strong." His tongue played at the corner of his mouth as it dropped open thoughtfully. "I can smell the heat in it from here."

"A gift worthy of a king," Terran said, but there was no emotion in his words. It was a rote comment, practiced perhaps or memorized a hundred years ago and repeated for centuries. "She has a fighter's heart."

I had to work to keep the surprise from my face as I realized he'd used a feminine pronoun in reference to me, and I wasn't sure if I'd heard him refer to me as anything but an it prior to this moment.

Ferranus bared his teeth at Terran in a fulsome smile that might have looked friendly if his teeth weren't so sharp. "She might be a lovely diversion this night before I tend to the strain of my duties here." He pulled his hand back to rest on his sash. "You have served your king well, old friend."

The way he said old friend elicited a low growl from Terran that made him step back hastily, as though he was both surprised and upset that the sound had been audible.

I glanced nervously sideways at him. I wasn't sure what was keeping him from collapsing to be honest, but I imagined it was the same sheer will that had him eyeballing Ferranus as though he hadn't just growled at him. As though he wanted the king to challenge it, and god forbid, I knew it would be Terran's final challenge. He looked like a waft of sour breath could knock him over.

"She is a gift worthy of your harem, my king," Terran repeated, earning a snap of the king's head.

"I decide who enters my harem," he said. "But perhaps you don't know that seeing as how you abandoned me on the eve of my first Days."

If it meant something to Terran, he ignored it. Instead, he dropped a few short words into the air as though they meant something as important as the king's declaration of abandonment.

"We've arranged for a trousseau as well, to make her stay a welcome and exciting one for you."

To Terran's credit, that made the king do a double take. He looked from Terran's face to mine and back again. The edges of his pointed ears turned pink.

"Hers is the trunk that sits even now in my throne room?"

Terran nodded. "As you said, we are old friends."

This time, I saw the king lick his lips and didn't bother to hide it, and I got real nervous about what might be inside that trunk besides the pouch of cursed objects and the books I'd buried in a pile of clothes.

"Your king might be inclined to think your protests of belonging to the Sentinels is not so much a protest as it is a hope. This gift is a grand one. Might you be interested in returning to your past position? Is that why you come to the Days on this century to face me after so long? Is this why you offer me such a delectable gift?"

I was aware that Terran was doing his best to get me into that harem and not off into some blockaded area where the king would decide to dig those sharp teeth into one of the spots he'd lingered on when he'd surveyed me like a piece of prize meat. But damn, he was also giving me far too much of his weight as he considered the question. I could barely hold him up any more.

Surely, he'd noticed the dagger the same as I had. I almost hoped Ferranus would try to wrestle me into a corner somewhere away from this damned be-spelled ballroom for a taste. I'd make use of that blade. And quick.

It was taking so long for him to answer that the king's expression clouded over. No doubt he expected a quick answer and being made to wait in front of his entire court and realm was taking a toll on his temper. And yet, Terran took that time. He made a noise that might have been a simple throat clearing, and I waited for him to speak.

Except when he did, none of it made any sense.

At first, I thought he was speaking in a different language, one filled with consonants and grunts. I glanced at the king, thinking he would understand what in the hell Terran was saying.

But he didn't. Not any more than I did. His expression changed from mild irritation at being kept waiting to an expression of horror that had me staring at Terran in confusion.

A moment later, the leader of the Shadow Court, the Fae who arguably held almost as much power over me here in Fae as the king, clutched at my arm in a spasm of muscle so fiercely it could only be described as a death grip.

I tried to shake him off at first. Bewilderment crowding out any other reaction.

And all hell and chaos broke out then.

Chapter 27

Terran collapsed onto the floor, writhing in what looked like an incredible amount of pain. Mist, thick and swampy and stinking of sulfur, crawled out of his nose and ears and where his mouth gaped open.

It took me several seconds—too many—to realize he was dead.

It took the king much, much longer.

For those moments he just watched mesmerized as the mist coiled in the air above the huddled form at his feet. His gaze followed the mist as it spread out like a swarm of locusts, buzzing, clicking, humming. It created a canopy over our heads that blocked out the glorious chandeliers and torchlight and left us in a noxious gloom.

I smelled ozone and sulfur. My skin prickled with a familiar sensation that took me long moments to realize the last time I'd felt it, I'd been in Terran's dungeons. Whispers brushed the back of my skull of horrors dealt and wounds suffered.

For a moment, all those blows and strikes I'd suffered there that Blade had spared me, all razored through me at once.

I staggered beneath the shock of it. My arms threw themselves over my head in a vain effort to block out the memories and the pain. The sound keened through me like an electrical wire.

Something awful was coming. I could taste it on my palate. This awfulness spiraled into a funnel, spearheading its way toward Ferranus and I only had time to wonder: so what happens to the weapon's wielder if he's already dead.

The answer came in half a heartbeat.

In a movement so swift, I barely saw it, Ferranus flicked his hands over his head.

A crack of thunder and a mewling, like a kitten sliced through the air. It met the swarm of magic head on, holding it off.

I peered around me and caught sight of Heuil jostling for a better position in front of the crowd of Fae waiting for their endowments. A wash of image information came at me then, and I took it all in, deciding to sort it out later, because right then...right then things were going all wrong, and I didn't want to be caught in the line of fire.

The little half trow jerked his thumb toward his shoulder as he hefted the token above his head. From beside me, the king let go a curse that sounded as surprised as it did angry.

"The bastard tried to kill me," he said beneath his breath.

At his words, spoken so softly anyone might have missed it if they weren't listening and standing close enough to smell the wine on his breath, a rush of wind picked up. Swirling from beneath Terran's body, it seemed at first to be more of the magic still spewing forth from his orifices.

Then, someone behind me started to shriek, the pained cries rising and collecting other pained screams until it became a din that made me want to stop up my hearing.

Hands clapped against my ears to drown out the noise, I swung around. Someone grappled for my elbow as I did and I shoved back at them so violently, I staggered. The sensation of thin, hard-boned sausages rolled beneath my feet.

Grimacing, because I knew I'd stepped on Terran's fingers, I hopped and skipped away, completing an awkward duck and run as I went. I forgot about who was trying to tug on my arm.

All I thought to do was bring up my fists. Make myself a small target, move and dance like water on a hot skillet.

But I wasn't prepared for what confronted me as I spun to put my back to Terran, to the King, to Ruby, the mercenary on the dais.

As frightening as those things were, the sight of dozens of lesser fae, no hundreds and beyond, collapsing all around me, was worse. As if they'd turned to rabid beasts caught in traps they couldn't escape, they tore at their clothes, gnawed at their own hands and arms, and in some cases, their own legs.

Sweeping the room with a glance, I noted High Fae had begun to shrivel, their skin losing luster first and then wrinkling like grapes turning to dried raisins.

All that energy was blasting upward in a wind so great it scooped out every breath I tried to take in. I had to suck at the air from the side of my mouth to catch enough to feed my lungs the most meagre of breaths.

I knew what was happening. I think everyone in the room did.

Ferranus was leveling his magic on his subjects like a vengeful demon.

A body slammed into mine, throwing me off balance. Like a rookie, I'd not jumped clear of the danger when I saw it begin. I tripped over Terran's body because I was still standing too close.

One of his eyes had fallen from its sockets and I had time to bat it away before someone stomped on it, squishing it into a smear of blood and tissue three feet from me.

The king's booted foot, I realized as my gaze journeyed up from the instep to the calf and finally to the owner of the foot scraping the goo from his boot onto Terran's shoulder.

Gorge rose in my mouth as I clawed my way to my feet. One thought rang through my mind as loudly as a clanging bell. The king was oblivious in his rage at Terran, and we were all going to die.

In a flash of inspiration, I stooped to pull the cloak from Terran's dead body. It was fetched up, stuck beneath his considerable weight.

With a curse, I put my weight into a shove at him, rolling him over so that his empty eye socket leered at me. I shuddered as I flipped the cloak from his shoulder, then yanked, pulling the rest of it free.

I bolted upright, pushing myself to my feet with the cloak fast in my grip. A swirl and it was over my shoulders and tucked between my legs in an old-fashioned loin girdle. Planted my feet apart, falling into the defensive stance of a linebacker.

Let it come, whatever the hell it was, let it come.

In the periphery of my vision, those Fae holding the tokens looked on with placid expressions, waiting, it seemed. All except Heuil.

He was gesturing wildly at me. Something behind him, I thought. He wanted me to notice something behind him.

It took a single glance to realize what it was he was trying to tell me. All the Fae who possessed the tokens were male. And they were not base fae. To me, they looked like High Fae who didn't need a token to access magic. He was the only lesser Fae in the group of one hundred.

A second glance told me I knew some of them. I'd seen them at Terran's dinner. The juniper man, who had considerable power already, held his token clutched to his chest and stared quizzically at Terran's body, his face a strange mix of satisfaction and fear.

Above us, the swarm of magic pushed back against the king's magic, growing until it blocked out the gorgeous ceiling, dampening the light. The wind bloated into full force, pushing at me. It no longer emanated from below Terran's body, but all around us.

And in the middle of it the king stood, his face hard and angry. Strain etched itself onto his magnificent features in deep furrows.

Once more, someone grabbed my arm, and this time I dropped to a squat, putting them off-balance. I struck out with my fist, aiming high in a defensive block.

It connected. I felt the reverberation of bone on bone, yanked my hand back in pain because I'd not delivered a good, clean punch. I swore. A voice I knew drifted toward me and I dropped my head back to look up.

Stone. At last, the traitorous bastard had decided to show himself. My chest burned at the sight of him.

"Bastard," I said. "You fucking bastard."

All the chaos around me was nothing to the rage I had in me over his betrayal. It was just him and I in that room and I knew it would be him or I who walked out of it. No matter what happened in between.

With a smoothness of movement that would have made Gideon proud, I whipped the cloak off and snapped it at his legs the way a Gladiatrix might have done to take down her opponent.

It caught his legs, but he somehow managed to extricate himself faster than I could move on him. His brow furrowed. His head canted sideways at me.

"Ava?" he had time to say before I raced for him.

I tripped on nothing, as though my feet had tangled in a net.

I went down hard. The buzzing of magic filled my ears like a flood of water. I looked up to see Stone standing over me. My lip curled back as I took in his hateful face. The spell. The spell had rebounded on me. It would protect Stone as surely as the king.

I swung my gaze to the chamber, where so many fae were still chewing on their appendages, roiling on the floor. The chaos spread backward as though the king's magic was taking its lovely time making everyone suffer.

"Ava," Stone said. "Come with me."

"Fuck you."

I scrambled to my feet. Rage had me so entwined in its embrace, I didn't care what would happen to me so long as I got one good swing in. I'd grab the king's blade. I'd swipe out with it at Stone.

My trajectory had already shifted toward the king when I heard Heuil's unmistakeable voice. Screaming a word I should understand. One that companioned my name. He was yelling at me.

The king dropped his gaze to my face right about the moment Stone grabbed me from behind. If my hand was out to snatch his knife, it didn't get there. I had time to see Ruby's gaze level itself on me. The shadows swirling around her gathered darker.

Stone got me first. He yanked me around and I heard Heuil's voice clearer. I understood what he was saying.

"Run," he screamed.

Run. As if there was somewhere to go.

My eyes scanned the throng, searching for his familiar face. It had disappeared in the rush of Shadow Court members clustering together like cattle against a hail storm. For a moment, I thought they might have done something to the little half trow, but a flash of his clothing suggested he was on the move through the throng of his fellow token holders.

And then I knew what was really going on.

This wasn't about Terran initiating a backup plan of some sort to assassinate the king because he didn't think I could succeed.

This was about the Shadow Court and the tokens. It was about Stone being MIA for so damn long only to show up now. It had everything to do with the disappearance of

Terran's food taster and the way Stone had passed his father his cup to drink from just that morning before we'd departed.

This wasn't about the assassination of the king. It was about a coup on the Shadow Court.

The king stood in the midst of it, arms outstretched at his sides. A waver of energy surrounded him, pooling out from his hands, his solar plexus. Behind him, Ruby was coming at me in a hailstorm of black cloud.

I had time to throw my arm over my face before something...someone slammed into me and that storm closed around a familiar looking back.

He wore ragged clothes and scuffed boots and his gilden token was clenched so tightly in his fist that all I could see was his white knuckles before he was consumed by Ruby's mist.

I staggered backward, numb from confusion as I watched the shades do its work on him. As though he and she weren't truly residing in the same realm as the ballroom, but of another, he morphed and split apart and screamed with noiseless sound as whatever was in that shadow of hers took pieces of his flesh. Sometimes I saw the hooked beak of an owl digging into his shoulders, sometimes wings flapped against his face.

Heuil. He'd thrown himself at her before she could get to me.

A sob stole its way up my throat as I swung around aimlessly, trying to sort through the next steps. Trying to figure out what came next. Grief bowed my knees. I clutched my hands to my chest, realizing I was once again naked.

Just as I remembered why I'd gone for Ferranus's knife in the first place, I sensed a presence behind me. I knew someone was there, watching me. Although I shouldn't have been able to sense it amid the throngs of Fae everywhere, yelling, shouting. Crying.

But I did.

I might wonder later why Stone didn't strike out at me. I was vulnerable as a naked newborn bird fallen clear of its nest. He could have killed me in a heartbeat without a stitch of magic, shoved me into Ruby's ghastly embrace and let me die.

Perhaps he didn't have the energy to do so. Maybe it was the way his body looked like it was about to split open, like the skin of a roasting boar.

All I knew was that he didn't. And because he didn't, I turned my back to him. I could have vengeance or I could do what hunters all over the world did on a daily basis.

One instant was all it took to make the decision, and I was racing for that damned mercenary. I fully intended to screw her head straight off her body before she succeeding in killing Heuil.

I couldn't be sure if she had pulled herself back into the realm because she saw me coming or if she'd finished with Heuil and felt confident her magic wouldn't turn on her but I slammed into her shoulder as solidly as if she was a stone wall.

She dropped the little trow to the floor. My bare feet slid over something viscous as I wrestled to take her down.

She took the hit like anyone would at first. Surprised, she fell backward, leaving the little half trow on his back and trying to roll over. The gilded token was bloody by now, still clutched with determination in his fist. I tried not to think it was grasped so tightly because his fingers were frozen around it in death.

I had one moment when she was solid. That was it. Then she wasn't.

Wrestling her was like trying to run through fog and brick all at the same time. It felt very much like I was breaking into my atoms and striking them into life over and over.

Then, mercifully, all chaos abruptly ended.

The room went silent. The howling wind, the suffocation of an energy that was highly unnatural, all that stopped.

Ruby immediately backed off to stand with her back to the dais, her hands clasped, military style, behind her back. Freed, I ran for Heuil and fell to a crouch by his side.

Whatever was going on in the chamber was second to seeing if he lived. And if he did, to getting him healed.

I knew I was lying to myself the moment I took in the swelling on his face. She'd done irreparable damage. The gilded token lay pinched in his fingers as his hand lay flung out on the floor. I leaned down, ear to his mouth, listening for breath.

A heartbeat. Two. Then three before I caught the barest of movement of air. Placing my hand on his chest, I felt for movement. His ribcage barely rose, but movement of any sort felt like a victory.

"Come on, Heuil," I murmured as I grasped the hand holding the token. "Come on. It's not over."

"I'm afraid it is," someone said from above me.

The king. I'd all but forgotten the chaos and din of the ball. I blinked at him for too long, so long that his expression grew pinched.

"Stone of the Shadow Court explained," he said. "I've pulled back my magic and gave the Fae their health again."

Confused, I looked past him to the room around me. The high Fae had regained their luster. The base Fae were quietly reassembling the clothes they'd torn at during their mania. They all looked shell-shocked but hale.

"Stone?" I asked in a quiet voice. "I don't understand."

The king held out his hand. "Yes. Stone of the Shadow Court. Surely you remember the Fae who brought you here. The Fae you danced with. Terran's son."

At Terran's name, his face clouded over.

I peered past him to where Stone stood with chin held high. His skin no longer looked like a boiled beet.

There was no sense of fear in Stone's face as he watched me. Perhaps he'd never seen Heuil. Maybe he couldn't know the half trow had insinuated him as a traitor.

I swallowed, gathering my thoughts and my resolve. Stone had bought my abduction. He'd pretended to care about me. I wasn't sure what his intentions were, but I did know what the king's were.

I knew more lives than Heuil's was at stake here.

Stone? Stone I could deal with later. I'd pretend the same as he had. And when it was over, I'd take his eye teeth.

I lifted my gaze to the king, pulling the best blink-eyed stare of confusion I could. "I remember," I said.

"Good," Ferranus said. "Unfortunate as it is, my old friend wanted me dead, but you, Stone assures me, are nothing but a pawn in the ruse. He assures me you are still a worthy blood gift." At that, he smiled. As though nothing had happened.

As though he hadn't just tried to bake and roast his subjects because he'd thought his old friend had tried to kill him.

Mad. He was indeed mad.

I flicked my eyes to Stone, narrowing my eyelids. Was this his way of getting rid of me without having to do the work himself?

"I still don't understand," I said.

The king sighed. "Terran of the Sentinels is dead," he said in a tight, impatient voice. "Stone informs me he has been ingesting poisonous magic from the City of the Dead with the intent to let the protection spell from this room claim both of our lives." His nostrils flared. "Old grudges. They are a wearisome thing."

"I am sorry," Stone interjected, bowing so low his voice was barely audible. "It seems he has been planning the hit for some time. Had we believed he'd planned to sacrifice himself to the chamber's spell, we would have stopped him."

I glared at him, unnoticed as he waved at the host of Fae I'd thought belonged to Terran, but now realized, were his. I noticed nothing he said was a lie. Careful and deliberate wording, but not complete falsehoods.

Bully for Stone for navigating his own takeover. For arranging the death of his own father without so much as raising a hand to him. I wanted to be sick. Not because I was a friend to Terran, but at the depths of his treachery and insincerity.

"Terran of the Sentinels misjudged my power and overstepped his own," Ferranus said in a tight voice, drawing my gaze back to him. "As he has always done. And now he has paid the price."

CHAPTER 28

"By letting the spell turn his own weapon on him," I said, shooting a glare in Stone's direction. "Cunning man indeed, if not foolish. Even a kamikaze warrior would make sure he hit the target with his sacrifice."

The king thumbed his chin. "Male," he said. "Fae don't use human terms." He canted his head at me. "But you are smart to understand the complexities of the situation. I didn't expect that in a human woman."

Only a fool wouldn't understand the situation, but I didn't say that. I wanted to say he expected too little, but I didn't say that either. What I did was smile blithely, ignoring the dead Fae at my feet and the tension rising between Stone and I as I fought to keep calm.

At last the tightness in Ferranus's face disappeared, and he angled his body toward Stone.

"It just goes to show that a Fae with my power can still be pleasantly surprised after all these centuries," he said, dismissing me. "As his Second, I presume you will take his place in the Shadow Court."

Politics. As if a young Fae wasn't dying behind him. "Pardon, Your Majesty," I interjected, drawing a glare from the king that I also ignored. "My friend is dying." I jerked my chin toward Heuil. "He needs help."

"Your friend is fae?"

I nodded. "I have few here," I said with a pointed look at Stone. "But he is one, and he has a token."

That did it. It wasn't just a test, because I wanted Heuil seen to, but I had to know if my suspicions were correct. And judging by the way Stone's attention flew to where Heuil had managed to roll over onto his side finally, I knew he had arranged to have his men acquire all the gilded tokens but one. The one Stone himself had given me.

Just what he planned to do with them all or what he'd done to the true owner was none of my business. But Heuil was. I wouldn't see him dead for Stone's ambition.

"He has a token," I said again. "Terran led me to believe they are important."

"Indeed," Ferranus mused aloud. "They are very important."

He waved toward the mercenary, who stepped into his view without looking my way.

"Bring the young male to me," Ferranus said without looking her way.

The mercenary retreated and came back with Heuil in her arms. He looked fragile in her hold, draped over her arms like limp bit of fabric. I felt sick at the gray look to his skin.

"Half trow," Ferranus said in a voice that held more than a blush of disgust. "I haven't endowed a trow with magic since my first Days."

I had the feeling that was somehow intentional, but he flicked his wrist toward the mercenary.

She laid him at the king's feet and stepped away, her eyes roaming the room from within that swirl of shadow that crept over her like a kaleidoscope.

The king nudged him with the toe of his boot and Heuil moaned.

"His endowment should be his healing." He nodded to himself as though he'd made a decision after much contemplation. "Take the token from him." He drew back with a curled lip, avoiding too long a look at the poor half trow.

I stepped up without thinking and the mercenary was in my face in seconds, blocking my view of the king. My fists clenched at my sides as I faced her.

"I would think a king of such power would have nothing to fear from a mere human woman," I said, not daring to blink for fear the female would attack. "Surely there are more powerful beings to worry about than a mortal."

It was the king who answered. "I am not afraid of a mortal woman," he said from beside me, and my breath let go in a soft sigh. "Leave the gift alone."

I waited until the mercenary stepped back, but I noted she didn't go too far. Her gaze skimmed past me to where Stone was standing and, for a second, her eyes softened. I had a terrible urge to look at the traitor. I resisted. This was about Heuil. He needed help.

"His endowment should be what his token gives him," I said to the king. "Your mercenary harmed an innocent subject of your realm. In view of all those who would give you their magic."

He sent me a sharp, displeased look. "Terran has told you more than just how important the tokens are."

I shrugged. "I have ears," I said. "I can hear. I can also hear the mutterings of your court as they pull themselves back together after an attack from their monarch."

"I was under attack," he said.

"And now you are not." I inched closer, my eyes pointedly downcast. I didn't want to go too far, but time was slipping away.

"Healing takes much energy," he said. "I must save my power for the Endowments."

"If you will not heal him, perhaps another can." I was thinking of Erachne and though I dearly wanted to scan the room for her, I didn't dare look up. One miscalculation and poor Heuil's life might be forfeited.

I still wasn't looking up but I didn't need to see his face to feel the tension in it. He wanted to look good in front of his court. Not because of ego, but because he needed them to give him access to their magic. That's what these Days were all about. He wouldn't risk acquiring all that power for one small Fae, and yet this one small, valueless Fae might turn the tables.

It was a good reminder that power wasn't always about the strongest or the biggest. Sometimes it was in the hands of the one who had the most to lose.

"Please," I said, loudly enough that my begging caught the attention of several lesser Fae. I heard them shuffling around me. From the side of my vision, I was sure Pan nudged one of the nymphs beside him. He picked up the word, echoing it loudly.

One by one, the lesser Fae gained courage from one another. They began to chant with me. Please. Please.

At last, Ferranus heaved a sigh. "Alright," he said. "But I will not deplete magic that belongs to my subjects to heal one half trow. Another shall do this healing."

He looked up, panning the room with a lidded gaze. "Who here has the magic of healing?"

No one moved. No one spoke up.

"I have given my word," he said. "But I will not take your due from you. I require someone with the healing magics before this small trow expires."

The silence in the room was enough to crack an egg. I spun on my heel to face the crowds, and as if some magic had been conjured, the doors to the ballroom flew open, pushed aside by the face I most wanted to see.

Blade strode forward with such menace, that fae all around him hustled to the walls to make room. I was sure I took a step toward him before I checked myself. I forced myself to watch, my heart in my throat as he moved so swiftly, so fluidly, he was like water color bleeding into paper.

He was beside me far too fast for him to have merely walked. Perhaps I'd lost track of time as I drank in his form. I was aware I'd started to tremble.

"Ah," the king said. "My dark enforcer. I wasn't expecting you for days yet."

Blade sketched a brief but formal bow as I gaped at him, my mind reeling.

"Your Iron Grace," he said. "I had a visitor who suggested a mortal woman here—a gift for you—was inappropriately coutured for a meeting with a king."

His smile moved over his face so expertly I began to doubt this was the fae who had sworn to kill the fae before I stepped through the veil. Now I was beginning to understand how he'd planned to do it. The wiley bastard had told me he was well placed, but I'd never for one second thought he was the second mercenary.

As if he was noticing me for the first time, Blade pivoted to look me over. There was hunger in his eyes as well as fury at my nudity. It took several seconds for me to realize he was holding something out to me.

"I'm presuming this is the woman," he said. "With your blessing, I will offer her something to put on so the rabble will not drink in what should be for one male's eyes only."

The king sucked in a breath as Blade shook it out, and I did the same as the material unfurled.

It was the cobweb gown I'd seen in Erachne's window when we'd visited her on the Shadow Trail. I nearly reached for it except for the snap in Ferranus's voice when he spoke.

"That was the gown my beloved wore on our wedding day," he said in a tight voice. "What right does she have to offer it to a mere mortal?"

"Erachne would never risk your displeasure, Your Iron Grace. I purchased this garment myself weeks ago for my mate," Blade said without taking his eyes from my face. "I assure you this is a newly spun garment."

The king laughed. "You purchased a wedding gown for a mate you have yet to meet? You are a dreamer, Dark Enforcer."

"A hopeless romantic," Blade said, holding my gaze so intently, I swore it was the only thing holding me up.

The king let go an indulgent chuckle, thinking Blade was making a joke. I wasn't sure he wasn't.

Blade laughed with him, but it was short and mirthless.

"The whole of the Iron Realm knows it would take a partner of great courage and grit to mate with the likes of me."

I blinked, knowing that tears were welling in my eyes. He was here. That was all that mattered because now everything would go right. My throat grew tight.

At that, he finally tore his eyes from mine to regard the king.

"I'm willing to dress your gift in the wedding gown I bought for such a rare female, my king. It would please me to see this woman in it as she stands before you."

Oh, so very sly and wily. Not a single untruth. And so beautifully, masterfully executed I was left gasping for breath.

From the side of my eye I could see Ferranus fidgeting.

"We have more pressing need of you than dressing a mortal," he said. "A fellow fae has fallen. He needs healing magics."

"Then let me take care of him," Blade said with a dip at his waist as he angled toward Ferranus. "This mortal woman can pull a gown over her head by herself, I'm sure."

He looked back at me with a wink.

Ferranus snapped his fingers and a page raced to his side.

"Take Blade to the half trow."

The page paled visibly. He didn't argue, but he didn't go racing off like he should. The king's lips pressed tightly together, thinning them out so they nearly disappeared.

Seeing it, the page nodded, bowed, and backed away. He nodded to Blade, who narrowed his gaze momentarily at the page before turning to me again.

With a gentle movement, he draped the gown over my arm. As his fingers brushed my skin, I felt a hum and a warmth that under the right circumstance would have had me melting against him.

And if I thought he believed me a damsel, still, who needed rescuing, he pulled his other hand out from his pocket and dropped a chain between the two of us, and reminded me what he thought of me.

"Erachne said you dropped this," he murmured. "She thought you might want it back."

At that, he slipped my necklace over my head. It settled between my breasts and I noticed he'd put me between the court and the king, shielding me from view.

The nudity didn't bother me, not really, but the act made the tears gathering threaten to spill. I lifted my chin and sucked them back. Like a warrior. An assassin.

"Thank you," I said, as I clutched it as it hung. It felt hot in my grip, the residual heat of his hand still lending it warmth.

He clicked his heels and gave me a bow, much deeper than he had the king, before he pivoted on his heel.

"Now, where is this little fae?" he asked jovially, but there was a strain in his voice and in his posture that maybe only I heard and saw.

I took the opportunity to pull the gown over my head and draw the king's eye to my breasts and ribs and hips as I arched back to do so, a languid movement that even if I wasn't a seductress, was plenty enough to capture his attention.

Sure enough, Ferranus's gaze remained glued to my chest, suggesting he'd watched every second. I ran my palms down the gown, feeling how soft it was, like angel hair. It hugged every curve of my breasts and hips and the flat of my stomach. I didn't need a mirror to know how I looked.

Without taking his gaze from my chest, the king angled his chin in the page's direction. "He will take you to the half trow."

Blade shot one, lingering look back at me and his entire expression said more than words could. This was my dress. He'd bought it for me. And if he'd been saving for some special occasion, he obviously thought that occasion was now. I didn't regret the king seeing me in it when I knew Blade had seen me in it long before I'd put it on.

By the time he prowled away, leaving me to the king, I wasn't afraid. I was surprised even to realize that I had been before he'd entered. I lifted my chin and faced Ferranus as he extended his hand to me.

"Come, Blood Gift," he said. "It is indeed a beautiful gown and the realm should see how a gift should be adorned to be opened by a king."

I took his hand, and at his touch, I simply levitated to the dais. His arm slipped over my waist and he spun me around to face the room. Seeing the room from this height, this angle, I was astounded at the amount of Fae the room could hold, even with being spelled.

Ferranus squared his shoulders and lifted his chin in the manner all good speakers used to aid in projecting their voice.

"Your king has heard your cries for mercy on behalf of a poor half trow. My dark enforcer will see he is healed sufficiently to accept his endowment of magic."

A reverent muttering moved through the crowds, and then outright cheers. The king smiled with half his mouth. He was pleased, but not because they were pleased. He was pleased because he'd thought he'd navigated a tricky river filled with white water on a raft peppered with holes.

I peered up through my hair to see the king gesturing toward the back of the room where the pages stood at the broad copper door. Daring to look back over my shoulder, I saw them pull them open.

"Until the trow is healed, you will find resplendent cheer in the food and drink, for we have all the time we need, my friends, to enjoy our lives."

At that, he gestured that I should as well. He ran his hand up my back to find my bare shoulder blades and I felt a trail of fire light beneath my skin.

"And now," he said in a hoarse whisper. "Now, I shall taste of the luscious Cleopatra and see if she is indeed fit for a Caesar."

A gentle pressure on the small of my back bade me follow him.

I was aware of eyes all over the room following us, some of them burned holes in my back. Some merely felt like a brush of curiosity. I caught sight of a copper door on the far end of the room behind the dais, and as the pressure of his palm on my back guided me there, my heart began to race.

A heartbeat of time took my gaze to where Terran still lay curled on his side. Two pages hovered over him, apparently trying to decide if they should move the body or leave it as a warning.

His one remaining eye was open, almost watching me. I might have felt his gaze fall to where my hands were clasped over my hips, wringing together as they grew eager for a blade. I might have imagined that gaze shift to the king's belt where a blade rested beneath a sash. Easy to grab for. Easy to extract.

And we were heading to a room where neither of his mercenaries would follow. I looked back over the room, scanning the crowds for Flint and Kit's changeling. He had her by the hand, penned in behind several of the Shadow Court.

I smiled a secret smile. Power wasn't always in the hands of the mighty. Sometimes it was in the hands of the weak. And sometimes it was in the hands of those who had nothing to lose.

A taste, he'd said. I was quite sure he might try for more than that because he needed to restore the energy he'd lost. In fact, I was counting on it.

He thought me a mere mortal. Someone without power. Someone he didn't need to be afraid of. But he didn't know I was Ava Ashe, hunter of monsters and protector of the innocent. That I knew, finally, what the secret to real power was.

I might be mortal in a realm of kings, but in this moment, with the king's hand on my back, I knew he needed something from me.

And that could be more powerful than anything else.

—the end for now—

***

Dearest Reader:

Yes. That's the answer you're looking for, right? That I didn't just leave this horrible cliffhanger sitting there without a way to resolve it. Yes. There is another book in the main story arc. You can download that now if you're using an ereader or look for it in paperback. And yes. You will see more of your favorite characters, some you may even have forgotten. And Yeppers. I am so very very grateful for your dedication to this story as I tried my best to write something that pleased me, that kept me going during the tough writing stints, that also would please you too. I often saw you in my mind's eye and especially as I penned this cliffhanger ending. And YES. You were grumbling aloud and cursing my name as I imagined you. LOL. Thanks so much for all your encouragement as I wrote this series. For each email, message, and social media post, I thank you from the bottom of my heart.

If you want to keep updated on the series and characters and what they might get into next, feel free to **<u>join my readers' group.</u>**

ciao for now,

thea

Author Thanks

Stories like this, that span several books, start to gather dust bunnies of all sorts. Plot holes, grammar booboos, spelling issues, consistency problems. It takes more than my poor eye to find them and I have several loyal readers who help me out and deserve much thanks.

Caroline Jenkins is a hoover when it comes to spelling and grammar and inconsistencies. Kerry Taylor and Evelyn Dotson too.

Julie Pederick and author, Debra L. Martin have done so much to help me shape the story, I don't think it would have been the same without their input.

Then there's readers like Crystal Amason. She is the first reader to make me feel like my tales were worth reading. Thank you, Crystal. I hope I can continue to write stories you enjoy.

I really appreciate you all.

-thea-